SAVING
RUBY KING

SAVING
RUBY KING

CATHERINE ADEL WEST

PARK
ROW
BOOKS

If you purchased this book without a cover you should be aware
that this book is stolen property. It was reported as "unsold and
destroyed" to the publisher, and neither the author nor the
publisher has received any payment for this "stripped book."

PARK
ROW
BOOKS™

PLEASE RECYCLE
THIS PRODUCT IS RECYCLABLE

Recycling programs
for this product may
not exist in your area.

ISBN-13: 978-0-7783-0509-5

Saving Ruby King

Copyright © 2020 by Catherine Adel West

All rights reserved. No part of this book may be used or reproduced in any manner whatsoever
without written permission except in the case of brief quotations embodied in critical articles and
reviews.

This is a work of fiction. Names, characters, places and incidents are either the product of the
author's imagination or are used fictitiously. Any resemblance to actual persons, living or dead,
businesses, companies, events or locales is entirely coincidental.

This edition published by arrangement with Harlequin Books S.A.

Park Row Books
22 Adelaide St. West, 40th Floor
Toronto, Ontario M5H 4E3, Canada
ParkRowBooks.com
BookClubbish.com

Printed in U.S.A.

To my grandma Viola and my mom, Georgia.

Mom, you're here to see the book. Grandma, you're not. But without both of you, I wouldn't be here and this book wouldn't have been written. Thank you for everything and more.

KING

SAUL KING SOPHIA KING
(FOSTER)

SARA KING ???

LEBANON KING ALICE KING

RUBY KING

POTTER

ANDREW MORRISON THERESA MORRISON
(WILLIS)

THOMAS POTTER VIOLET MORRISON

JACKSON POTTER SR JOANNA POTTER
(WHITAKER)

JACK POTTER JR LAYLA POTTER
(J.P.)

SAVING
RUBY KING

"Neither is there salvation in any other: for there is none other name under heaven given among men, whereby we must be saved."

Acts 4:12

PROLOGUE

ALICE SYNTHIA KING

Ruby wants more than I can give her, but that's how children are. They expect you to fix all things, figure out all things and love them always.

And, sometimes, you can't do any of that.

Sometimes you barely love yourself or not at all, sometimes you barely drag yourself out of bed and function in a world that has nary a clue nor care you've abandoned the dreams you had for yourself. Instead you raised a child who loves you but resents you because of the mistakes you made.

I'm stitched together by the lies I tell myself and the lies people want to believe about me.

Chicago wind is unique in its relentlessness. It lifts the bottom of my coat and whips my skirt around my knees as I walk outside. Leaving this place of prayer, of unanswered requests, I'll drive the few miles from my church to my home that is not a home. I'm praying when I open the door that Lebanon isn't there or, 'if he is, he's drunk enough to be in an unconscious heap on the couch. Maybe Ruby will be home if her job hasn't kept her overtime. She hates it there. Her green eyes are dull, and her voice holds no emotion, happy or sad. She comes and goes more ghost than person, but of course we're all haunted.

Maybe we can talk. I can show her my new quilt, royal blue with gold stars and ivory trim. My finest creation yet. Maybe I can make her smile. Maybe I can smile.

"Alice! Alice! Sweetie, you're just in another world, aren't you?" Ms. Anne yells from the top of the crumbling steps. She ambles her way down and I walk toward her. She clutches my left arm for support. I try not to grimace and breathe slow because that arm is sore and bruised. I think back to Lebanon's angry face when I dozed off to a story he was telling me about the bakery.

"Sorry. Just thinking about the sermon. It sure was good, wasn't it?"

"Yes, it sure was. Reverend Jackson preached up a storm, but at least it didn't last long. Can't do them long services like I used to. And Lord knows—"

Wind drowns out the last of her sentence, but I pretend it didn't. I pretend I hear Ms. Anne's words, that they're important and I smile and nod.

A few more people leave the church and walk past us, all warm smiles and hugs. I know these people. For decades. If you ask them, if you ask Ms. Anne, they'd say we're good friends, more than that, they'd probably say we're all family. Church family. And we're here for one another, we love each other and the Lord God unconditionally, but they'd be lying. I'd be lying. Although if there is one thing you can sometimes find in lying, it's comfort, warm and complete and blind.

"How're Lebanon and Ruby?" Ms. Anne looks at me.

"Just wonderful! Lebanon is working hard at the bakery and Ruby adores her job. She's at some fancy law office downtown. Just so blessed. So very blessed."

Ms. Anne searches my face like all old black women do when

they want more information than you're willing to share. She examines my tired eyes and the thin folds of brown skin around them, my mouth, the pursing of my lips. "Your arm sore? Your face looked funny when I grabbed it."

"No, ma'am. It's just fine. Probably acting up 'cause of the sewing I was doing today."

"Really, Alice?"

"Yes, ma'am. I'm fine."

I gently remove her hand and begin walking a few steps to my car so I can drive home, toward whatever I will find there, peaceful or ugly.

"Hold up, darlin'! I'm gonna walk with you 'fore I try and take this bus. Doctor said it's good to exercise this new hip."

"Now, you know I'm not gonna let you take the bus home, not when you live right next door!"

"I'ma be fine. I don't wanna be any bother."

But Ms. Anne knows I'll fuss until she's in my car. Christian or not, it's simple decency.

I slow my pace to accommodate Ms. Anne's stunted stride. "Alright, since you are insisting, and we both could use the company I'm thinking." She waddles up and grabs my right arm for support instead of the left one this time, and smiles this smile, invasive and knowing, though she means it to be warm and kind.

I'm careful as I cruise on East 73rd Street, turning at South Lafayette Avenue then toward 79th Street. This route I've taken countless times, the stores and streetlights, the blocks and roaming bodies in this part of the city are as much of a fixture to my routine as church itself.

In fifteen minutes, we're close to home, on Bishop Street, and Ms. Anne starts singing a song, an old gospel only she remembers, probably one she heard many times as a child, but one I don't know, because many of these songs are lost to time or atrocity or apathy.

Ms. Anne sings about the River Jordan, how a man is going

to cross to see the Lord on the other side. She softly croons to me and the empty air until we arrive at her house.

The wind picks up again, pushing against us as we make it to her door.

I try to shield her from the onslaught, but it doesn't seem to make much of a difference. As I press my body closer to Ms. Anne, her voice, her song, reaches my ear. The man is in the middle of the River Jordan. The current is taking him farther from the other side, but he's still trying to reach the Lord. The man is afraid he won't make it.

Our houses, two brick bungalows, are nestled near the end of the street. Ms. Anne's house is lit from the front, golden shadows of electric light stretch themselves down the block. My house is dark except for an anemic glow from my sewing room window. I help Ms. Anne to her door as she finishes her song.

He saved me from my poor self; No more do I gotta roam.
I got my home in Paradise, Yes, Lord, now I got my home!

Ms. Anne fumbles a bit with her keys before her grandson LeTrell comes to meet us helping her inside. He's tall and broad framed, dwarfing his grandma. For all his seeming power, he gently guides Ms. Anne and smiles his thanks at me.

Turning back to the wind, I walk a few steps to my place, trudging through the invisible wall of air making it almost impossible to open my door. Parts of Ms. Anne's song cycle through my head, the lyrics simple, almost too easy to remember, but the words and how they're knit together, telling a story of hope, of victory—that's what makes them powerful. It ignites that spark, the one I barely possess, the one my daughter, Ruby, may have abandoned altogether. But maybe I can still unearth what little power or breath or whatever that's still good I carry within myself.

The key sticks between the lock and won't budge, but I realize it's the wrong key. I put in the right key and it smoothly turns. I'm humming the song, that music has given me some courage, a way to try to again cobble together a plan for me and Ruby. A way to escape Lebanon and find hope. Hope that we can be better versions of ourselves or those versions of ourselves harboring no lies or fear or regret. Perhaps that's too much to wish for, but it's the only thing taking me past this door and into this place. *He saved me from my poor self; No more do I gotta roam.*

I got my home in Paradise, Yes, Lord, now I got my—

CHAPTER 1

RUBY NAOMI KING

NINE DAYS AFTER ALICE KING'S DEATH

My hands are clinched into fists. They're always sore when I wake up. It happens more and more now. It's like when I sleep, I'm trying to grab hold of something I'm going to lose anyway, but it doesn't stop me from trying. Or maybe my hands are sore because I'm trying to catch things like the past or flying bullets or ghosts. My hands reach out so impossibly far, and the pain comes when I fail, everything still slipping through my fingers.

Maybe my hands are sore because Lebanon slapped me, and I slapped him back and we fought.

Without Mom, we'll batter each other because we don't have her between us, to keep the peace, pray the prayers, take the hits and slaps and punches. What will happen to me without her?

How can there be a *me* without *her*?

Mom's supposed to be nagging me right now about getting up for church. I'm supposed to give her money for the mortgage payment, because she can't rely on Lebanon for money. Mom's supposed to tell me the skirt I want to wear is too short. I'm twenty-four years old and should by now make my own decisions, but she needed us to look a certain way to not attract any attention.

There is a picture next to the light in a glass frame. Mom is holding me. I am crying, scared of the small flame atop the birthday candle on my cake. She's telling me it's going to be okay. I have a picture memorializing the one thing Mom probably will never be able to do again—protect me.

My cell phone rings. I have twelve missed calls, all of them from Layla. I don't want to speak to her. I don't have anything new to say about how I feel. I don't want to explain to her that words won't help or heal or comfort, but she'll call again and again.

Layla's relentless.

This is fine if you lose your purse or want to grab front row seats at the Rihanna concert, but I don't want this kind of energy aimed at me now. Her fierce stubbornness results in endless calls, a panicked need to know if I'm okay, that I'm alive.

"Why haven't you been answering, Rue?"

"I had a Mom and she's gone. I don't need you to take her place."

"Rue I didn't mean—"

There's crackling on the end of Layla's line. The sound of car horns and the manic rumble of her car's engine make it hard for me to hear her. "You're already on your way to church?"

"You know Reverend Jackson Potter expects me there before everyone else."

"Well, you *are* his daughter."

"Are you coming today? Is your…father bringing you?"

"No. I don't think so, not for a while. Lebanon will probably be there though. I don't want to be where he is if I can help it. Being in this house with him is enough, really, it's more than I can take."

"What does that mean, Rue?"

"I didn't mean anything by it. I'm not like *that* anymore. Okay? I promise."

My wrists throb, a hot pulsing, an itch. The skin is still raised and puckered like thin lips, kissing the tops of frail veins. Through the phone, I hear her car radio playing music. I try to diffuse Layla's concerns for me. I try to make her laugh. I try to spare people my pain. It's the polite thing to do. I'm good at doing the polite thing. Mom taught me very well.

"Are you playing secular music?"

She chuckles. "Look, even God gives Bruno Mars a pass. He's probably coming to Chicago this summer for a concert. We can go. We always have a good time you and I, some good music."

"You're right. You're right."

"Just…just pick up your phone when I call you, Rue."

I sigh. "I was sleeping, girlie. Just sleeping."

The sputtering of her car's engine ends. The Bruno Mars song shuts off mid-baby-come-back refrain.

"So, we'll talk soon? After I get out of church?"

"Sure, whenever you want. I'm up now."

"Okay, love you, Rue."

"Love you too, girlie."

I hang up and lay my phone on the chipped and scarred mahogany nightstand next to my Bible, black and leather bound. I blow dust off the top and hold it in my hand.

The book is in perfect condition. Its spine still firm and intact, the thin pages not yet yellowed with time. Mom bought it for me as a Christmas gift three years ago. Placed under the green plastic Christmas tree strung with white lights.

Lebanon came home that night and laughed at the gift, reeking of cheap whiskey and cheaper beer. Mom cried and locked herself in her sewing room and didn't come out until the morning. He's an asshole, an abusive asshole, and my father, and I don't know why Mom ever married him.

After Mom's funeral, when we were alone in the house, Lebanon told me, "God doesn't act like some long-lost father waiting, rooting for us to do the right thing. God's the bully with the magnifying glass and we're the ants." He said this with tears in his eyes. I don't think he felt the tears. He didn't wipe them away, they just cascaded down his face, then he got up and stumbled down the hall to their bedroom.

How did this even happen? Mom should've been in her sewing room that night. That's where she always was, but there was a special Friday service so, of course she had to go, she couldn't *not* be at church. And when she came home, someone killed her.

I would have given anything to save her. But why couldn't she save herself? The both of us? She wasn't the kind of person to leave someone she saw as weak. She had too much faith. It's what we learn in church, that if you have enough God in you, you can pray to Him and He can move mountains and shape circumstances and do great miracles on your behalf. You just have to believe enough. And Mom believed God would change Lebanon, but some people can't be saved. You can't pray away evil. You can't ignore its destruction. But Mom certainly tried all of that, and now I'm here and the one person who deserved a bullet more than anyone I know is here with me.

I toss aside the Bible and shrug into my lavender bathrobe. I don't want to leave my room, but my hands are sore. Running them under hot and cold water helps. With light footsteps, I remember the weaker portions in the floor, avoiding them. I don't look at the pictures on the walls: the forced smiles, numb posturing, Lebanon's hand on Mom's shoulder.

I'm shuddering, but I keep moving.

The sink is full of dishes. Dried spaghetti, collard greens, sweet potato pie and peach cobbler residue cling to each fork, plate and cup. I'm expected to clean the dishes. Mom would do so without protest. Docile. One trained to serve. Breathe and serve. If Mom were here, there wouldn't have been a dish in the sink. The black granite countertops wouldn't be sticky with dried coffee. The kitchen would sparkle and smell of bleach and the gardenia perfume she loved to wear.

Leaving the kitchen dirty is my rebellion. Rebellion even in its smallest forms can eventually birth great change. With change comes hope. So, for now, letting the dishes rot in the sink gives me some small satisfaction.

I turn on the water rinsing my hands as steam rises, swirling and disappearing. My fingers and palm stay under the faucet. It burns, and I don't move. My caramel tone becomes an angry red. The water beads differently on my scars than on my smooth skin. I let the heat cocoon itself around my body, willing the warmth to move from limb to limb, head to toes.

I welcome the pain and deserve it. Atonement for sins, for empty nights and flesh and sweat and flashes of light and metal and actions that cannot be taken back. My tears stream, and I don't recognize their salty wetness until they hit my shirt. Removing my hand, I look at its temporary redness with a practiced detachment. Feeling the pain, but not acknowledging it.

Turning the knob and allowing the water to run for a few minutes, I leave my hand under the water, feeling as it gradually turns cold.

A small window two feet above the sink offers blue-and-white tones slowly emerging from the night's shadow. I flex my fingers and they belong to me once again, doing my bidding without fight or pain. Basking in the relief, I don't hear Him, but tremble when He speaks, "Good morning."

I swallow my scream.

LAYLA VIOLET POTTER

Rolling my neck side to side, I try to relieve the tension in my shoulders, the ache will soon make it to my head and beat between my eyes. I squint, removing as much of the sun from my vision as I can.

Loud sputtering noises escape the engine of my rusting 1997 Chevy Malibu that I call the Black Stallion. I lightly close the door. I don't lock it because, hey, if you want to steal a fourteen-year-old car, you have more problems than I care to count, and I've got enough of my own.

Ruby tried to sound like herself on the phone. She cracked jokes and changed the conversation because it suits her to not talk about painful things. It must suit me too, because I let her do it, I didn't press her, didn't say, "No, Ruby! We're going to talk about what happened…now!" I didn't say, "No, Ruby. You're going to come with me and we're going to find somewhere safe for you because I see the man your father is. I see Lebanon and know you need to leave."

I didn't do any of that. I just told her we should go to the Bruno Mars concert, like that would change her situation in any real way.

Why didn't I say *something*?

Even at the end of March, the air still bites and nips like a hungry dog. The Chi Town spring sun is deceivingly bright. I sing "Every day is a day of thanksgiving" to the concrete beat of my boots.

I want to believe these words so much that I sing them a little louder hoping the measure of volume will equal my measure of conviction. Maybe God hears me better when I'm not so much in my head. And to be honest, I have a *lovely* alto voice.

Stopping a few feet from the entrance of the church, I scan the block. Only a few passersby make their way up and down the street. Not many people up this early on Sunday. Most are sleeping or coming home from parties I would've loved to attend if I didn't have to be *here* by seven o'clock in the morning.

A couple of cars are parked in various points on Indiana Avenue, in Bronzeville, a whole black world within a city; a world with only our people, who arrived barely a century ago in innumerable droves during the Great Migration, living in cramped tenements with the tenuous hope of more freedom than what was doled out down south. And now there is a weird dichotomy of stilted gentrification and unpredictable violence, and yet there's tangible opportunity if one were to look beyond hasty misconceptions and blatant prejudices.

Long arms grab me from behind and lift me up. I scream. My lungs burn and blood rushes to my ears. I kick and flail and twist.

"Damn, Lala! It was just a joke! You actin' like you was gonna get kidnapped!"

I turn and punch my little-big brother in the arm as hard as I can. I hope it leaves a bruise.

He's laughing, bending over thoroughly amused at my near heart attack. "Come on, Lala. I was just playin'. I was just playin'."

J.P. couldn't say Layla when we were younger, just Lala. It stuck. Black people always seem to go by nicknames. They are as official as a birth certificate or driver's license. It's the funny and the abiding puzzle found in sticky sets of syllables, ancient and varied, affixing themselves to a person, a hundred-year-old, multirooted cypress tree, finding its depth and permanence in a grove of many lives.

My brother's tall, muscled frame goes in for a hug. He wraps his massive arms around me again. I remain stiff for a few seconds, and then wrap my arms around him. I let go and then punch him in the arm again.

It's not like I could stay mad at him for more than a few minutes.

Still clad in his post office uniform, my brother parts his lips in a half-moon-bright smile showing the small gap between his two front teeth.

"You're not coming to church today?"

"Nah, sis. I've had enough church for this week, this weekend, hell my entire life! Besides, I just got off a double shift. I'm going home, get some sleep," he says rubbing his bald head with his heavily muscled arm.

"You know our father, the good ole Reverend Potter, is gonna give you hell for not coming to church today."

"Oh the holy and devout Reverend Potter can try, not like it's gonna work." He laughs.

"What are you doing here, then?" I ask, my heart finally starting to beat a normal rhythm inside of my chest.

"I'm dropping off the programs for this morning. Didn't get a chance to do them earlier 'cause of Auntie Alice's funeral."

My brother raises his head and cranes his neck toward the sky. "Shitty circumstance, but it was a nice homegoing service. She'd have liked it."

"Yeah, I guess she would've. The sermon and songs. It was nice. Maybe it's what she would've wanted, but she never said much about what she liked or didn't."

"Yeah Auntie Alice was quiet, like Ruby. Is Ruby gonna be at church today?"

"No." I look down the block again.

"Stop biting your bottom lip, Lala. It's gonna get ashy as hell doin' that."

I shrug.

J.P. sighs. "She needs time. We all do after something like that, but especially her, now she's all alone with her father. It's gonna be rough."

"That *man* is not a father."

"I'm not tryin' to debate with you, Layla. I'm only telling you what I'm seeing is all."

"Give me the programs."

J.P. cocks his head and raises his left eyebrow. I always hated the fact he can do that and I can't.

"I'll give them to Dad. You go home and get some sleep. Only one of us needs to piss him off today. It's my turn."

"Hmph. You looking for a fight, Lala. You always wanna be the one to go at it with Dad."

"Give me the damn programs, J.P. Go home."

My brother hugs me one more time.

"How much you wanna bet Dad hasn't finished his sermon yet?" I crack a smile.

"Sis, I'd be stupid to take that bet. You know he hasn't finished it." J.P. laughs and strolls to his car, an electric-blue Ford Mustang with a white racing stripe down the middle. The car smoothly turns over. He sticks his arm out the window, throws a peace sign and drives off.

I'm alone again on the block. Calvary Hope Christian Church stands before me, a sandy limestone juggernaut. At the bottom of the church, deeply chiseled, is the year of construction, 1891. I crane my neck up, to see the top of the bell tower. Every time I do this and try to take in its great expanse, I feel the same: a seven-year-old girl whose life cannot be separated from this structure, only defined by it.

The small ache in my head is constant. My jaw is tight. I'm frowning. My jaw aches only when I frown. Momma always scolds me when I do that. She says it makes me look older than my age.

Walking toward the newer building, I reach for the keys in my pocket. The wind always seems sharpest on this side of the church, next to the empty field littered with a buffet of trash and old car parts. I grab the key to the church without even looking at it. I know the shape and weight of the brass and insert it into the lock. I shake it until the tumblers give way, and the lock finally relents.

★ ★ ★

During the late spring and summer, the urban pasture is lush and green, wildflowers sticking out and defiantly displaying their beauty among the junk. But for the moment, the haphazardly discarded items are all one can see and the potential is obscured.

I understand how the state of the deserted pasture is a reflection of my community. I understand how remaining behind walls of worship and offering plates and gospel music does nothing to change my side of the city. I understand how religion without action makes it worse. But even good people grow complacent. And it comes at a high price. That's how Auntie Alice died. Good people doing nothing.

Elder Alma stands in front of door, tall and broad with a warm smile. "I heard you struggling with the door. I was gonna help, but you always figure things out, baby."

I smile. Old black people, elders, always figure you need a lesson about struggle because they had so much of it in their lives. Maybe they think it makes us stronger. So they'll teach, but they won't coddle. They'll oversee, but they won't hover. I'm not annoyed at Elder Alma. She wasn't trying to be mean. She was being herself. You can't ever fault people for being themselves. Unless you're my father, Reverend Jackson Potter Sr., then you can fault people for anything and everything under the sun. Must be nice.

I open the door reading REVEREND JACKSON BLAISDELL POTTER SR., and he is hunched over his oak desk staring at a dog-eared sheet of paper. A yellow notepad with a few lines sloppily written on it sits untouched in front of him. Old football trophies and a degree from seminary school are prominently perched on the shelf behind him.

Beside him is the old Bible, falling apart, the spine bound and rebound over many years with tape. The desk and the Bible I see almost as much as I see him and I think they are so much a part of him, each one cannot exist without the other.

The lamp gifts a cloudy circle of dirty golden light. A new desktop computer sits behind him, but my father refuses to use it. He prefers the old-school method of writing by hand. His handwriting is horrible. Momma calls it "chicken scratch" in that rich soprano voice of hers. Even when she's talking, it seems like she's singing so when she's insulting you, it still sounds like some wonderful compliment.

Knocking lightly on the door, I catch my father's attention. He quickly folds the piece of paper, sticking it into the old Bible and acts as if he's resuming the task of writing. "Yes?"

"Still working on today's sermon, Pops?"

"Touching up. Only touching up."

"Church starts in about two hours. Will you be finished *touching up* then?"

He's lying and I know he's lying, and I want to call him on it so he knows I can't be fooled like the other people in this building, but I don't.

He looks up from his paper. "Stop biting your bottom lip."

I let my lip go, a light throbbing the only evidence I was biting it in the first place.

"I have the programs. J.P. is headed home. He won't be here today."

"You know, I don't expect much from you and J.P.—"

"Spoken like a parent who expects too much."

"Watch your tone."

"I'm alive and so is J.P. I'm *assuming* that's the best news a father can expect. His children are alive and thriving."

"My children can thrive *in* the church," he retorts. He turns his attention back to his unfinished sermon. "How's Ruby?"

This is my cue to stick to pleasantries, but I'm not doing that. I made that mistake already with Ruby. "She's not coming to church either. I'm worried about what she'll do, living alone with Lebanon."

Dad puts down his pen and sighs long and heavy. "Maybe give her some space. It's a difficult time for her. For all of us."

I roll my eyes. "Give her space? That's the last thing she needs right about now."

My father stands up, cocks his head and clenches his left jaw. "For once, just listen to me, stop being so disrespectful. Give Ruby some time to grieve, to be alone with her family."

"The last of her family is buried in Restvale Cemetery."

"Layla, she has—"

"No one, Dad. Ruby has nothing and no one left, except us."

"She has her father."

"Who drinks and beat her Mom!"

"Layla!" My father stalks from behind his desk. It still terrifies and amazes me how fast, how stealthily he can move. "Leave this alone. I'm telling you for the last time," he whispers. His eyes are dark and his fingers are meaty and firm around my right arm. He doesn't shout. Shouting draws attention and listening ears. We're a perfect family and we can't have someone in the congregation witnessing a fight, people talk, rumors swirl. It's best to leave our dysfunction in the home and out of the church.

"Let go of me." Shame slowly creeps into his eyes. I no longer feel my heartbeat through the flesh of my right arm. "If I listen to you, if I leave her alone too long, it'll happen again."

"What will happen?" My father's face tightly creases and then relaxes with the bleak understanding of what I mean. "She won't...do *that*."

"You don't know, and you didn't find her the first time. You didn't see—"

"Turn on the lights and start laying today's programs on the seats, please. Thank you."

There are times when Dad plays the role of someone truly listening. He nods, but he's already forming a response because his mind is made up. It's been that way for years in my calculation and it won't change. He's shut down so I shut down. It's a silent waltz, a graceful movement of questions and nonanswers perfected over many years. That is the end of the conversation. That firm "Thank you" is as good as him saying "Get out." There's no reasoning or persuading.

He's set and so am I.

I close the door harder than I need to.

"Layla, I *just* fixed the hinges on that door yesterday. Can you let a man enjoy his work before you undo it?" Timothy Simmons smiles as he scolds me.

"I'm sorry. I just…"

"Come here, Layla," Tim says as he gently takes my hand and leads me to an alcove nearest to the bathroom, a small space where prying eyes can't reach, and he puts his arms around me. His embrace provides a calm to the uneasiness I've felt since Auntie Alice's murder. I listen to his heartbeat for a minute and try to time my breathing along with it.

"He never listens, Tim."

"You can make anyone do anything, Layla. Remember when you convinced me and Ruby to sneak out with you so we could go to the Usher concert?"

"We had a great time though."

"Yeah, I thought about it a lot after I enlisted. That night. We didn't have problems or pressure. My dad wasn't a drunk. Ruby's wasn't mean. Yours wasn't—"

"A pretentious jerk."

"Layla!"

I laugh and Tim does too, despite his better judgment.

"My point is if you can convince us to sneak out on a Saturday night before church, you can make your Dad listen."

I let go of Tim and raise my face to kiss him, his lips are soft, melting into mine with warmth and ease. I can stand here and kiss him all day, but there's much I need to do before the service starts. The light click of heels in the hallway causes him to break our kiss. "Make him listen, Layla," says Tim as he leaves the shadow of our small, sacred space.

Tim is wise, but not when it comes to the ways of my father. Jackson Potter never listens. He won't listen to my words and he can't see what I see in Ruby, how she is slowly folding in on herself and turning brittle like fallen leaves. It's true that the church can cocoon Ruby, but that protective layer can suffocate her, too. I'm all too familiar with that kind of pressure.

Nevertheless, Ruby and I are bound by these walls and these pews and the cracking stone and chipped wood. When we were small, we ran down the halls, our patent leather shoes slapping against the old tile in the basement as we played games or laid our backs against the old mint-green wall and held hands and talked about what we wanted to do when we grew up. Neither one of us became what we thought we'd be.

The Sunday after Auntie Alice died, there were so many rumors moving back and forth in Calvary Hope Christian Church. So many people eager to know the details, some feigning concern for Ruby and Lebanon, others asking if they needed someone to help them clean the house or cook a meal. Sister Washington thought her nephew might know someone who saw something. Sister McKay believed she saw someone running from the house "real suspicious-like." But no one, *no one* could give the police any facts or actual leads. They brought pies and cakes and looked at the dried blood stain on the living room floor.

I was the one who held Ruby until she cried herself to sleep in my arms, felt her body shake so hard I thought she might fall apart, flesh and bone, in my hands. I told her it was going to be okay, though neither one of us believed it then and still don't. I made her eat. I call her every two hours, because I know her potential for destruction in a way no one else at this church, save a few, understand.

In this way, Ruby and I are bound together. We are bound by her blood and her survival. Sometimes, I don't know how

I can bear the weight of it, of what I think is one of the truest relationships I'll ever know.

My phone buzzes in my pocket. A text from Ruby. Beverly Café. 1:30 p.m.

I feel a pang in my chest.

I try to call her. No answer.

I try again. No answer.

I try again and again and again.

No. Answer.

CHAPTER 2

CALVARY HOPE CHRISTIAN CHURCH

In this world, all things have a presence, a subtle realization about life and the humanity around them. Though I don't possess a traditional body with arms and legs and a brain, I have, over my years in being, come to witness a collective series of events and lives blending in a sometimes gentle, but often garish, rhythmic pattern and hum. It produces what some overly educated philosopher might call a consciousness.

Within my walls and rooms and arched wood roof, I hold the laughter and sorrow, hope and regret, love and hate of a people who escape into services and music and speaking in tongues and dancing and prayer. My form was created fierce and strong by rough, scarred hands long since passed from this earth. The men who built the foundation, placed each of my limestone blocks ever upward, laid the floors and crafted the windows, praising God through their trades and perhaps thought they bartered their way into the pearly gates with their bodily offerings. Maybe they did.

Two nine-foot bloodred wooden doors with creaky, black

hinges are set on each end. Open square eyes with no pupils, I stare into the pockmarked street. The winter was not kind to my paint. There are cracks on the steps leading to my entrance. Once small hairline fractures, they are now open crevices, gap-toothed remains of grimy gray concrete puckering up toward a gray sky.

My rear corridor forms an L shape, a rusting blue metal door heralding the third entrance. Though bumped and nicked, it is still somehow sturdy and not falling off the hinges. God's grace shines in the smallest of things. Constructed during the 1960s, my addition is a lighter shade of brown, but still melds itself perfectly against my older stone in mottled tans, coffees, gingers and hazels.

Some of the church elders still call it "The New Building." Sunday school, Bible studies and smaller church meetings take place here. During the week, all seven rooms hem and haw with church trustees brainstorming ways to reconcile decreasing offerings with a need to minister to a community of which they are increasingly afraid. Here, children learn their books of the Bible, their young mouths unable to yet form the complicated syllables of the longer books like Leviticus or Deuteronomy. The usher board debates among each other the best tactics with which to welcome new members to the church. So many conflicting agendas, so much to accomplish, but some things remain the same no matter the measured progress.

People enter and pray, think, wrestle with thoughts not shared with others. They are the little balls of radiance, pulsing, illuminating energies sustaining me. Those times of quiet and light are the most precious, filled with grace and uncomplicated honesty. Silently and fervently, I protect the words that tumble off lips or the tears that fall down cheeks. Desired or not, I'm heir to their memories and I pluck out moments, those that are forgotten or want to be forgotten, those that are happy and hopeful, sad and incomplete. Looking inside and out, my time and position fixed on this avenue, I see things are better and worse, people are smarter and more foolish. I don't have more hope and I don't have less.

I don't remember birth. I remember *being*. My history etched in numbers at my base, my memories are the whispers and gossip and conversations of congregants old and young and dead. But in the very atoms that make stone, stone and wood, wood, you can find me. You will never hear me speak. I have a feeling a few people, Elder Hughes in particular, would ask me only for the numbers to the next lottery jackpot anyway. But I'm not a genie. I'm a collection of decaying bricks and crumbling mortar. I'm not all-powerful and all knowing. I am not God. I just am and people just are.

That is the bulk of it.

"I didn't want you to come here. They did." Sara gestures to the hospital staff milling about outside of her room.

She birthed me, but she doesn't love me. I don't think she can love. She can't hurt me anymore with her words. She can't beat me with her hands. She can't touch me. She's only my mother. That's all. I repeat this and breathe deep.

"Say what you gotta say," I fire back.

"I'm sorry 'bout what happened with Alice, son. We know the world is a dangerous place, don't we?" She tries peeling the orange sitting on the table attached to her bed. Her dark brown fingers shake. "I mean people ain't even safe in they own houses anymore. But the Bible says, 'It rains on the just and the unjust.'" She shakes her balding head; a few stray gray hairs cover her white pillow.

"You're quoting the Bible now?"

"Just sayin' bad things happen to good people more than it ought to, I guess."

My mouth waters, like it does right before I take my first drink of the evening, happy to let my problems melt away with a little liquor, but I don't have a drink in my hand. I want one. My body wants it, but I'm not at home. And Alice isn't at home.

"Are you sorry, I mean *really sorry* something bad happened to Alice?" I ask.

"Course I am! You wasn't the only one who felt some sort of responsibility to that girl! When Naomi told me Alice was coming to Chicago for college, I promised to look after her. Couldn't even do that right."

Sara takes her mask and breathes in the oxygen once, twice, three times. Her collarbone rattles around, sharply jutting out from her skin. Her eyes hard set and drilling into mine. Naomi was one of Sara's few friends she'd do anything for. I still don't know how she got Sara's love. What do you have to do for that? What do you have to sacrifice?

"Well, I don't know what you promised Naomi you'd do for Alice. None of my concern anyway. I wasn't even there."

"Yeah, 'cause your ass was in prison for killin' that boy… What was his name?" she asks, clumsily clawing at the fruit.

I snatch it from her hands, making short work of skinning it and placing the wedges in front of her. "Syrus. Syrus Myllstone," I reply.

It was January. Before I met Alice. Before I had a business and a family. Before I became a good Christian man, I was sent to prison for killing a boy no older than me. The few times I've seen Sara in these last years, she always brings up my time downstate. Trying to hurt me, she dangles my past sins in front of my face as if she doesn't have to answer for an abundance of her own.

"Considering the job you did raising me, it's a wonder I didn't kill someone sooner." My stomach tightens. I swear I can smell the stale musty air of our old apartment, remember my stiff fingers cutting around the moldy bread to the edible parts.

"I did the best I could," Sara retorts.

"Your best? Damn, Sara, I'd hate to see your worst."

"Did you better than my daddy did me."

"Least you knew your daddy."

"Shut up, boy. Just…you don't know so shut up talking about the past. Don't do us no good, and I ain't got enough of a future left to relive it."

Next to her bed is a vase of dying roses and the picture of her and two girls. I can't see the other faces all that clearly. It's black-and-white, kinda blurry in a dirty silver frame. I saw it only one other time on her dresser next to some raggedy doll named Louisa. I snuck in her room trying to find a toy Sara took in one of her fits. She hit me when I touched the picture. She didn't have any pictures of *me*.

"Why your fists clenched?" Sara asks.

I shrug. Often, I don't notice one way or the other what my hands tend to do.

"Alice brought my picture to cheer me up. Make the place feel a little like home is what she said. She was a good wife. Not that good of a cook from what I remember, but a good wife to you at least."

Sara chuckles empty and cruel. "Anyway, seeing as how they figure my old ass is gonna die from this cancer, they want some kin they can talk to and make arrangements. All I got is you, my son." She coughs, a hard, phlegmy sound from her lungs. She grabs for her oxygen and takes big, deep gulps of air.

"I can see about talking to someone, but I got somewhere to be, Sara."

She puts the mask down and sits up. "You disrespectful as hell, boy. I'm your momma."

"If you acted like one, I might call you one."

"If you was worth a damn, I might've claimed you more. Only thing you ever was good at was whining. If they gave out awards for that, you'd have at least been good at *something*, might have these hospital bills paid."

"I provide for my family well enough."

"No the hell you don't. You don't provide for me!"

"I don't owe you a damn thing! Plus, I do better than you ever did."

A wheeze and a smile cut across her face. "Tried to tell Alice about you before y'all got married but she had stars in her eyes and a baby in her belly. Still thought she could find a way to make her dreams come true. Dreams just childish. Thinking she could make people good. You can't make people nothing. They are what they are."

Her eyes are unfocused while she talks to me or more precisely at me; I could be air and she'd still ramble on. It's probably the drugs they're giving her. They make you loopy, like

you're talking to the past and present. I don't know if she's be-
rating me or a ghost.

"Lotta good you did for her in the end. She prayed. She went
to church and pretended things was fine and you stood by and
acted like you was a good person, a holy person and people in
church pretended right along with y'all."

"So, you asked me to come here to fill out paperwork and
talk shit about me and Alice?"

"Umm. I—I'm just saying you ain't important. I ain't either.
You're money in the collection plate. If you honest with yo'self,
the real reason you even go is to make people think you a good
person. It's the only reason anyone goes. You go and dress up
nice and pretty to cover up all the ugly things you do. Like God
even hear us anyway. Remember, he the bully holding the magnifying glass—"

"And we're the ants. Yep. You know everything."

"Hmph. You just mad about what happened to Alice."

"What do you know about any of it?"

"Just what I saw on the news. Caught Jackson on the TV
talkin' to a reporter. He looked nice, downright regal. They
say they ain't ruled out any suspects yet." Her eyes hold mine
searching for something deeper, an answer she won't get from
me. Not today. Not ever. "You don't gotta say nothin' to me
about it. What goes on in your house, stays in your house. What
goes on in my house, stays in mine. Am I right?"

"Yeah." It's the only thing I *can* say to her. Remembering that
night. Ruby holding Alice in her arms as a small pool of blood
became a red sea. The sirens and the questions. The bulging
eyes and flapping mouths up and down the street.

"How's Ruby? Not like she even know about me. Don't know
why I'm even asking after her."

"You think I'd bring Ruby around you the way you act?"

"I'm still her family," she fumes.

"She ain't seen you since she was five."

"Alice and you invited me to her birthday party. Well, Alice did—I know your ass didn't want me there."

"You drank too much like you do and damn near ruined the party, slurring your words, falling down everywhere."

"I don't remember that."

"I do. I remember. I'm happy Ruby never saw you after that."

My throat burns. I walk up to her bed. She stuffs the last wedge of orange into her mouth, a bit of juice leaks from the left side of her mouth and she smiles. Like we're having some pleasant conversation. Talking about good ole times.

Sara's hooked up to all manner of machines, tall and short, skinny and wide. Blood and medicine and oxygen pumping through collapsing vein and deteriorating bone. But no doctor can remove whatever it is that made Sara so angry, so mean. No cure for that. It just is. Malignant.

"Well, Alice still came and saw me. Careful she was, careful about what she said and didn't say, careful how she moved."

God, just let her shut the hell up. *Please!*

"You always was a little shit. A little shit who thought the world owed him—"

I grab her sunken face with my right hand. I tighten my grip ever so slightly and watch her eyes grow wide. "The world didn't give me anything I didn't damn near kill myself trying to get. And even when you're here, even when you're dying, you can't even pretend to act like you give a damn about me. So stop talking about shit you don't know about."

I let her face go. She massages her jaws staring at me more like an enemy than a son, but we are more foes than family.

She hisses, "I talk about what I goddamn well please! You don't scare me. I seen monsters like you before. Ain't nothin' you can do to me. Nothin' you can do to Alice anymore either. You tore her away bit by bit. You're good at that."

"Like mother, like son."

"Bastard," she mumbles.

Sunlight doesn't shine on this side of the hospital yet, but I make out my reflection in the window to the right of Sara's bed. Gray pinstripe suit, white dress shirt and a coral tie adding a pop of color. This shirt isn't as crisply pressed and starched as I like it. Alice always ironed them better than I could. She knew I could be difficult when I didn't get my way. But we gotta fight for everything we want. Sometimes kill for it. Everything. A nice suit. A friend. A good job after a five-year bid for manslaughter. A life.

Fight and kill. Those are your weapons. That's how you live.

"Hello, Mr. King?" A doctor comes in the door, chocolate-tinged skin with a white coat. "The nurses told me you were here. I wanted to stop by and introduce myself, Dr. Liza Savoie." I barely hear the click of high heels on the floor as she extends her hand to shake mine.

Walking over to Sara she gushes, "I also wanted to check on my favorite patient before the end of my shift."

I've never known Sara to be referred to as a "favorite" anything. Ever. Maybe favorite pain in the ass. Favorite drunk. Favorite hell-raiser and child beater.

Dr. Savoie scans her chart; thick lips form a smooth grim line, and then a tight smile.

"Let's talk about the latest results and our options," she begins. "First, I'm sorry to say, but the cancer has metastasized to your liver and both kidneys. Now, we can continue with chemotherapy. However, with the current pace…"

"How much time I got?"

"I can look at some other options, Ms. King, if you'll allow me…"

"How much time?"

"Two months. Probably less."

Sara takes Dr. Savoie's hand and, with more care, fake or otherwise, in her eyes than she could ever muster for me, says, "I made my peace with my God. I'll take whatever comes."

I've never seen Sara in a church. I've never seen her touch a Bible. Never heard her mention God's name except to take it in vain. But it's something to say to a doctor who thinks this old woman is someone worthy of saving, and if she can't be saved, someone whose memory is worthy of keeping. And I see how good Sara is getting people to believe she's vulnerable and sweet and loveable. Human.

We're both good at pretending.

Sara never gave me much, but she taught me the shit that can help you survive in a world where dark skin and no money are liabilities. How to make people think you are what you're not. Getting others to give what they wouldn't willingly if they knew, *really knew*, who you were.

"I truly wish I had better news, but I'll be back tomorrow so we can go over some more options including hospice care, if you want to go that route."

Sunlight streams through the window now and I make out the thin watery film of tears as Dr. Savoie shakes my hand again and hurries out of the room.

"You give niggas a damn degree, they ass get all siddity. Using them ten-cent words to say you gonna die."

And like that, she's back. The real Sara. The one that doctor will never see.

"She seems to really like you so why you gotta be like that? You understand what she said. Why you care what words she uses?"

"Shit, my time is short. Don't use five minutes to tell me what you can in one."

Sara's mouth puckers and she draws the thin bedsheet closer to her chest. "Women like that think they got something 'cause they wear a white coat and got a title. Just wasn't place for that nonsense when I was younger. No place for dreams. I coulda done that. I was smart. Momma always told me I was smart."

Dr. Savoie wasn't that much younger than Sara. She probably

went through a lot to have a white coat with her name on it. Saying this wouldn't make a difference. Truth plain in front of her face rarely does. That's why she had liquor I suppose. Easier to deal with your life at the bottom of a glass full of whiskey.

"Mmm-hmm, bet you're gonna say your daddy said the same thing. Poor smart, sweet, innocent Sara."

"Shut the hell up! You don't know what you talking 'bout!" Sara's body tightens, she grimaces and hits a small plastic button attached to the twisted artery of tubes and her body relaxes. Whatever liquid concoction she released takes hold quick. She tries to yell, but she's whispering. In her head, Sara's probably calling me all kinds of names like when I was a kid, but she mutters, "Don't talk about…him…no right." Her eyes glaze quickly and close. Her breathing is uneven and she whimpers like some wounded animal. And I'm at peace. Not because it's quiet and she isn't grumbling whatever cruel nonsense comes out her mouth.

I *might* be happy. Maybe not so much happy as I need Sara dying to mean something more to me. I'm scared it won't. That'd make me even less human than I already feel. Who doesn't feel something when their momma dies?

Me and Sara are tethered by time and hate, by blood and broken promises and dreams, and even more fractured beliefs of who's guilty for what's happened between us. Without Sara, who do I blame for…being me? Are children supposed to forgive their parents for the horrible things they've done? Alice begged me to see Sara, to listen to her story, find some understanding for why she is the way she is. Alice wanted me to do this for the sake of our family, for "our little girl Ruby," she said. And I never listened, because my anger was righteous. It still is.

But what if I'd have forgiven Sara earlier? Would I have been different? I don't know what a better man is supposed to look like. But maybe I wouldn't feel like I'm almost underwater without my wife, so lost when I look at our kid who has that same look in her eyes for me, the same one I have for Sara. And I know that girl can do something about it. And the hate Ruby has for me is the same flavor I have for Sara. Salty with a little bit of smoke.

I have no answer to who Sara is to me and why she is the way she is, why I am the way I am, because whatever haunts her, haunts me. What I should do with her. There's no action for this situation that seems whole enough to provide relief for the inside of me, the parts constantly churning and moving.

The nurses' station is perched just outside of Sara's door. Some of them type. Some of them are on the phone. Dr. Savoie calls my name right before I make my escape. "Mr. King, can I steal a few more minutes?" She shrugs on a long black wool coat. The muted clack of her feet ringing in my ears. I do my best to muster any semblance of sadness or sense of loss or anything a son about to lose his mother would feel. Something other than relief.

"Mr. King... I again want to..."

"What's up, Doc?" I chuckle. "I'm sorry, I just..."

"It's fine. I've heard it all." An easy smile graces her face. Like the kind Alice had when we first met. The one I hadn't seen in years until I witnessed it a final time in her open casket.

"Mr. King, your mom needs you. She's a fighter—"

"That she is, Doc."

Her eyes go wide for a brief moment as she continues, "I know she puts up a tough front, but Sara's scared. Having someone there for her, to hold her hand can make these next days easier, for both of you. Maybe *easier* isn't the best word, but I...well I hope to see you more."

"Sara doesn't need anybody." I can't snatch back those words after they escape my mouth. "What I mean to say is she's tough and she deals with things the way she deals with them, and sometimes it's alone. That's her way. It's best to leave her be."

Her mouth opens to respond, but she thinks better of it and squeezes my shoulder.

"I appreciate your help and you being so nice to her," I say.

She smiles that smile again. "Well, you know your mom, but we all need someone. Connection is a human thing. We all recognize that especially if there's something...propelling us to an inevitable conclusion."

Sara is right. Dr. Savoie uses too many words.

"What I mean to say, Mr. King, is to visit her if and when you can as much as you can handle. I'm sure your mom will appreciate it and, in the end, so will you."

She glides to the bank of elevators beyond the clustered desks and computer screens, past the glossy pictures of doctors pretending to care for patients with rosy cheeks and hope in their eyes. I start to follow when I hear my name again. A nurse with flat dark eyes and golden skin motions me to the desk.

"Mr. King, we still need the rest of your mother's insurance information."

"I'm not sure what it is. I don't really handle that."

Alice begged me to visit Sara before all this. In that cramped, dirty apartment, where my childhood was broken off into my blood on the floor, and the men in her room and the light in the refrigerator with no food.

"Well, do you know who does, because we have to contact them in order to maintain care and we can't do that without—"

"Money. Yeah, I get it. What's the balance?"

"I don't have the current information, sir. Accounts Receivable would deal with that."

"Give me an estimate," I say, my voice starting to rise.

The nurse's tiny nose goes slightly in the air and she closes her eyes though I can see the slight roll of them under her lids. "Sir, as I said, I don't have the current information. So anything I say..."

"Goddamn it! Just tell me what the hell I need to know!"

The rest of the nurses' eyes cut in our direction, a pack of wolves ready to protect their own.

"Mr. King, I'm gonna need you to lower your voice!" She smooths her crisp uniform as if it had wrinkled from my shouting. "If you don't have your mother's information, there are programs that can subsidize her care. Medicare. Medicaid. I'm sure you can visit one of those offices and they can help you. I'm trying to let you know what's coming."

"Help? Yeah if that's what you call it. I'll get my own subsidy or grant or whatever," I say softer.

"Of course you will." The fake politeness drips from her thin lips as a smile mars her ashen face.

Death isn't the hard part. It's the money it takes to die. Money I got tied up in other things and doesn't deserve to be spent on Sara, on a mother, even if she's my own.

But we all need a backup plan and I have the church. And I ain't planning on praying for money either. I just have to ask for it. Church folk, folk like my wife, Alice, would say ask in Jesus's name. I don't have to ask Jesus though. I just have to ask Reverend Jackson Potter Sr.

Problem solved. Prayer answered. Ain't God good?

JACKSON BLAISDELL POTTER SR.

Three lines and forty-five words. I have no idea how I am going to minister to my congregation. My left shoulder is tight and I want to pour a glass of whiskey and drink until my body is slack and slumped and I no longer have the energy to think how much my daughter, Layla, disrespects me. She pushes and pushes until you give her what she wants. That, or you better move to a remote location where she can never, *ever* find you.

All I want to do is protect and provide understanding, and I can never figure out how to do both. Perhaps because to protect I must omit, blur lines and control what I present myself to be in front my church. And to my family.

This chair is too soft. I can't get comfortable. I stare at the mostly blank notepad. There is one sermon I have in reserve, but it's one I can never deliver so I'll leave it tucked away safely, in my Bible.

Rushing footsteps shuffle past my door and voices whisper bits of gossip about a funeral for a God-fearing woman, a woman whose life was taken too soon by a beautiful city with a lot of ugly, broken parts.

Some in our church and others who live on the twisting blocks of neighboring apartments whisper that Alice probably stored away money in the house and that's what the murderer wanted. They always saw her scurrying about with stacks of papers and folders. Maybe those papers held some secret accounts. Others hear Lebanon turns a good profit at the bakery, so he probably also had thousands or tens of thousands stashed somewhere in the house.

It's foolish listening to idle gossip. There's never knowledge gained, just temporal excitement.

Many people believe it was a random act of violence, and our lives, black lives, are like that. Unforeseen patterns shape our fate. And on the South Side of Chicago, we exist with a unique kind of knowledge of how fragile life unfolds among these clustered rows of brick, cement and asphalt.

I need answers like everyone else. The problem is, I'm not supposed to be like everyone else. I'm supposed to know or at least act like I know.

Addressing her murder in my sermon puts upon me a pressure I haven't felt in a long while. Reconciling myself with the fact Alice is dead is proving difficult. I'm dealing with my own guilt, my eyes overlooking bruises pancaked over with makeup and long-sleeved blouses on ninety-degree days.

What are the odds that Lebanon just abused her, but didn't kill her outright?

The odds are low. They are very, very low.

Persuading others to put their faith in a God that didn't protect a good person is not easy, but forgiving myself could prove damn near impossible.

Lost in my meditation, I don't notice as the door creaks open and he strolls in. Doesn't knock. Doesn't care. Doesn't respect the title on the door.

Nothing about Lebanon is friendly or shouts *friend* to me anymore, but that's what he's *supposed to be*, that's what he was to me at one point long ago. That's what I still want to see in him, what I need to feel in my bones, but those are cold, like the windowpane rattling against the gusts of wind.

"Need a favor."

"They're never favors. You just come in here and give orders like you run this place," I say.

"Dramatic as always, Jack. Damn! I don't ask if I don't need."

"Stop cursing. Have some respect for this place, and my place in it."

"Your place."

The door remains open and the hall, though at this moment empty of walking bodies, isn't empty of listening ears. He follows my every move as I rise and close it behind him. I move deliberately, every limb and muscle careful not to incite suspicion or anger.

"You do that, you know? You tiptoe around me like Alice does, did. I hate that."

Did he hate her or something about her so much that he took her life? I piece the night together as I remember it. Layla getting the call from Ruby. Her rushing out, her momma and me following behind. Blue lights, yellow tape, brown bodies and a redbrick house with rigid white bodies cycling in and out. Lebanon's eyes filled with tears when people looked, his body shivering with grief when eyes wandered over his frame. But when people didn't look, those few moments when something else grabbed their attention, the tears and the grief briefly seemed to dissipate.

"This is a private conversation. Listening ears and all," I respond.

"Sure. Whatever you say, man. Now about that favor."

"No. Whatever it is, I got things I need to do. And you need to be with Ruby right now."

"Don't tell me about my family, Jackson. Worry about yours."

"Don't let this robe fool you, Lebanon. Watch your mouth about my family."

Wind rattles the windowpanes. Lebanon stares at the picture of me and my father on my desk and picks it up, the hard glint in his eyes softening a moment. I couldn't have been more than six or seven in the picture, and I'm looking up at my father maybe the way all children look at their fathers at one point in their lives, with a mix of love and awe. He was telling me to look at Momma, but I refused to look at anyone but him. I had what some called a charmed life. Blessed. Then one night two officers came to the door of my home saying my father, Pastor Thomas Potter, died in a car accident. Some criminal trying to outrun the cops caused a good man to not come home. The guy who killed Dad died too, so I suppose there is some justice in that.

"Uncle Thomas was a good man."

"Yeah, he was."

"You're a good man, too. A good pastor."

"Now you want to sweet-talk me into doing your bidding." I sit back down behind my desk and begin writing, trying to compile something, *anything* for a sermon I have to deliver in an hour or so.

"Nah. I don't have to do that. You're gonna do what I ask, but this picture reminds me of something...something good and I wanted to acknowledge it, I guess."

He sets the picture reverently back down on my desk. My breath catches and I'm still caught off guard by how much I miss Dad. You don't forget those who mold you or how disappointed they'd be if they saw how misshapen you've become in this world.

"What do you want? 'Cause you want something, and I got a sermon to finish up."

"I saw her today. Sara."

I drop my pen. "It's been..."

"Over ten years. Since Naomi's funeral. Only time I'd ever seen Sara cry."

"But why?"

"Sara called me. She's dying, wants me to help her make arrangements. Crazy right?"

"Isn't that something you've always wanted? Her. Dead."

His dry, bitter cackling bounces off the walls. "I've wanted a lot of people dead," he responds while looking straight in my eyes. "Anyways, hospital says it needs money."

"I'm not sure how you think I can help."

"Church is about charity isn't it?"

"Meaning..."

"You're really gonna make me beg, Jackson, Reverend-Pastor-

Apostle-All-Good-All-Knowing Jackson Potter Sr.? I mean instead of charity, I could make church about confession," warns Lebanon.

I stop scribbling and glare at him.

"Come on, man. I was kidding," he teases.

"No. You weren't."

"What happened stays with us. You go out there, preach, be their god."

"I'm not a god."

"Don't seem to mind sacrifices like one, Jackson."

I swallow hard with no comeback for this statement. It twists like a knife in my stomach. Now, I'm back there in a dirty hotel room staring at a painting of vast wilderness with no way out. Pleading to God to forgive me. Wanting to tell someone what really happened to a boy named Syrus, but my voice and self-preservation keep me silent.

Lebanon saunters to the bookcase running his fingers over etchings and trophies, stock paper with my name in loopy letters embossed with gold print.

"You accomplished so much when I was locked up," he says.

"I don't know how you think the finances work here, but it's not just my eyes on the paperwork." I pretend to write again. "Can't you figure out your own problems? You always come to me to clean up your messes."

"Remember who started that tradition, Jackson."

I could reach across my table and punch him, bloody that nose, mess up that pretty high yellow face women seem to love. I remain in my chair. I try to count slowly and let my rage escape in uneven breaths. "We already helped with Alice's burial costs."

"And you can eventually help with Sara's, but for right now I need some money to pay a hospital bill. Come on, Sara was Aunt Violet's friend too, right?"

"Yeah Sara was Mom's friend. Still is for whatever reason."

"Probably the same reason we still friends."

"That's what you call it?"

Lebanon smiles big and wide. That perfect row of teeth. I know what's coming. He'll ask the impossible of me and I see my life in this moment as if I can reach out and touch it, and I know to go right, but I'll still propel myself left. Because I still owe him.

Damn it.

"Tell whoever you have to tell, whatever you have to tell them. Make the check out to the bakery like always, Jackson. It should be for $9,000 at least. Meet me by that spot after church, the one your dad would take us to. Be there around 2:30 p.m."

"I have to be at another service around that time."

"And you'll make time for this. Me being happy is important to you and for you, Jackson. Remember that."

The door creaks open and he walks out.

I still possess the three lines and forty-five words I managed to cobble together before Lebanon's arrival. I am bereft, defeated in this moment, laid naked to all the things I know about myself and that he knows about me, but I'm alone in this circle of dark winter nights and infinite debt.

I unlock my drawer and write the check.

CHAPTER 3

CALVARY

September 17, 1960

A young girl walks into my hall wearing a yellow dress with white flowers. She wants forgiveness. She wants solace. She wants resolution. I can't give this to her, but I can provide a place where she is safe and where the night holds no fear, only stillness.

Hands grasping together so tight, the only word leaving her lips is, "Please." This drastic begging, calling out to God in the heaviest of her pain, her fear—listening to these pleas is my ministry.

I cannot comfort, nor put human arms around a body, but I can *be*. I can *stand*. I can hear their cries, feel their despair and be present with them.

The young girl in the yellow dress thinks about home. She thinks about her mother, who died when she was nine. She gave her a rag doll with black buttons for eyes. Her mother said the doll would protect her when she was hurt or scared, or if she needed a friend. She thinks about her father's hands, how they are rough and how they grab her in the night. How he puts them over her mouth and how her tears hopscotch over his fingers, never falling to her pillow. She thinks about how those hands tear and grasp and touch and she thinks about her hands and her pretty yellow dress with the white flowers, and she looks down at her fingers now gently cupping her belly.

Please. Please. Please.

LAYLA

Though the heat coming from the vents in the floor of the worship hall provides some relief, the morning's chill even now stubbornly stays under my skin. My internal temperature has more to do with feelings than the mercury level on the thermometer. By now I should be toasty and relaxed, but this coldness is my unshakable companion for now, and each time I close my eyes, I see Ruby as she was a week ago, crouched and small in a detective's car, rocking back and forth. I bent down and all she could say was "Momma" over and over. I touched her hand and it was sticky. There was blood on it and then blood on mine.

There were onlookers from the doorways of various houses. One small neighborhood devoured by night and flashing blue lights. Nosy people hungry for details. Reporters say this is a tragedy, but always mark their tones with a rehearsed cadence about violence and the South Side of Chicago. It's a wasteland, but a place where they can test the exploitative extent of their craft and leave. We're a minute blip on someone's television. Sixty seconds and my friend is ruined, or ruined even more than she already was.

My parents arrived soon after I did. Mom was bereft but she was not crying. Hers is an expected grief, the sadness that comes from losing someone close to you, someone who's been sick a long time. She knew she'd lose Alice to Lebanon and it would be ugly.

Mom kept Alice's secrets. She took calls in a midnight hour, soothed and coddled, pleaded, begged and threatened, but could never convince Alice to do the thing she really needed—to leave. She'd make plans for Alice. Called dozens of shelters. Slipped Alice their pamphlets before Sunday School, like valuable contraband in a prison yard. But Alice always had a reason or a plan of her own. Alice hoarded pamphlets, ones about family counseling, crinkled, torn and dog-eared. They'd whisper in the basement of the church. And me and Ruby would listen, hidden, clasping our hands together, both hoping Alice would see. That she'd know the best thing to do was abandon hope this one time and leave with Ruby—to Tennessee or Tuscany, it didn't matter. They just needed to go! But they never did. The people at church glossed their eyes over bruises and swallowed the poorly explained reasons of why these things *always* seemed to happen to Alice. "It ain't any of my business," was a common refrain. But now, they shake their heads and cry their tears, wondering how this could've happened. There are only whispers around Auntie Alice's life and what was happening and how she could have been saved.

That night Dad stands there and does what he always does: acts like the pastor. He prays for Ruby, skin and clothes stained in her mother's blood. He speaks to the people on the street. They attend the church after all. No one daring to say anything true or shoulder any of the responsibility as friends of Alice.

The detectives mill around, go in and out of the house, ask us questions. They are faceless with white skin and harsh, measured voices. Respectful, but businesslike and distant. They see this too much. Especially here.

Live white faces. Dead black bodies.

There have been burglaries in the past few weeks around here, they say. Auntie Alice probably startled a burglar before they could take anything, they say. Ruby found Alice and it was too late by then, they say. Open and shut. Tragic. They're still going to canvas the neighborhood. There are some suspects they have in mind for this. They'll be in touch, they say.

One of the detectives hands me a card made of cheap stock paper. Lebanon stands on the street smoking a cigarette. He gives the detectives the song and dance. Lebanon says he was on his way home from work. He says people saw him leave, but the bakery is only ten minutes away by foot. Lebanon easily could have done it. But should I say anything?

Tears come, salty false drippings cascade from his swampy green eyes, down his high cheekbones. He loved Alice, his wonderful wife. What is he gonna do without her? He's convincing. One of the detectives puts his hand on his shoulder, swears they'll find the monsters responsible for this.

I want to believe I can feel Ruby's pain. I want to believe the pounding in my head, the bumps raised on my left arm are some cosmic sign we're connected, that she has the same headache and bumpy skin. We used to play this game when we were younger. We'd hold hands and close our eyes and guess a color or a number one of us was thinking. Ruby's hands were soft but grabbed mine with such force my skin turned crimson. Ruby was always right about my colors and numbers, but I could never guess hers. She would always say, "I'm not easy to read, Layla. But your heart is open, and that's why you don't need to be good at this. I just need you to be good at being my friend, and you're better than good at that."

I know what haunts Ruby is rooted in circumstances that I have yet to imagine like in our game. I probably don't want to know. I'm glad I'm seeing her this afternoon. I want to show her I'm here, that I'll do whatever I can because there's nothing more hopeless than believing you're alone. I'll show Ruby I'm still that good friend. Together we can come up with a plan to get her away from Lebanon, then she can finally be free. And I want to help her, in the way Mom couldn't for Auntie Alice.

I'll have to skip the second service to see her, but I have a plan: ask my dad in front of a couple of parishioners. He always plays the understanding father in front of others.

I always wondered why we needed multiple services in one day. There is only one Bible and only so many books in it. If you didn't get the message in the morning, will the sun going down make your hearing any better? Sometimes I think I've had enough worship for this lifetime and the next one. The one after that, too. Other times, when I struggle like I do now, I simply talk to God, no need to kneel or quote scripture or be all formal, just talk, and despite all my shortcomings, I know He's there and He hears me and I have hope.

God doesn't judge me. But my father sure does.

Laying the last of the programs on the cherry-colored cushions of the pews, I hear the reluctant groan of the wood doors at the main entrance announcing its first visitor. Not so much a visitor, but an inhabitant, a piece of the church as much as the bricks and mortar holding it together.

My momma, First Lady Joanna Lillian Potter, walks toward the front of the room still bundled in a black wool coat and black-and-white scarf featuring fleur-de-lis in a diagonal pattern. Her black hat reflects an elegant style, a double white band wrapped around the middle becomes a bow in the back and emphasizes a wide brim. My mom has a thing for hats. She has dozens. Most people would call it an obsession. She calls it a hobby. Her hobby takes up two closets at home, but this is a small indulgence she allows herself and, living with my dad, one of the few she can afford.

When TV pastors brandish their fine-tailored suits and gold-plated pinkie rings, I kinda wonder why Dad couldn't be *that* kind of pastor. The one taking five offerings and only half of one goes to the church. I guess I should be glad money isn't his driving force, but I don't know what motivates him.

Looking up at my mom, I smile.

Her long black hair shows veins of soft gray throughout. A flawless brown complexion easily camouflages her forty-nine years.

I hug Momma in a specific way. I don't really embrace her, rather I simply bend my five-foot-eight-inch frame and rest my head on her shoulder. She isn't a tall woman. She teases she gave me and my brother all of her height. Despite being at least three inches shorter, her arms encircle my body and she easily holds my weight. My nonhugging ways elicit the same response every time: laughter.

"I don't get it, Mom."

"What, baby?"

"You married Dad. No gun to your head. Why?"

Mom chuckles again, but her voice, its dulcet measure, reveals a small sadness of a marriage filled with love and disappointment. I know this laugh. I know its undertone of acquiescence in parts, but earnest belief in others.

"Why doesn't he ever listen?"

"I can't begin to explain the whys of your father, sweetie."

She lets me go and says, "He is a good man."

This is as much of a statement as it is a prayer.

I unlock the rest of the church for the people who will enter its doors needing a word from God or, like me, a relief from the relentlessness of my thoughts.

RUBY

Save yourself, baby.

I knew it would happen. Soon. That he'd see me and what I'd done. That he'd want me to surrender to him because of who he is and what he knows. He wanted me to bend like Mom and I refused. I wasn't going to clean the kitchen. Wash a dish. Sweep a crumb or clean a countertop. I wondered how many days before he'd start in on me since Mom isn't here. He can't explode his rage and fear on her anymore. I was next. Now I know. Less than ten days, which was longer than I thought.

The sand-colored tile floor is hard and cool against my right cheek. A familiar taste of blood lingers in my mouth. It's not always metallic, and it can be kinda sweet. Witnessing Mom recover from His tantrums, I don't get up too fast. I let the air settle again around me and feel the slight hum of the new refrigerator through the floor when it cuts on and off. I count three cycles before I try to get up.

I take a deep breath and crawl to the sink. It provides enough leverage for me to hoist myself up. Legs with the sturdiness of rubber bands somehow guide me to my bedroom.

I text Layla. Beverly Café. 1:30 p.m.

Afterward, in the bathroom, I study the slightly raised and bruised skin of my neck. His fingers are no longer around my airway, but I still feel them clenching, squeezing, tightening. I flailed, kicked, fought, the edges of my vision turning the deepest black.

To clean the kitchen like he demands is so simple. Don't fight it. Just perform.

"It's your house. You clean it."

Those two sentences when they leave my mouth are *freedom*. They are the words I wanted my mother to speak so many times. But she can't so I will speak for the both of us. It's the only way I find a purpose. It's the only time I feel brave, just for a moment.

The knock on the front door comes in three soft coded taps. I brace myself on the wall and make my way to the living room where Ms. Anne waits in her white housecoat with the red and purple flowers.

"He slammed the door. When he slams the door, I know there's trouble. What happened?"

It's the stupidest question. *She knows what happened.* She's known since we moved here when I was six years old. And before I meet Ms. Anne's face, I already know the pity I'll see in her dark brown doe eyes. Those eyes scanned Mom's swollen cheek or bruised eye. She'd avoid the cause and instead spout off a remedy. What'll help ribs heal faster, what ointment will cover up this scar or mend that wound. She could've used her fingers to dial the police, pick Lebanon out of lineup, but she used her fingers for other kinds of healing. She kept the same secret my Mom did. She's a nice woman who helped Mom through her mess rather than out of it. Maybe Ms. Anne didn't know any better.

She's from a different time.

These things probably happened to her and her friends. They probably bandaged each other up because what were they going to do? Go to the police? They barely do anything for us now, only come after the crime is done not before. And forty or fifty years ago? A man beating on a woman wasn't their concern. And black women—no one cared about us. They don't care about us now. I don't think Ms. Anne knows what to do except what she's been doing most of her life. Lebanon isn't a threat to her. He's just another man. Like her husband was just a man. Like probably her friends' husbands were just men. Black men. These women didn't need any more burdens on their shoulders, because they were already carrying a heavy enough load.

"Sit down," she orders. I sink into the couch and she shuffles down the hall into the kitchen. She comes back with a warm towel and plucks two small bottles of holy oil and cocoa butter from her left pocket. "Child, what did you do?"

I'm Child. Not named in her eyes because my decades on this earth barely register two, and her decades push past eight.

"I don't know," I reply. "I don't know what I did."

"Anything seems to set that man off. Could be that time he spent locked up that made him mean like that. Your momma said she always thought that's what made him lose his temper the way he did with her."

"She didn't talk about it with me. Not that part. Him being in prison. Besides, nothing should excuse what he does. Nothing. It doesn't matter if he was in jail. I know——"

"You're young. You don't know! Life sometimes justifies lots of things for you. Now hold still and let me look at you."

Ms. Anne prays. She prays God heals me, then mutters men are no good; that they aren't built to love, only built to damage. Then she prays for God to mend her heart. Her fingers, light yellow sausages, massage my neck. They touch the same places Lebanon bruised, and I'm tired of her praying. I'm tired of knowing all the names of God. Those names are broken promises. Like the times Lebanon said he wouldn't touch Momma, but something always found a way of upsetting him and he'd break.

"It's enough. I'm good now," I tell Ms. Anne.

"Just give me a little more time else them markings gonna stay a lot longer than you want 'em to." She picks up the towel and places it around my neck.

I snatch it off. "Let everyone see. I don't care anymore!"

"Child, just——"

"Go! I'm not covering anything up. Not like Mom. Not anymore… Just go. I know you mean well, but I don't need your kind of help, Ms. Anne. Just go. Please."

She says nothing else, gathers her holy oil and cocoa butter, and shuffles out of the door.

There's no ointment or prayer that can heal mean. No one to deliver me like the fairy tales in storybooks or churches.

We look to others to save us and we must save ourselves.

CALVARY

Violet, Sara and Naomi in their jean overalls and colorful hair scarves begin to slather my halls in this horrid shade of green. "This paint makes me think of Caribbean waters," Naomi says. "Just floating with the sun hitting your skin. The color's relaxing."

Though very different, the three girls are harmonious when together. Familial blood does not bond them. There is something deeper shared, maybe past lives or common troubles. Whatever small and pure miracle, these girls found one another and became as close as the Old Testament Hebrew boys from the Book of Daniel. Despite their shared knowledge of how empty and cruel the world can be, they are sisters and fierce protectors one of the other.

From their earliest years, they learn together, play together, fight and reconcile. And there is a phrase that means how they love one another—"Forever and to the end." That's what they say instead of "I love you." When uttering this phrase, only they know what they mean. The three girls have something all their own. The world takes so much, sometimes words are all one can possess.

It is their secret to keep, one of many. Some of their confidences, schoolgirl crushes, skipped classes, are cotton candy light, sweet pink fluff, easily consumed and devoured in giggly pleasures. However, in the deep, uncompromising mystery of friendship, there are the things they keep to themselves for the sake of each other. Things, that for Sara, are acutely destroying her.

This damage is not quick. It is slow and painful as the stripping of thin layers of skin. Bearing this fire, this silent torment, changes Sara in ways her friends know. Violet and Naomi suspect something foul. Sara's father's hand lingers too long on her waist. Naomi saw him kiss Sara, like she was a woman. Naomi closed her eyes and quickly prayed, and opened them again. She saw the same thing. She told Violet the next day.

But what could the two of them do? What could they say to their dads? Their congregation? Naomi would be told she didn't see what she thought they saw. They'd be labeled troublemakers. Their families spoken about. Lord knows what would become of Sara! You can't go against a pastor, not with accusations of something so unspeakable.

So they suffer in silence with her, but try providing distraction and comfort and laughter and happiness whenever and wherever they can offer it. Painting my hallways this atrocious color is what they concoct for now, hoping they can get her to talk—if that's even a possibility.

Sara's brush batters my wall as she slashes up and down, criss-cross with no thought for technique. In her bag, a cloth doll named Louisa sits patiently with black button eyes in a pretty green dress and perpetual sewn-on smile. She takes the doll almost everywhere, a reminder her mother will always watch over her.

"Girl, do you have to take that doll with you all the time? We're almost twenty, people are starting to ask questions," Violet teases.

"It reminds her of Ms. Sophia. Leave it be," Naomi warns, her frame barely five feet, she rises on her tiptoes to reach the farthest corner on the northeast wall.

"Don't worry about what's in my bag," Sara says. "Worry about getting these walls painted like the pastor, my father, asked." It's the tone in which she said *pastor* and *my father* that causes Violet to grit her teeth. A few loose strands of Sara's light brown hair are ornamented by tiny speckles of green paint.

"I'd never choose this color," Violet continues. "This paint makes me think of mint ice cream that melted after it hit the ground."

"You like green!" says Naomi.

"Not *this* green!" Violet replies. "But this was the only color he agreed to. Like he's the king of England or something. It's green, who cares what shade we use for Revival?"

Every year for three nights, Revival was held at different churches in the Chicago community. This year it is held within my walls. Thursday to Sunday. Preaching and singing and praying will take place with renewed vigor under my roof. Revival is a tradition. It is a movement that sparks other movements of equality. Revival lures people out of gin-soaked taverns and dance halls with the opportunity of salvation for sins past and present.

Other people from churches within the city and beyond arrive to celebrate or mourn or release whatever pent-up anguish is harbored in their lives. These are people to whom the indifference of the world felt many times over is too much to bear. Brown bodies will arrive through my doors, seeking an impossible solution to injustices not provided by the nation at large. But the relief they feel need not be complete, just enough so that they can return to their normal lives with the strength to deal with the indignities large and small suffered because of skin color.

"Well, *he is* the pastor of this church, Violet. You know how big it is for Revival to be held here! So many churches are attending. We have to represent Calvary Hope in the best way possible," reasons Sara, her hand shoots to her hip, her dark brown eyes cutting toward her friend.

"*My father* being pastor would be the best way to represent this church," Violet says. "But it's a damn popularity contest around here. And we all know King Saul is popular."

"Stop calling him that." Sara's face tightens, her skin flushing red, her fists balled up at her sides. She hates that name! It was never meant as a compliment, but a warning. Sara remembers what happened to King Saul in the Old Testament. How he was a temporary king. How he eventually fell to David. Maybe if she was more righteous, maybe if she was more holy, maybe if she painted these walls the way her father liked. Maybe things would stop. Maybe Violet would stop being mad at her for things she couldn't change. And maybe her father would stop.

"He worked hard to get this," Sara whispers.

"You don't even believe that," Violet says looking at her. "Your daddy is light skinned with pretty eyes. Your daddy knows everybody on the church board. Your daddy, Reverend Saul King, is so perfect, huh?"

"You don't know anything, Violet," Sara says. "You talk so much but you don't know a damn thing."

Violet steps closer to Sara who drops her paintbrush, which luckily lands in the bucket, though a few splatters mar my concrete floor.

"Be nice," says Naomi who steps in between the two girls. "We're not gonna keep doing this. We're friends. Cradle to grave. That's how it is. That's how God wills it. Forever and to the end."

Naomi holds Violet's stare until she breaks it, bends down and resumes painting. Naomi then turns to Sara who again picks up her brush and returns to slathering my walls.

"Forever and to the end," Violet and Sara mumble.

"Now, it's a good color," Naomi continues. "This basement could use some lightening up."

"Like your face," quips Violet, who then flicks small droplets of paint to her right, hitting Naomi. Harsh looks and harsher words almost forgotten, Naomi and Sara run after Violet, laughing.

They speed through my halls, light cascading in cloudy shapes, never quite catching the quickness of the girls' movement, their jostling. Raucous pattering of shoes resonates in heavy thuds on my floor.

"What's all this noise?" a voice booms from the edge of the hallway tapering off into the worship hall.

Reverend Saul King looms in front of the girls, and Violet,

unable to stop herself in time, slams into him and tumbles to the ground. She quickly scrambles onto her feet.

Saul King isn't an especially tall man, he barely reaches six feet, but his compactly muscled body, honed by years of construction work, gives him the appearance of a modern-day gladiator clad not in armor, but a nicely tailored blue suit. His light skin and pretty green eyes cause flirtatious stares from women, hearty handshakes from men. When he smiles, all rumors about his character quickly dissipate like water on summer-baked sidewalks. But he's not smiling now.

"I gave y'all permission to repaint this basement 'cause Revival is tonight and we gotta make sure the church looks its best. I also want you to make sure this one," he says pointing to Sara, "stays out of trouble. Are y'all the bad influence I gotta keep her away from?"

Reverend King stares hard at the trio. Naomi and Sara tremble, hands crossed behind their backs, heads down. Violet looks at the Reverend in his eyes. Her father is the assistant pastor, second in charge, and she pushes King Saul at every opportunity.

"Violet, do I have to speak to your father? Better yet the church board? That wouldn't be a good reflection of your father's performance. They surely do listen to me, the church board does." Saul King smiles cruelly. "Also, it'd be more of a shame for you and young Thomas Potter to have to get married somewhere else, if I were to say something."

Violet grits her teeth and bows.

Reverend King pats Violet on the head, then turns to leave. "Good girls. Now this kind of lack of temperance, this arrogance of will is something that displeases God, is it not?"

"Yes, sir," they answer as one body. Sunlight cuts through my glass block windows.

"Will disobedience be tolerated?"

"No, sir," they answer, again as one.

Sara focuses only on her father's light brown shoes, how they make the same hollow tap just before they approach her bedroom door in the night. The squeaky twist of the doorknob. The smell of lilies from Louisa's black yarn hair.

"We're sorry, Reverend Saul. We were having fun and we got carried away is all," Naomi whispers. "Won't happen again. We promise. It's like you said in your sermon this past Sunday, 'God favors those who favor forgiveness.'"

"So you *do* listen, little Naomi."

"I treasure your sermons, Reverend," her soprano voice almost a whisper in my halls.

Violet smiles wide, hoping King Saul can't see from her bowed head the wide arch it creates in her cheeks. Naomi always falls asleep at some point during the sermons! So much so Violet and Sara take turns pinching her sides to keep her awake.

"Well, you're right, Naomi. As the Bible says, 'To err is human, to forgive divine.'"

Violet barely stifles her laughter. She's not sure if King Saul even cracks open the Bible except for Sunday mornings. That quote is from Alexander Pope.

"And what's this?" Reverend King strolls to Sara's bag. "You still carrying this doll around with you?"

"It helps me remember Momma," Sara murmurs, her voice barely floating past Violet's ears. He snatches Sara's doll from her bag.

"Put away childish things, Sara," he orders, his voice heavy with authority. "You're a...woman now."

Violet slightly raises her head and turns, Saul King's back and shoulders impeding most of her vision. Saul's hand rests on Sara's arm and then travels to her waist. Violet quickly whips her head back down farther into a bow. Her arm breaks out in skinny little bumps. Violet tries to float along in thought, tuning out most of King Saul's rambling. Moments later, she peeks her head up and sees him turning the corner away from them and out of sight.

Spent, the girls slouch down on the ground leaning against my walls.

"You know that quote 'To err is human...' isn't in the Bible—" Violet starts.

"I know!" Naomi whispers, her small hands covering her smile. "Didn't have the heart to say anything."

"My mom stopped correcting him," Sara offers. "She said you can't teach an ass to stop being an ass."

For a moment, the girls laugh hard and loud and free. Sara is laughing such, tears spring from her eyes, until Naomi and Violet realize these are no longer laughs, but sobs, angry and unbound. She's talking, but it's hard to make out what she's saying.

Naomi holds her and speaks softly, "What's wrong? You can tell us."

Sara lifts her head, her tears covering her face so that her skin seems to move with the liquid leaking from her dark brown eyes.

"I told him, no, but he wouldn't stop."

"You told *who* to stop," Violet asks.

"My father, the righteous and holy Revered Saul King. He wouldn't stop what he was doing, and Mom's gone so, I got no one, but y'all."

"What did he do?"

All Sara can do is look down. She can't say those words, what he did, to her friends. She doesn't need to. All she can muster is, "I been sick in the mornings. It's been happening for a while now. My clothes are getting tighter. I know what's happening to me. Momma explained woman things before she died. I know I can't hide this. He'll kill me if he finds out. I know he will. He can't have me around the church like that...too many questions."

They know. Her eyes tell them what Sara's father did and the terrible consequence.

For a while, no one speaks. They hug and cry. Violet, however, can stand feeling sorry for only so long before taking action. Standing up, she wipes her face. "We need a plan. You can't go back there, so we gotta figure out what to do."

"Where can I go? He's the pastor, above reproach, above everything I guess. No one's gonna believe me."

"I believe you," says Violet.

"I believe you, too. And we can help you. Let us," implores Naomi. "Now, my favorite aunt, Lennie Mae. She lives in Tennessee, in Memphis. She'll look after you. I won't tell her too much, but she's always been a kind spirit. She won't judge your situation."

"Tennessee?"

What is there for Sara in Tennessee? People she doesn't know, a different way of living, where her skin color is not a welcome sight in most places, an acquiescence, regression about black life and its meaning—and with this, she isn't comfortable. Chicago has its limitations, a place where white people have created this rigid little box for blacks. The inequality permeating the streets and neighborhoods is not ideal by any means, but it's livable. Down south, weight of segregation seems to be oppressive and immoveable. But what choice is there? Banishment to the South or the unknown dangers of her father.

Extending her hand, Violet orders, "Leave the rest to me. We're going to your house now, we'll get some clothes. You'll leave as soon as Revival is over. There'll be so much going on, King Saul won't know you're missing for a while.

"Time to go," Violet says. "Say goodbye to all this, to him. You'll never be back."

With those few words, Sara's decision is made, for a time. Violet thinks she has the answers, a set plan where God will allow everything to fall into that perfect and right place.

But Sara deep down in a place close to her blood and bone fears she will be back. That decision is made for her, too. Something will always bring her back to these walls, to her father, someone evil, but evil isn't new. It doesn't disappear. Men like him don't disappear, but maybe with Naomi's and Violet's help she can. Maybe they're right and she can leave. She must believe something good for once.

Walking to the end of the hall, they reach my entrance door leading to the densely packed street. The three girls look back at my half-painted basement wall, then at one another. Violet utters, "Forever and to the end." Naomi and Sara, respond in kind, "Forever and to the end."

They close my door.

CHAPTER 4

RUBY

FOUR DAYS AFTER ALICE KING'S DEATH

Funeral homes are funny places. There are fresh flowers and pictures of dead people in gold frames. This tries to pass as good taste, but it's creepy having painted eyes stare at you while you decide on whether your mother would like to be buried or cremated, which shade of white would she have liked her casket, brass handles or silver or chrome.

Why are there so many kinds of white? Do the creepy eyes think I have good taste?

Walls and ceilings consist of light brown, tan and bronze. Mom likes these types of colors; well, she liked them or would have liked them. They are boring and she is boring, *she was* boring. Boring was safe so boring was pretty. She finds, *she found* reds and yellows and pinks too loud, tactless for a "proper home." Different kinds of brown she likes, *she liked*.

It's been only four days. I still remind myself everything about her is now past tense, not present.

Layla asks all the proper questions in her most professional voice. I call it her "white girl" voice. That practiced, over-enunciating dialect we all must speak to be considered worthy of someone calling you intelligent or, worse, "articulate." She's great at *that voice*. Not too high or low, easily conversational, nonthreatening, nonregional and unstained with color or humanity.

I use this voice at the office, but I'm not as good as Layla. She probably perfected conversating like this in all the college classes teaching her philosophy and economics and sociology. She probably talked to her white friends over coffee and impressed her white professors who probably thought she could barely read the book they gave her, let alone understand it. I bet they thought she was the first person in her family to go to college, like in all those movies and television shows they enjoyed. I'm sure her "white girl" voice quickly eroded any idea of ignorance. Well, it probably didn't do all that, it probably just made them feel comfortable enough to invite her to their house for dinner. They probably even used the good silverware and only checked once or twice to make sure their valuables weren't stolen.

Why are there so many pamphlets on dealing with grief? They always use terms like *acceptance* and *family*. The safety cards in the backs of airline seats are more helpful at this point. I wonder what the funeral director would do if I bent my body and put my arms over my head.

My life is one big crash landing, isn't it?

I need more than a folded-up piece of paper to tell me how to deal with a dead mom, a demon posing as a grieving father and a color palette making me want to blind myself. But I have Layla, and I'm grateful, for a voice, for a friend, for something that doesn't consume me whole.

I hear Mr. Hawthorne, the funeral director, talking to me. His practiced somber voice, low tone, brown-black eyes sad but greedy for the insurance money his place surely needs to keep interring the dead for a hefty profit.

I find the worst in people. I think it's a gift.

"I'm sorry. I didn't hear you," I say. I try to take a deep breath, but the room smells funky, like butterscotch candy and fake pine trees.

He repeats, "Will you be droppin' off the burial outfit for dear Alice?"

Mr. Hawthorne didn't know my mother, but he calls her *Dear Alice*. I never heard Lebanon ever call her *dear* or *sweetheart* or *baby*, say *I love you*.

Layla hands me a tissue. I'm crying. Didn't feel it, but I don't feel much anymore. Maybe that's another gift.

Save yourself, baby.

"I'll take care of that," Layla replies.

"Very well, very well," he says.

Mr. Hawthorne stands. A well-tailored navy blue suit doesn't hide his broad stomach, but the material gives the appearance more so of former football player than man who sits on a scooter puttering down Walmart aisles. Fingers sheathed in skin a few tones lighter than an Oreo cookie grip my hand and solemnly repeat the six words I've heard dozens of times the past few days: *I'm so sorry for your loss.*

Layla's rusty black car slumbers in front of the Hawthorne Funeral Home. No one stole it. We're not that lucky.

"Let's grab something to eat. I'm starving," Layla suggests, her short camel-brown coat outlining the curvy silhouette of her frame. I wanted that coat, but I'm two sizes smaller.

"You're always hungry."

"You're always a pain in the ass."

She smiles so I smile. She hugs me and I return her embrace. It's the only true comfort I allow myself. I don't really deserve it or love or forgiveness. I deserve to be the one on a cold metal tray with brown-gray skin, filled with chemicals.

Mom should be here with Auntie Joanna choosing caskets and handles and planning a service I'd probably hate. Maybe Mom and I could've been here together planning out the service for Lebanon and I could have him buried in an old polyester jogging suit, plan a small service where no one would come and mourn him; put him in a small plot with no headstone—a final screw you. But he's not dead because life's not fair, and because God is as real as Santa Claus or rap stars who write their own lyrics or a father's love or maybe love itself.

The sun has yet to appear through the labyrinth of bloated slate clouds and the inside of Layla's car is slow to warm.

"Where do you want to eat?" she inquiress.

"Flowers. I want to go take care of the flowers first."

I can see her eyes dull a bit, but she tries to hide her slight disappointment and hunger and replies, "Sure. Whatever you want, Rue. You know what type Auntie Alice liked?"

"Gardenias."

LAYLA

Christy makes her way up the cracked stairs of the church. I stand out front and wave. I should've called and canceled. Said I had a bad cold, the church had a flood, something other than there was a murder and I needed to be there for my friend, my sister, Ruby.

During the commencement celebrations at my college, I invited Christy to visit the church. It was a vain attempt to keep her in my life and I didn't think she'd take it, but she did, and then she chose the one Sunday that couldn't have been more inconvenient.

Damn it. The pounding in my head now matches the muffled bass of a passing '80s Caddy with large rims, the words from the music lost in the vibration of the rattling frame.

With outstretched arms, a high-pitched squeal and a twitchy smile, Christy trots up in her heels and hugs me tightly.

"Oh my God, I missed you tons!" she says.

"You brought your dad?"

"Yeah, he said he wanted to come and be among the people."

Her father slowly scans the block at least three times before ascending the stairs with a smile and a handshake.

"Mr. Sikorska, so nice to see you."

"It's 'Senator,' dear. Will the car be okay out front like this?"

Already I hear the anxious superiority in his voice. I know he doesn't mean for it to come out, but there's an inherent assumption in his question, about where I live and that dividing line between State Street that to him separates the haves and the have-nots.

"It'll be just fine in *this* neighborhood, Senator."

His snow-white Lexus is parked near the end of the block. That car could probably feed three or four families in my neighborhood for a year. This bothers me just as much as the Senator's words and constant glances.

I remember hugging Christy goodbye at graduation last May, on campus with fresh air and elm trees. She got her degree in advertising, and I finished my graduate degree in journalism. Everything lay before us—changing the world and making fortunes within our grasp. I was going to use my education to right wrongs and become a troubadour of justice and truth. But beginning troubadours make very little money so I settled on a career in marketing at a boutique firm downtown. Christy's father, a state senator who now, according to the news, aspires to become a US senator, handed her a cushy job in his main campaign office. Her future already set. Her education already paid for. Her life laid out. No worries.

Must be nice.

A round face with a pug nose and a barely tamed crown of blond hair slicked with gel, he says, "So happy to be here."

"Happy to have you," I respond.

He again looks down the block to make sure no thugs have stolen the car or stripped it for parts in the three minutes since they've arrived.

"Sorry we're late. I got a little turned around. We normally don't go past 35th Street," Christy blurts out.

The Senator closes his eyes, slightly shaking his head.

"You're pretty much on time. We haven't even started Praise and Worship," I say.

Christy squints her eyes and I can see the question forming before she asks. I break down Praise and Worship in the simplest of terms for my friend: "It's basically songs and expression of thanks, some shouting, maybe speaking in tongues if Mother Wheatley's in the mood. It's the warm-up before a main event. It's loud, but happy. It's meant as a release from, well everything."

"Oh my God, this is going to be so much fun! So real. So different."

Christy is my friend. But it's not like with Ruby. There's a shallowness to our bond because I can't open myself and all my experiences to Christy. When Auntie Alice died, I should've been able to call her for emotional support, but I didn't. What would I have said? "Oh yeah all that crap you probably believed about where I live, where I come from, well it happened, someone close to me was murdered." It probably would've been a confirmation for her.

"So how long does church last?" Christy questions.

"As long as it has to sometimes," I respond. "Generally, about two hours, maybe more. It really depends."

"Geez, that's a while. We're out of Holy Name Cathedral in an hour."

"Well, Saint Sabina actually lasts a little longer than that I think."

Christy's ocean-colored eyes grow wide. "I totally forgot about that church."

"Yes, Christy." Senator Sikorksa adds, "African-Americans have a rich tradition when it comes to religion and let's not forget political action in church. It's not limited by denomination or category. All that money I paid for college, I'd expect you to know this."

"Of course, Daddy," she replies.

"It's fine. You're smart in other ways," he laughs and so does she, a sad, forced laugh at a joke at her expense.

He smiles again. "You know before the festivities, would there be time to speak with your father, dear?"

There are a million reasons why this is a bad idea. Two men with big egos and easy lies rarely lead to progress. But my father can take care of himself and entertain this charlatan. It wouldn't be the first time. But whatever favor the Senator seeks, hopefully Dad will be able to resist this one time and do what's best for the church.

LEBANON

"Why are you back so soon? You were going to church," the girl asks.

"You need to watch your tone. Your momma was too busy spoiling you and didn't teach you manners. You know that's why we got into that little argument this morning."

She pulls down her shirt collar. "Oh, you mean this?" Long markings reach around her throat, like my fingers are still there. I don't look long and continue to search for the debit card so I'll be able to deposit the check Jackson's gonna give me. He will give it to me.

"Look, I got a little beside myself. I can admit that. But when I tell you to do something, do it. The world ain't here to indulge you."

The girl stares at me in my own room like I'm an intruder, like I can't be in the home I pay for, in the place where I put food on the table. Her eyes are my eyes, but I don't know where my eyes came from. They could be my daddy's but Sara won't tell me. She's laying in a hospital bed dying. Sara could tell me something, show me she's a mother before she dies. Instead, all she does is look at me like the girl. I'm angry all over again.

"I need that damn debit card. Help me find it."

She turns her back to leave. I grab her arm, not realizing how hard.

"You're hurting me!" I tighten my grip a little more to let her know I mean business, that this isn't a game for me.

Sometimes when I get angry, it's like I'm outside myself and watching as I do these things. It comes in waves, this rage, big crashing waves, and I'm drowning in it and I can't breathe, and it's like I'm reaching for her, for someone to pull me up.

"Let go! I'll help! Let go!" she yells.

She's not like Alice. She doesn't whimper or get sad. I release her, she goes to the bureau searching around the open jewelry box and there under some old bills lies the card. She thrusts it at me and quickly walks out of the room. And instead of throbbing, bruised flesh, I grip thin, lifeless plastic.

My hands shake. My face in the mirror is twisted into something ugly, and I'm Sara. She looked this way after she hit me or blacked an eye or snapped a bone. Her eyes were faraway. I wasn't even worth her staying with me in that moment of pain. Sara would leave, and her hands would take over. I was still a little there when I'd take my anger out on Alice, or when I hit the girl. But I didn't do it a lot. I'd try to leave when I felt my rage bubble up, but people can push you and you do things you wouldn't do. I didn't hurt Alice or the girl as much as I feel my anger. It pulses almost constantly, like the blood in my arm. I can still be a good person and have those bad parts if I can make up for it. You can do things, awful, terrible things, but you can make up for it.

Breathe deep and think about the sun. It's not shining outside but it is in my mind. It's bright and gold. When my eyes open again, I see Alice's pearls poking out of the drawer of her silver jewelry box, the shimmering beads telling me what I need to do. I measure the size of them in my hand. They're delicate, the strand holding the bone-colored beads together. Doesn't take much to crush something so pretty, so fragile.

I find the girl at the kitchen table and lay the pearls in front of her.

"Your mom liked this necklace. Most expensive thing she owned I think. She'd probably want you to have them."

She doesn't touch them. She doesn't cry. She doesn't say thank you. I could've sold them. Kept them to myself, but I offer her something Alice loved and…nothing. She remains a pillar of salt.

A sharp knock on the front door pulls my attention away from this light-skinned, ungrateful girl. I almost ask Alice to answer the door before I realize she's not here to do that.

Two detectives stand outside of the door. Cantor and Jurgensen. They told me their first names the night Alice died, and I remember them. Not that I really need to. No point. All cops look alike. First, they're mostly white. Second, they have this air about them, not of authority. No, it's more an air of invincibility, that must be tied to the gun they wear on their beltline. They know they won't be held accountable for their actions. America doesn't need ropes and trees anymore to kill us. They have cops and the legal system to do its dirty work. You can't trust anybody, your friend, your mother, your daughter, but in my experience that goes triple for cops.

Sara was right. You're either the bully holding the magnifying glass or the ant.

"I'm actually leaving," I say trying to close the door behind me, but Jurgensen barges his way past my threshold. Even in the disappearing sunlight, I notice the wrinkles framing his face, a strong jawline, hidden by too many burgers and pastries; thick gray-and-chestnut hair covering slate-blue eyes.

"Well, are you coming to tell me you have some suspects or something? It's been over a week."

"Mr. King, finding the person responsible doesn't quite work out like you see on television," Cantor chimes in, a slit of dulled white teeth forming a tight smile.

"This isn't entertainment for me and my daughter, so excuse me if I think you're coming here to tell me you've got someone in custody."

"Of course, of course." Cantor's hand clasps my right shoulder and slightly wrinkles my suit, wispy red wrist hairs match the burnt copper mane on his head. The tan line of his expensive watch falls back to the tailored cuff of his shirt.

And that's it. If jail taught me anything, it's how police operate. They're nice at first. They act like they're my friends and they want to help me find out what really happened. Then they take my words and twist them, and they keep asking me things and saying no this didn't happen. I'm lying. I'm hiding. I'm worthless. And then come the fists. Then come the shouts. And the kicks. Then come my cries, and I don't even know it's me crying out into a room, in a place where it's just me. But, yeah, they're nice at first. Like right now.

"We have a few more follow-up questions. We won't take up much of your time," Jurgensen says scanning the living room, the pictures on the walls.

The light scraping of the chair in the kitchen steals his attention. The girl gets up and heads to her room.

"It'd be nice if we could talk to your daughter, too," says Cantor, his long nose twitching in the direction of the girl's shadow. He walks farther into the living room and stops two steps from the faded imprint of Alice's blood on my oak floors. These men enter and roam my house, and I must take it.

I step in front of Cantor. "She's not feeling well. Told her to lie down so you'll have to talk to her some other time." His eyes, green like mine, narrow a bit in challenge, but he thinks better of it and backs off.

"We're not meaning to intrude. We just want to clear up your whereabouts from that night."

That night, that collection of seconds and minutes bleeding heavy and slow like Alice.

"Why don't you have a seat, Mr. King?" Jurgensen says. It was an order he posed like a request to me in my own damn home.

Alice picked out that couch barely a month ago. I sit down as if I had a choice.

"I know it's hard to relive that night, but we'd appreciate it if you would take some deep breaths and recount your steps. That's all I need you to do. Connect the dots for me. It'll give us a better understanding, help us put together what happened," Cantor requests and it almost sounds like he's trying to help.

"Detectives, I told you what I told you that night. I left the bakery around 9:00 p.m. Then I came home and found the girl—"

"Your daughter?" asks Cantor.

"Yeah... She was holding Alice, begging her to stay, hold on, but she was gone, nothing behind her eyes anymore."

Cantor scratches something down in a notepad. "You know that look, Mr. King?"

"Yeah, I do. Suppose you do, too."

"Would anyone want to hurt Alice? Most of the items taken weren't worth very much. They even left a laptop in plain view. That's strange," Jurgensen says. He forces a smile.

"Alice interrupted them, and they killed her. They fled," I propose.

"That's a neat little summary, Mr. King. You got it all tied up in a little bow for us, huh?"

"That's what some of the cops was saying to me that night. Makes sense to me. What do you want me to say?"

Cantor looks back at Jurgensen waiting for some kind of permission, some signal from his partner, and Jurgensen nods.

"Look, we did some digging. I'm wondering why you haven't mentioned this." Cantor places a folder on the table. I open it, but I already know what's there. My mug shot. A statement with my shaky signature. A judgment that damned me years ago and damns me now. I remember the musty smell of the courtroom, how the proceedings were dry, mechanical and took about ten minutes. Ten minutes standing in front of a judge sent me to jail for five years for Syrus Myllstone's murder. My lawyer said he knew the judge so it could've been way worse, but everyone wanted to clear the case and be quick about it.

What's another black man dead? What's another black man behind bars? That's where we all end up anyway—dead, with some kind of ball in our hands or paraded around in front of reporters and carted off to cages. History comes around to visit sometimes and the repeats ain't always pleasant. That's what they think about us: we're entertainment or sacrifice of some sort.

I realize I'm not leaving unless I answer their questions, until they like the words coming out of my mouth. It puts another notch in their belt and another black man in chains, like I used to be.

I shrug my shoulders and answer, "I don't much see how my past has to do with what happened to Alice." They think they know about that night years ago and who I am as a result of it, but they only know black ink on a paper form. They don't know what I sacrificed.

"You okay, Mr. King? Your face is all red. You want me to grab you some water?" Cantor gets up, walks to my kitchen and produces a glass of water in a couple of minutes. How hospitable of him.

"We don't bring up the past to be cruel—" he continues.

"All people know is how to be cruel. Most of y'all cops think cruelty is something special you have."

Cantor sighs and finishes, "We need to know if what happened all those years ago might've had something to do with your wife's death."

"I don't think that has anything to do with Alice. Like you guys said, the night Alice died, it was probably a burglar. Now, you think someone wanted to kill her because of a mistake I made as a kid?"

Jurgensen scratches the side of his nose and says, "So murder is a mistake now?"

"It seems to be a mistake when y'all kill us in the streets."

Jurgensen lunges forward, but Cantor grabs his arm. The movement causes the vase on the coffee table separating us to slightly wobble.

I don't budge. This man with his nice clothes and thin smile don't scare me. Nothing much does anymore.

"We're just…looking at all the possibilities," Cantor says,

slowly rising and walking behind me. His hand back on my shoulder. "You're a religious man, Mr. King?"

"Suppose I am."

"Me too," Cantor commiserates. "It's not always the best combination—a cop and religious. But it provides comfort. You know, men of faith, like us, we can also be men of logic. We've still got to make sense of why something happened. We can't help but to ask questions, you know. Like, what if I decided to become a teacher? What if I'd taken Bishop here instead of Ashland? What if you'd gotten home a few minutes earlier from your shift at the bakery? What if the missus came home later from church?" Cantor leans in close and whispers, "What if it was *you* instead of her?"

The coffee he drank lingers on his breath and singes my nostrils a full minute before he sits back down on the couch next to Jurgensen who glares at me.

"We want answers, Mr. King. I'm sure you do, too," Cantor coaxes.

"Yeah, I want answers to lots of things—most of 'em you can't give me anyway. I told you what I told you and the girl isn't feeling good so you can either come back another time or take what you got and roll with it and find out who did this."

Cantor walks toward the door. Jurgensen's backside remains on my couch. "We're not done here, Mr. King. There are things not adding up. Like why did it take you so long to get home? I didn't think bakeries stayed open past nine at night."

"Seems to me you know a lot about bakeries," I fire back.

"Listen—"

"No you listen, Officer Jurgensen…"

"It's *Detective*…"

"I told you what I told you. I was only late coming home cause of paperwork. There's a lot of it since I took over the bakery, more than I thought."

"Not so good with numbers, huh? Yeah, some people said

your wife was smart like that. Understood where all the pluses and minuses went."

"That's the only reason I was getting back that late. If I finished sooner…then maybe, maybe… I don't know. I just know where I was instead of where you're trying to put me. Now, I gotta go to church. I'm already late." I stand up and head toward the door, opening it.

All their questions and suspicions eat up precious time, time I need to get to church, time I need to get my money, time I need to fix my life and get these detectives out of it.

"Church is more important to you than helping us find who killed your wife?" Jurgensen says, his tone trying to cut me with each word.

I meet Cantor's eyes. "Well, men of faith answer to someone higher. Perhaps, God can give you answers He didn't give me yet."

"You know how this can look to someone like us, Mr. King? It looks suspicious. *You* look suspicious," Jurgensen presses.

"Well, I've learned over the years I can't change how people look at me so I'm not trying now."

I close the door, and I know the kind of hell I've possibly brought down on myself, but I'm good with fire and fists and bullets and blood.

CALVARY

The little boy curls into the smallest ball, almost willing himself to disappear. He wriggles through the opening in my fence and finds my third window ajar. One of the deacons leaves it open so stale water from the previous day's rain won't leave such a pungent odor Sunday morning. The little boy pushes and shimmies down into my dank basement and, with featherlight footsteps, walks up the twelve stairs to the first floor and into the worship hall. His steps are sure in the sable embrace of evening.

The moon provides cool light, casting hideous shapes of the pews and the gold-plated altars spanning the right aisle on one side and the left aisle on the other. The little boy comes here a few times a week and always sits in the same place, the seventh row in the middle aisle. He prays. He's not scared of the creeping shadows bending around him because he knows real fear.

I find the place in the little boy's mind.

He hides behind a door in the corner of a basement where the dim bulb's light cannot reach. Most children are afraid of the dark and make-believe monsters, but for the boy shadows and darkness are welcome companions. And the monster in his life is not imaginary.

She is real. *She* is looking for him.

The little boy can hear those elephantine footsteps maiming the silence in the house.

"Get yo high yella ass out here now!" she'd shriek.

The little boy prays, "Make me good. Make me righteous. Keep me Lord in thine arms, forevermore. Amen."

This prayer. This prayer doesn't work. It never works, but he thinks maybe this time it will. Maybe *She* will become nice and tell him why she's angry all the time. He knows *She* loves him. It's beneath the layers. *She* can't see it, but he can. Just look harder and find it and they can be a family, the boy hopes. The boy prays. The boy lingers in the blackness.

The footsteps. The dust from the splintering floorboards showers him and he muffles a cough. He can feel the tightness in his chest from being here too long. He's going to cough again and *She* will find him. The footsteps are coming closer, and he knows what will happen. He can already feel the slaps and hits and kicks. He starts to shake.

The little boy can feel her hate, but he can't understand it.

She opens the door at the top of the stairs. The rough thump, thump, thump of rushing movement down the stairs. Water dripping into the stagnant puddle of the dead gray cement floor a few feet away. *She* is searching for him. Three doors open and shut. He's the fourth door. The bulb's light finds him and so does *She*. The monster.

She pummels him. He yells. Neighbors ignore the cries, bury themselves deeper in their own shallow tasks. If I had the ability for tears, I'd weep. I can't give the boy answers, but I give him silence and maybe he can use that as a foundation for peace.

JACKSON

"You've got quite the nice little church here. Good people," Senator Sikorska says as he strolls through my office, his compliment sounding forced to my ears.

"I wanted to come by and show my heartfelt support for someone such as yourself, a leader, a pillar of this community," he continues.

My Bible lay just out of reach. Good thing. I'd probably lob it at his head.

"Mr. Sikorska—"

"Senator."

"Yeah, can we speak a little later? I'm in the middle of finishing up a few things, if you'll excuse me."

The Senator sits down in the chair, unbuttons his jacket, folds his hands and smiles oil-slick.

"Yes, you're a busy man. I'm a busy man too, but this is such an opportunity to establish a friendship. Much like the one our lovely daughters have."

I cover the check to Lebanon on my desk with my mostly empty notepad.

"Let's get down to brass tacks, Reverend Potter. You're a man these people trust. They listen to you and what you tell them. You have a valuable resource, and I want to urge you to use that resource so these people can choose someone who can help them."

"That someone being you?"

"I could see how the people of this good state and this church sometimes need others to lead them in the right direction come election time. I simply want your help, guiding that choice."

"And what if you aren't what's best? I can't say you're offering anything more than any alderman or mayor or senator has offered. None of whom seem to deliver on anything other than lining their own pockets and serving their own interests."

The small muscles in the Senator's left cheek twitch. "Well, I can't say we are any different than a pastor or a priest."

Reaching forward, I slide my Bible down and pray the Senator thinks long and hard about his next few words.

"Think of it this way, you do so much for the community, and I can help you continue to do that. Black men in power are something this community needs, right? I mean look at that Obama! I admire him a great deal, a great deal. Look, all I'm saying is I can be a valuable resource to you. Robust social programs for a blighted community, new construction for low-income housing, expanded funding to law enforcement to put these low-life gangbangers in prison where they belong."

"You sound like a political ad."

He laughs heartily. "Hazard of the job, I guess. Look, your church is nice, but I see it. I see the crumbling steps, the paint covering up the water marks from rain and snow. I know you're a man under a lot of pressure. Wasn't one of your members recently murdered?"

"Yes," I whisper.

"I saw you on the news. Tragic, just tragic to lose someone like that. That's what I want to help with. These kinds of problems can be solved with someone like me at the helm with your support. I can help direct communities like yours toward better days, usher in some of those better days now."

He reaches into his suit, retrieving an envelope and laying it out on my table. "If you were to look in that envelope right there, you'd find enough to start repairing that roof, or those steps. I almost broke my neck coming up them a few minutes ago." He laughs again, the sound empty.

"Are you seriously offering me a bribe for my support?"

"This is my own money, from my own bank account. It's a donation, a tax deductible one actually. Just think of it as, what do your people call it? Tithes and offerings."

I imagine Jesus fielded the same temptations from the Devil

alone in the desert. I imagine he entertained it, but he told Satan to get behind him. He discovered a resolve and a character I search for at this moment. I glance at the check hidden underneath the notepad.

The money I could give to Lebanon. I could replenish the church's account. Make those repairs. But at what cost, what true cost? To be his puppet, just as I'm sometimes Lebanon's. Finding myself beholden to someone against my will is something I've lived with and it's torn me apart, shredded my dignity and tainted my honesty. And I can't bear that anymore.

I slide the envelope back toward the Senator.

"I thought you'd want to be part of the solution. Change is coming to these neighborhoods, Jackson. Progress."

"Gentrification," I retort.

"Progress has a lot of different names."

He places the envelope back into his jacket pocket, sighs and stands, buttoning his jacket, and extends his hand. I shake it with the sole intention of washing my hands after he leaves my office. He grips it a moment longer and applies the slightest added pressure. "You're a smart man, Jackson. I want to urge you to think, *really think*, about friends and enemies. We need protection from enemies. All of us. Think of me as a friend, and I'll think of you as a friend. That envelope will be here whenever you want it."

He lets go and places a card on my desk with his name etched in expensive gold lettering, his personal address and a handwritten cell phone number.

"Do whatever you think is best Senator, and I promise you I'll do the same."

Whatever lingers in his gaze is lost on me, but he finally leaves my office. As I try to gather my thoughts, Elder Alma Locke bursts through the threshold with unsigned papers in hand, a list of orders to dictate and appointments to keep. I take Sikorska's card and shove it in my desk.

"Morning! Now I got a couple little things here. Pastor Alman's church is celebrating their anniversary and that starts at three o' clock…"

I know these appointments and the obligations I have to keep, the hands I have to shake, the favors I have to exchange, and I wonder if I'm all that different from the Senator. He peddles unfulfilled change. I peddle a God for prayers.

Alma waves her hand in front my face. "Where you off to?" She chuckles.

"Just got a lot of things on my mind, Elder."

"Yes, yes. The Man of God doesn't get a day off and what did I tell you about that Elder stuff?"

She prefers Alma. She likes being an elder, but she faults people in church for being hung up on titles and not paying more attention to the Lord's business.

An inch or two shy of six feet with a full-figured frame, Alma runs her finger the length of my desk and looks around with a subtle disapproval of what she perceives to be disarray, but I believe to be a reasonably well-organized space. "I'll be by to tidy up later on."

Alma unconsciously hunches her shoulders taking careful steps toward me, not wanting to hit or bump into anything. She moves like the office and the world are too small for her. She lays the gas and property bills on my desk. Opening the envelopes, the amounts cause me to go cold in my very bones. The combined total with Lebanon's check barely leaves enough for the rest of this month.

"We have that other monthly donation to the Lazarus House. I sent that check off yesterday."

That tithe I give of my own accord every few weeks like clockwork. That amount further drains the church's coffers. The dwindling resources, the pressure and need to appear as if things are fine and that I have more to offer those around me: more love, more funds, more meat and bone. The Senator flashes through my mind. …*think about friends and enemies. We need protection from enemies.* The Senator's help, his ability to bestow grants to a struggling church and community, that'd resolve my mess, fix the stairs, fix my life and my lies. It'd also create a host of new problems.

"Don't look so worried, Reverend Potter. Jehovah Jireh. God the Provider," Alma consoles, her beautiful, snow-white, short-cut afro complementing the soft wrinkles in her face which fold themselves into the corners of her mouth and eyes.

I nod in affirmation, but not one part of me believes God can magically put money into a bank account thin on funds and heavy on debt. My secrets drag me down, and this church, the church my daddy once shepherded, down with them.

I hand Alma the check for Lebanon. I try to keep my tone even, not let my voice waver. I try to sound like the pastor of a church. "You need to sign off on this expense for the King family."

The easy smile on Alma's face gives way to an expression of light panic. "How do you expect me to justify to the board giving Lebanon this amount of money? We've already gone above and beyond for him—"

"I don't care how you justify it, Alma. Call it mercy!" I wish I knew the depth of that word, *mercy.* I know regret. I know shame. I know fear. I know fear so damn well.

"Mercy?" Alma's brow furrows in defiance. "You can't help that man with everything! Other things, other people in this place demand your attention, too!"

"It's not just about Lebanon. It's for medical expenses, for his mother, Sara, she's sick. It doesn't look good and her being in the hospital during this time, after Alice, it's only right we help them in any way we can." I rise from my desk and walk over to Alma, placing my hands on her shoulders. "Alice was your friend wasn't she, Alma?"

"You know she was, Jackson." Her breath catches, and she dabs at her eyes. She walks to the small window that lets in no light and stares at trees with no leaves and the garbage that the wind rolled into the lot next door.

"It's really about helping Alice, giving her family some relief with what they've been through these last few and terrible days. Mercy."

"I know Alice," Alma says. "What she gave up. What she begged me and Joanna to never talk about."

She walks back over to me. "You know, too. You know what he did to her, and you *still* help him. You don't blink. And now you wanna talk like you have some direct line with Alice in Glory, and she wants you to help the man who beat her down and brutalized her? I mean he could've been the one to kill—"

"Enough!" I didn't realize how loud I was or how I must've looked, but it was bad. I know it was bad. Alma shrinks back the tiniest bit. Shocked I raised my voice. I've never done that. I've never disrespected her, but this is not a normal day. I can't fake normal anymore.

"We all stood by, Alma, and there's another side to the story," I say, softening my tone, pouring as much honey into my voice as I'm capable of at that moment. "There are things they both suffered. Things that don't go away with love or prayer or good intentions."

Alma takes my hands and gently squeezes them. Her onyx eyes bore through mine trying to reach the answers I have locked away. The ones I want to share, that will surely bring down not only me but this entire church, everything I've built, and while that's something I deserve, it's not something right now I can abide.

"If you believe him to be such a monster, then why would he ask for money to help his family? He wants to help Ruby, Sara, too," I say without much conviction.

"Now you're just lying to yourself," she scolds and releases my hands. "Whether it's supposed to be for Ruby or Sara, only

Lebanon is spending that money. I know that like I know there were eleven disciples."

"Twelve, Alma."

The sharpness of Alma's glance cuts me. "Judas wasn't a disciple. He was a betrayer. I never counted him."

"Just sign the damn check, Alma. This will be the last thing I ask you. I swear."

"God is not a man that he should lie, Pastor. Numbers 23:19. You shouldn't be that man either."

I repeat, "Sign the check, Alma. Please." I give her the same look I did when I wanted an extra piece of cake at one of the church bake sales. I didn't need another slice of cake. It wasn't good for me, but she'd give in, like she was giving in now. I can tell. I know defeat.

"I don't know about you and Lebanon. You're supposed to be friends, but you're not how you were. Not like when you were younger. Not like before Lebanon went away. Y'all are both locked up somehow. Alice spent her life trying to free him, now she's gone. What's gonna happen to you?"

Alma signs the check in bold, scripted cursive. "I know it's not my place to say."

Standing up, Alma walks to the door and opens it.

"You're right, Alma."

She turns around and smiles.

I return to my desk and sit down. "It's not your place. Please help Layla with the programs. Thank you."

Alma's hopeful smile fades. She shakes her head and leaves my office. The way she looked at me, shaking her head. It's the act you'd bestow upon a child who can't seem to grasp the simplest lesson. And I realize it's pity. She feels pity for me.

I push and shove the entire contents of my desk onto the floor. I walk to my door and leave the mess for Alma to clean up later.

RUBY

I don't ask myself why those men showed up at the door. They're the same ones who passed in and out of the house the night Mom died. They presided over the dusting of prints, the cataloging of evidence and the collecting of my mother's body. My mother was placed in a black bag and loaded into a white van while I sat in a police car covered in her blood.

The door slams shut. I'm relieved. Lebanon is gone and I am left alone. That's the best way to be.

My neck still throbs when I think about it, and I'll have a bruise on my left hip from where I hit the edge of the table before I crashed to the floor. Lebanon always looks the same way when he hurts someone—surprised. Like he didn't know he was capable of such harm. It's the closest thing to sorrow or regret he feels. I think that's why Mom forgave him the many times he hurt her. Maybe she believed it wasn't really him who did it. Not his true self. It wasn't his fault. It was something she could pray away.

She probably thought she failed him. She probably thought she wasn't strong enough, or good enough or deserving enough to change him. She couldn't own up to her defeat and he couldn't hold himself accountable because no one else did. So we all suffered. Mom was a failure. Lebanon was a monster. I was a prisoner.

Save yourself, baby.

Layla called nine times.

Turning on the shower, I undress and notice blood on my shirt. It looks like raindrops. The water feels good on my body. It's my own kind of baptism. Christianity has to be the only religion where you can attempt to drown someone three times and call it salvation.

Each steamy droplet clears my mind before I step out and

dry off. The color on my neck has gotten worse. I'll go to my room and grab some clothes, ones with long sleeves and high necklines. I have an anthology of these teachings from Mom.

I hate looking at my eyes in the mirror because they are *His*. Contrasting with my deeper skin tone, they are vivid reminders we share the same blood.

Leaving the bathroom, I walk past the living room and notice a manila folder on the table. It's something the police left behind. I open it.

Lebanon stares at me, younger, vulnerable and scared and hurt. A black eye and a swollen bottom lip adorn his skinny face. For a moment, I see me in him, and I don't want to see that. I don't want to empathize with him. I don't want to believe I can reach him because then I'd be like Mom, and I can't afford her version of hope.

There are other papers, ones listing a charge for murder, an arraignment, a plea deal to involuntary manslaughter. All of this in 1979. I didn't know. I didn't know he murdered anyone. Yes, I knew he spent time in prison. It would have been hard to not know that because people talk. But he killed someone. We were living with a murderer this whole time. This dark side of him was always lingering under the surface like a riptide.

Violent people do violent things, and in the end, someone pays for it. A smile grudgingly crosses my lips at the picture of his wounded face, knowing he can hurt, but be hurt in return.

Those bruises, the cause of them, isn't hard to explain. I've only heard about this, from news sound bites and front-page articles in the *Sun-Times* or *Tribune*. Men being tortured, being freed after hasty convictions, spending decades of life in a prison cell. These aren't fantasies made up by a marginalized sect of society. The men are real and the horrors experienced to this day hang over the city. A legacy of law and order remain frayed in the very communities police are sworn to protect. Black people don't trust the law because there is no accountability for when the law fails us. We know heroes are capable of evil things. Fathers are capable of evil things. Every person on this earth is capable of evil. Maybe Lebanon didn't commit this murder, but I doubt it. I'm certain he deserved every punch and kick, every wound and cut, every desperate cry for taking a life.

You reap what you sow. You always reap what you sow.

I leave the folder on the table and walk past the guest bedroom. We never had guests, so Mom used it as a place to do her crafts, to get away from *Him*. It was her protection. Her sanctuary away from church. I open the door and for a brief moment, hope to find my mom there. I don't. I hope to find forgiveness there. But that's not there either. So I sit down at her desk. My knee bumps against it and I hear the smallest jingle. I open the drawer and see an envelope. I open it and I smile.

CHAPTER 5

CALVARY

People spread out around my sanctuary, brightly colored little beetles, clicking from one pew to the next. Greetings are whispered. Hugs are given and light, lipstick kisses are planted on cheeks with care. Movements are not as they were, there is less freedom and more caution among this group. And though there are many, Alice is not here. This is what the people speak of, her absence, not of how brightly the sun shines, or of how crisp the air is this late in March, but how one of them is no longer here to enjoy these things. How they just saw her. How they can't believe what happened.

I always found it odd how the impermanence of life is something that surprises humans though it is something they know with certainty—that death will come for them all. There is still shock among them, sorrow, fear. Their mourning as fresh and distinct and varied from person to person, like snowflakes.

"It was a good homegoing service they gave Alice," Sister Ellison says, a blush-colored hat framing her lightly wrinkled face and graying hair. "Everything just laid out so pretty."

"Mmm-hmm." Sister Cullen nods in agreement, an ankle-length lavender dress highlighting her ecru-tinged skin. "Standing room only. Even saw a couple of them news cameras in the back, too. At least they still covering the story. You know most times them news crews do one story on us only when something bad happens and leave. At least they might keep the story up a little while longer."

"Just don't make no sense. We ain't even safe in our homes," Sister Ellison laments.

"You know one of them reporters said something like residents are on edge after what happened to Alice. I almost laughed. We black in Chicago, we born on edge."

"You know you ain't never lied. You ain't never lied," Sister Cullen affirms.

They laugh.

"Speaking of liars, look who walked through the door," Sister Ellison announces. She jabs Sister Cullen with her right elbow.

Lebanon King strolls down the aisle, eyes avoiding the two women's gazes. A few people gather around him, offering their condolences and both Sisters look on with a mixture of curiosity and suspicion.

Sister Ellison sits down in the third row of the right-most pew as is her self-designated seat and has been for almost fifteen years. Everyone knows to *never* sit in this spot. She opens her Bible. Sister Cullen sits down beside her doing the same. It is a code, a tool they both use. Under the guise of appearing to read and debate God's word, they're able to discuss other church business and scandals. The pretense of holiness they believe keeps them safe and others unaware of their true and sometimes petty intentions.

"Now all these reports saying it's probably a burglar, but Lebanon knows more than he's letting on," says Sister Cullen.

"Maybe he wants to find the man himself. Do justice his way."

"Didn't the Lord say, 'Vengeance is mine'?"

"That's all well and good until it's someone you love," counters Sister Ellison.

"Mmm-hmm, true, but did he love her though? We both saw Alice with them bruises from time to time, and you know *no one* is that clumsy," Sister Cullen says with raised eyebrows.

"Yeah but it ain't our business anyway and people got enough drama without inviting other people's into their lives."

Sister Ellison lays her Bible down. "Just feels empty, you know? I mean Alice was quiet, kept to herself, but she was good people. Good people. Lord knows we need more of them in the world than we got."

Sister Cullen slightly turns her head, to see Layla escorting the Senator and Christy to her family's pew.

"Layla, sweetie!" Sister Cullen calls. Layla dutifully marches over to the two women whom she's known since birth, unsure what they have on their minds.

"Hey, baby. Is Ruby coming today? How's she doing?"

Layla's stomach churns. Her left arm breaks out in small bumps. Finding ways to answer questions, keep Ruby's confidence, but maintain respect for elders in the church, is a difficult tightrope walk.

"No, ma'am, I don't think she is, but she's doing as well as can be expected."

Both women nod and wait for more, some detail, some tidbit to help them fill out the facts or fantasies playing out in their heads.

Layla says nothing else. She simply smiles and calculates how much longer she'll have to stand there for both women to realize all she's willing to share is what's left her mouth.

"You should probably go back and attend them visitors," Sister Cullen advises.

"Yes, ma'am." Layla turns from the two women and exhales.

A light breeze enters my halls. "Still smells like them gardenias from Alice's homegoing. I ain't never seen that many flowers," says Sister Cullen.

LAYLA

The wonderful thing about some songs in the black church is they are simple, repetitive and you can replace one verb with another making for a completely new rendition. The word *praise* turns to *love* turns to *thank* and so on. If the choir director, Levi Morrison, is particularly feeling the spirit, this song can go on and on—and on.

A gay black choir director is a stereotype, but it just so happens Levi *is* gay, but no one talks about that. Everyone knows. He doesn't swish and sashay. The *S*'s at the end of his words don't give him away. But he refuses to cower in who he is, and he has an undeniable gift for music. Everyone knows a church with a good choir puts people in the pews and keeps them there. If anyone can get the choir to hit those notes, Levi can. I asked him why he works at this church or any church, and he told me he serves God, not man, and he's gonna do what God told him to do. Screw everyone else! This was over dinner one night with him and his partner, Danny.

Strained vibrations from the organ reveal it's in need of a serious tuning, but Deacon Baldwin manages to still bring forth semblances of heavenly chords through gifts either bestowed by Jesus or a deal with Satan. The tin and boom of snare and drums; the jingle of tambourines; the firm, melodic thrumming of bass guitar; multihued brown hands clapping on beat; our voices high and low and sharp and soft convey a deep longing. We sing tragedies dredged up from our homes or our ancestors or some faraway and long-ago place; this beauty in who we are and how we worship is inextricable from the music and weaves itself back and forth, to and fro. This congregation of feeling makes the music shake the very walls of Calvary Hope Christian Church.

A bobbing sea of wide-brimmed hats in pink, purple, orange,

yellow and every other color of the rainbow slightly obstructs the view of my father sitting in his high-backed oak chair. He's moving his head from side to side, metronome steady.

Sharply arched wood beams seem to rattle just a little, but they will hold. The church will stand. It always does.

Christy sings an off-key alto and happily claps along, trying to keep the count with the choir in front. She remains slightly offbeat. Senator Sikorska stands next to Christy, stiff and hawkish, something like a smile on his lips. Watching my white friend struggle to grasp movement and tempo and coolness and swagger, something my people possess with ease, I do my best to not feel superior.

This feeling. This warm deliciousness like melted butter on freshly baked bread—this is pride. It is the kind of elitism I imagine white people like the Senator feel and practice all the time. This thought is insipid at the very least and most likely racist, but I allow myself these moments because I spend so many others feeling less than or proving why I am just as good as the next person by working twenty times as hard. Now the bitterness will settle in my spirit. And these thoughts, these flashes of consciousness, all rotate within milliseconds while I still sing my song and keep the beat.

I don't notice much if any discomfort on Christy's face and that is good. The Senator would smile through a five-alarm blaze if he thought it meant another vote, so his expression means little to nothing. Lebanon King sits one row behind me and I can see him over my right shoulder. His eyes are not on me, but I feel them probing nonetheless.

Levi masterfully coaxes the last notes from the choir and the fading melody echoes throughout the room. My father always rises from his chair sure and steady. A true shepherd. His voice fills a place like this, commands empty air and measures and shapes it into rapt attention. The timbre of his tone, the poetry of his words, the act of his ministry can mesmerize. That means he's a good person, doesn't it? God wouldn't give this ability, this gift to just anyone, right?

Not once has my father glanced at his notes, but whatever his inspiration, divine or human, the people are responding. Hands up and waving, *Mmm-hmms*, *Yes Lords* and *Amens* are punctuated by the occasional shouts or brief speaking in tongues.

After the service, people mill about the church's halls and pews catching up on gossip or plans for the week. Senator Sikor-ska glad-hands different people practicing his "I really care what you have to say" face. I half expect a camera to film this; good B-roll for a political ad he'd air in a month or two. Without the minority vote, he's toast.

"I'm sorry about your friend, Layla," says Christy.

How does she know about Ruby?

"Geez your eyes got big!" She laughs. "I'm not that out of touch. I saw it on the news. I recognized your dad," says Christy. "You mentioned Ruby a lot at school. Wasn't hard to put it together. Are you okay?"

I stare at Christy, somehow amazed at her kindness and my ignorance of it. She knows what happened and still came when someone lesser might have given a lame excuse to back out. She might not come past 35th Street much, but for her friend, she did so when it counted.

I hug her.

"I didn't wanna say anything in front of Dad to give him an excuse for me not to come. He'd come anyway. Needs the face time, the votes," she whispers.

"It's that obvious?" I ask, surprised.

Christy gestures to the Senator. "My father is not a complicated man. He wants power. It doesn't matter how he gets it. It's what he cares about. People are second. A very distant second."

"I know what you mean." I stare at my father, Reverend Jackson Potter, behind the pulpit speaking with ministers and deacons.

"Dad underestimates me," says Christy. "Sometimes, I think

you do, too. With him, it's arrogance. With you...with you, I think you want to protect me in some weird way. Shield me from things you don't think I'd understand. You've done it since we met."

"I don't mean—"

"I'm not asking for an apology, Layla. It's just... I know you're going to try and do everything you can for Ruby. You're all or nothing, girlie. I adore it," Christy takes my hand and squeezes it. "Just be careful. Our strengths can be our weaknesses, too."

"You sure you don't want to get up in that pulpit? Sounds like you got a word or two."

Christy laughs. "No, no, no. I'll leave that to your dad."

The Senator strolls up, planting himself beside Christy. "It's time we say our goodbyes now, dear. I have a few other engagements. Layla, so nice to see you again. I'm sure I'll be back soon."

Notorious for courting favor in urban communities during elections, white politicians often look painfully out of place and horribly off rhythm in an ocean of brown faces, uncomfortable being the minority in the room, aching to return to neighborhoods and suburbs where everyone looks like them.

It's awkward to watch this. It's funny too.

I extend my hand which the Senator takes. His hard smile appears as he looks at Christy, then to me. "Thank you again for the invitation. It was a fruitful experience."

My eyes search Christy's and now I see it, a subtle cunning in those Caribbean-blue orbs, one she hides behind the fake smile she returns to her father.

When we embrace, Christy whispers, "Remember what I said, girlie. Call me anytime. If you want to grab some coffee, talk, whatever."

I know she means this, and I smile. "Same here."

CALVARY

Layla walks back through my wide corridor, and I listen to the resonant tap of her footsteps. Her step is heavy and I easily deduce from her jumbled, heated thoughts she is more than a little reluctant to speak with her father. Through my glass windows, sunlight playfully shapes itself into sparse remains of rainbows on my ugly chipped mint-green walls. If I'd arms and fingers, I'd paint my halls a more cheerful blue, but I remember green was the favorite color of the girl who painted them decades ago with her only two friends.

A door with a hinge in need of oil gives way to Jackson and his billowing black robe, bestowing the appearance of more girth and height. My friends the shadows and the light enjoy playing games and manipulating perceptions. Jackson's mind also churns in thought, moments, regrets, words he'd take back if he could.

Jackson stops and looks at the wall, a shimmering ray of sun carving out the spot on the floor with a raised tile. He steps on it knowing the tile will remain level for a time, but the unevenness of my floors, will cause it to rise again. Layla tripped on this tile once when she was four years old. She fell and cut her knee. There was blood and tears. But there was Jackson, too. There was her father who scooped her up into his arms and Layla held on to him as if he were the only solid thing keeping her afloat. And Jackson swore he wouldn't let anything else harm Layla though he knew it was a futile promise, a whimsical notion. "Daddy's got you. I've got you," he said to her over and over again until her cries turned to whimpers and then calm. And her smile, wavering, and her deep brown eyes puffy from crying, gazed into his and there was nothing else around them, father and daughter, but love and a bond neither one of them at that moment believed anything could break. They were wrong about that, but most people are wrong about the unbreakable.

However, some humans (and this about them I admire) will try to mend their love and heal their brokenness. This is what Jackson wants to do. Layla too.

But can it be done when two are so far apart?

Opposing forces, opposing motivations, opposing people, and most of all stubbornness keeping them one from the other at such times it seems they may never come together again.

Jackson walks through my halls whispering to himself, pleading in all sincerity, "God, just…help me," he whispers. "It's too much. All of it and no one knows. No one knows." Again, his mind drifts to a January night and a boy named Syrus. He thinks of Alice. His mind then turns to Lebanon, about the check he made Alma sign. One thought begets a regret which brings another thought which begets another regret and so on, his mind never loosed from the internal churning of his shame.

Layla's steps mirror her father's, an earnest plea for understanding and acceptance ready to tumble from her lips. She wanted people around while speaking to Jackson so he could exude that false, reassuring humility she needed on display to get out of a church service with a clear conscience and unhurt feelings on either side, but she must meet Ruby soon and there is no more time to rehearse and practice what she will say. No more time to wait for other people's grace to save her feelings or ego.

Only a few steps behind her father, Layla says, "Dad, I have an errand to run. It's going to take a little time. I won't be able to come to the service this afternoon."

Jackson turns around, his brow deeply furrowed, replies, "You're needed."

"No. *You're* needed. *You're* speaking. I have something important and I gotta go do something other than make you look like Dad of the Year."

"What's so important that you can't give some time to the Lord?"

"Considering the past twenty-four years in God's Army, I think He can forgive me one church service."

Jackson Potter's immense stature when angry seems to give him an extra three or four feet in height. At least it appears this way to Layla, who does her best to feel tall and powerful and not give the impression she's backing down an inch from this man. Like someone does with an angry, wild bear.

Jackson bellows, "It's not just about one church service!"

"Really? Please do enlighten me. I *so* need to hang on your every word."

"You know, there's this little part in the Bible about children obeying their parents."

One trait she got from her dad that she proudly flaunts is her stubbornness. She wanted to have the conversation on amicable terms, but now all she wants to do is piss him off. It's sport for her now. Layla's voice now matches the volume of her father's, but the venom bubbles and boils with each word leaving her mouth. "That line only works if I'm a child. I'm an adult."

"An adult that still lives under my roof."

"I'm more than happy to change that arrangement anytime but seeing as being pastor here means you make less than I do, you *might* need me to help with the mortgage."

That dig at his ability to provide for the household, that not so subtle hint of glee in Layla's eyes when she let those words leave her lips, enrage Jackson and he steps toward Layla. A Bible gripped in his fingers points so close to her face, a few inches separate the air and the spine of the book. She swats it away.

"I ask again. What is so important that you have to miss service?" His voice pummels and pounds the empty air of my hallway, near the spot where he once cradled his daughter in his arms.

"Trust me. It's worth it."

"I don't think so."

"So you wanna grab me like you did in the office? You wanna hit me? You aiming to turn into Lebanon—is that it?"

He won't touch her. The guilt about this morning still fractures him, and he knows there aren't enough apologies to make it right, but Jackson feels he needs to protect Layla, his daughter, his little girl. Though he can't speak the words, share the underpinnings for his motivation, he needs her to stay under the roof of the church, stay with him.

"What in God's name are y'all two going on about now?"

Behind Layla stands Violet, her voice the only physical testament of her presence as Layla's body blocks her from Jackson's view.

Jackson looks at his mother. In this moment, that command and strength vanish and he is a little boy.

Stepping between Layla and Jackson, Violet holds them both silent. "Let her go do what she needs to do. She's a grown woman. Treat her like one."

Jackson opens his mouth in response, but one look from Violet and he thinks better of it.

"Layla, you show your father due respect. Now, in the short time I've got left in this city, there is no more of this bickering. Am I understood?"

Both answer, "Yes, ma'am." Pitch-perfect and on time, the conductor of an orchestra couldn't have produced a better symphony of acquiescent melody. Layla and Jackson glare at one another. There is no great awakening or recognition and acceptance of faults. Just a momentary truce. Violet produces an immense wall against which neither Layla or Jackson will break themselves so Jackson walks the other way to his office and prepares to worship at yet another church service.

LAYLA

Left in the hallway, Dad stomping off to his office, the floor feels uneven and slightly lumpy underneath my feet. I don't immediately meet Grandma Violet's crystalline gaze, afraid of any reproach I'll find dancing in it.

"'A soft answer turns away wrath…'" she begins.

"'Grievous words stir up anger,'" I finish with a sigh.

Distant voices and light footsteps echo above us. Dusty boxes full of seasonal decorations are tucked against the wall. Grandma Violet guides me to the old, creaky pew where Ruby and I used to sit and talk after church was over, where I learned what life was like for Ruby and how my father, a man I thought could do anything, seemed powerless to stop bad things from happening to my best friend.

Looking into Grandma Violet's eyes I see love mixed with reluctance. "You are just like me." The lilt of her voice holds equal measures of pride and concern as she takes my hand in hers. Her magnolia perfume wafts in the air with dust particles. "I used to battle everything," she says. "Made me feel like I was fulfilling some great calling, but I learned you can't do that all the time. There's a time for war yes, but peace…that's the real prize. You need to figure out when to fight and when to be still, baby. Learn this lesson and learn it now. Learn it like I never could."

Grandma Violet reminds me of so much good, all the stuff I sometimes forget when I'm angry or upset. Her voice, the gentle offering of her wisdom, reminds me of how she talked to me when I was a little girl. I remember the sun's peekaboo filtering through trees in the neighborhood. Well-kept lawns. Girls playing double Dutch on the sidewalk while the boys play football or basketball in the street. Power lines and crowded homes. Candy houses on every block selling treats to kids after school.

Laughter and a rush to always be somewhere. The impatient cries of moms calling in kids for dinner after a long day's work. Grandma Violet's soft and wrinkled hands firmly holding on to mine and my brother's as we make it home from school. And her voice. There was always a tale or lesson to be taken from the stories she told me about her youth here in Chicago. But the stories, some wild and some sad and some funny, though I loved them, they were bleached, cleansed in places.

Grandma Violet loved Chicago. Said it was beautiful and big, bursting and violent and dirty and so very unfair at times. But what other part of the world championed fairness, especially for us with dark skin and eyes that have seen too much? Chicago was indicative of life for everyone, not just blacks. There *was* more freedom for us up north and we arrived with all the hopes and dreams that green lady with the torch promised. From the red clay pathways of Georgia, the long winding river corridors of Mississippi and ruthless heat of Louisiana we came. The Great Migration it's called, like blacks were geese or buffalo, Grandma Violet mused. The North was Jericho, it was Mecca, it was Nirvana. It was everything America promised and in wanting everything, people are always disillusioned with the results.

There weren't so many of those strange fruit harvests Billie Holiday crooned about on the radio and blacks were free enough to come and go as they pleased without fear of retribution from some imagined slight. Louis Armstrong once roamed these blocks, raging down red and orange streets with wintry blue jazz, music from his dull brass coronet to shining gold trumpet, harnessing rare talent with the likes of King Oliver himself! Richard Wright and Gwendolyn Brooks and Lorraine Hansberry stained paper with beautiful words of tragic circumstance and racial pride and sometimes Pyrrhic victory.

Invisible lines dissected black lives from white ones, and these lines were intentional and political and created with clear meaning. The unspoken rules and written laws define these boundaries. It's okay to be my garbage man but not my neighbor. It's okay to be my housekeeper but not my doctor. It's fine to paint my house but don't expect to see your work of art shadowing any great halls of museums. Be who you want to be as long as your potential doesn't eclipse mine. Know your place. Stay in your place. As a result, much of our majesty and power remained invisible to us—lost, entombed, obscured, hidden among the rubble of the past; in demolished buildings and omitted paragraphs in history books. The city Chicago was color-blind; people, however, were and are another matter.

Decades, some assassinations and a black president later, those lines are not erased but redrawn. Blacks for the most part reside on the South and West Sides and the whites are up north in trendy neighborhoods like Lakeview and Lincoln Square or in the burbs. The Asians have Cermak-Chinatown and the farther north you go of Ashland Avenue, you stop seeing soul food restaurants and murals of Martin Luther King Jr. and Malcolm X and start seeing taquerias and paintings of the Virgin of Guadalupe and the baby Jesus. It's a melting pot jigsaw puzzle with very distinctive boundaries. And those invisible lines still carve up the city, separating black, brown and yellow from white, opportunity and a void of such things.

Though much of Chicago has evolved—the city a living organism of growing glass and steel and asphalt—segregation and its impact hasn't stopped spreading borders of discord and violence. I suspect that this is the reason why Grandma Violet left for Tennessee. I never knew the exact reason. Grandma just said she had too many memories of this city, of this church and wanted to be somewhere different, try to live different. She left it at that. She left us.

She left me.

Having Grandma Violet here this past week for Auntie Alice's funeral has been a comfort, her steady presence a welcome distraction. When she's in Tennessee, there is one less barrier between my dad and me, one less translator, one less person to stop us from tearing each other down.

I want her to stay.

"That temper of yours—it's about as smart as trying to kill an ant with a hammer. I guess I'm guilty for giving you and your daddy that."

"Can he listen? Just once."

"Do you listen to him?" she says.

I have nothing. No smart-ass response.

Clutched in her hand is her Bible, old and tattered and held together by duct tape and prayers. I smile and follow Grandma Violet back into the main worship hall.

With church over, some people crowd around my father to congratulate him on another rousing and uplifting sermon and others speak to Lebanon, offering condolences and words of encouragement. Some like to be seen, some mill about to possibly hear another tidbit about what happened that night, now a little over a week ago. Gossip is an unfortunate language of the church, but in this congregation so many, men and women alike, are fully fluent.

Reds, blues, golds and greens of the eight stained-glass windows cast light across the mostly empty pews. Each thirteen-foot pane tells a story from the Bible. Most of them about Jesus. His birth. Feeding His many followers with only fishes and loaves. Death. Burial. Past the pulpit to the back of the church, a stained-glass window depicts Christ's resurrection. It is the biggest in the hall spanning twenty feet from top to bottom and seventeen feet across. I always feel warmth from the colors on this panel. Focusing on every little detail in this fragile piece of art is a great way to not think about the run-in I just had with Dad.

Next to the drums on the second platform of the church, Momma stands slightly above the remaining congregants. They would like nothing more than to approach her with their questions about last week, but most know better than coming to Joanna Potter with gossip in the first place. And in the second, Auntie Alice was Momma's best friend.

They know she is grieving, but hers is a private kind of grief. There are many forms, but two basic tenets involve those who relish in the attention mourning brings and those who wish to be left alone with their thoughts and memories and regrets. Momma is the latter.

I again walk out of the main hall, down the corridor and open the door leading to the alcove where Momma is perched.

I squeeze lightly on her shoulder.

"You know I thought when I got older, I'd dislike him less. Being older doesn't always calm your hate, but you can teach yourself to hide your feelings a helluva lot better."

"Sorry, Ma, when it comes to Lebanon, you don't hide your feelings as well as you think."

"I suppose when it comes to that *man*, I do not. All I think about is the last time I saw her. I keep thinking I failed my friend. I got used to that beaten down look in her eyes. I got used to ignoring the bruises. I got used to her not wanting me to be involved. I got used to a lot of things I shouldn't have gotten used to. It was convenient, baby. And now I have to live with that."

"Momma, it's not your fault."

"Thanks, baby, but don't." Momma sighs and it's the saddest sigh I've ever heard. "Maybe part of me was relieved to not bring some of her pain to my doorstep. For that, I will answer to the good Lord."

"Momma, God forgives, right? Maybe you should, too."

I feel her hands on my face as she whispers, "No."

She walks down the four steps to the first platform and makes her way down to stand behind Dad. He is still talking with Lebanon and a crowd of at least fifteen others.

Momma never had a good poker face. The firm line of her mouth. The flat sound in her voice. Not many people recognize this version of First Lady Joanna Potter, but I do. My father should also, but sometimes he's too wrapped up in himself to notice her feelings. Interacting with Lebanon King is the *only time* I observe Mom exhibit this behavior. It's as close to hate as I have ever seen from her.

I understand perfectly why Momma loathes Lebanon. But I want to know why my father remains so loyal? How can you see someone you claim to be your friend hurt someone in the ways Lebanon hurt Auntie Alice and still want to be his friend? I've never understood this and so I push back at the idea that we see only what we want. We mind our own business.

What goes on in your house. Stays in your house.

But. It. Doesn't.

It doesn't stay. It bleeds into the next home and the next block, the next family. My family. And then you question why your father would bend over backward to help a man who abuses his family.

Maybe I don't want to know. Maybe I'm like Momma. Hoping my compassion is enough. Enough to take calls in the middle of the night from Ruby. To plot and plan with my friend. To coax and cajole. To threaten and scream. Rip yourself apart to help a friend you love, and in the end, wind up desperate, heartbroken and defeated.

And even though I ask these questions in my head, I come up short on answers. What I need to know, what could help me, help Ruby, free all of us is the answer to this question:

What are the frayed bindings holding these people together when ties should be cut?

CHAPTER 6

LAYLA

Outside the church, five guys mingle on the west end of the street, pants hanging low, loud talking about their next reckless conquest, and a friend who was shot. Curses liberally added in between every other word tumbling out of mouths. This scene I'm glad Christy didn't witness. Most don't grasp the nuance of South Side living and all the work of representing this place not as a warzone, but somewhere with nice homes, friendly faces and untapped potential. Those guys on the corner are the South Side stereotype personified. What people imagine and fear when they listen to thirty-second news stories.

If we're to truly look at ourselves and not at our pain. If we realized our value and spent less time captive to hasty perceptions. If we saved ourselves, what could we become? They fear our skin and we fear our power. It's a perfect storm for destruction. Our destruction.

I'm always exerting time and energy and effort justifying where I live to colleagues and friends and strangers who believe they have the right to speak about where I come from based on hurried statistics, as if they're some kind of ordained experts on my neighborhood, *my side* of the city.

Shades of black and brown and tan, deep and light, intermingle throughout these streets with a different kind of testimony; a different kind of worship; a different kind of church, and prison or death, a different kind of hell. But sometimes it's too much. Wearied residents abandon Chicago, a place cradling both rich history and affliction, for Atlanta and North Carolina and Alabama. A reverse Great Migration of sorts.

The guys on the corner are too consumed with missed chances, lack of opportunity, relinquished dreams and hollow guidance. They're ready to prove manhood by lashing out with a gun, bad aim and the temperament of a child; they eagerly war among themselves for imagined domain and false pride.

A few of the guys on the corner I recognize. One of them went to my elementary school. We were in the same class. His name is LeTrell. He stopped coming around seventh grade. Then I started seeing him on the corner.

LeTrell spots me now and I smile at him. He at least nods. A small gesture, nothing big, but a recognition.

The headache returns. My temples throb in a familiar rhythm.

"Hey."

Even though I recognize the voice, I still jump.

"Damn it, Tim!"

"Whoa. Such language, church girl."

"Other than sneaking up on people like a ninja, did the army teach you how to annoy the hell outta people, too?" I say.

He chuckles. "That talent comes natural along with my good looks and charm." He comes from behind and embraces my waist, and I turn and kiss him.

"Aren't you afraid of someone saying something to your dad?"

"I don't care."

Tim lets go and searches my eyes with that deep, abiding gaze and replies, "What's wrong?"

"Is it too dramatic to say *everything*?"

Tim tilts his head to his left, unsure of how to reply.

"I just had a fight with Dad is all. About Ruby and everything that happened last week. Dad wants to bury his head in the sand. I'm sick of it. It's like he doesn't know how to help any other people except Lebanon King."

The sun, hidden behind the fluff of clouds, emerges again shining light on the church. Wind whips around our bodies, daggers of cold air cutting our skin.

"Did you know your dad was the only one who could get my dad to stop drinking for a while, get him to come home?"

I shake my head. I knew parts of Tim's story. The ones I pieced together from our childhood. The memories I made with him, the ones I make with him now. He was alone a lot in school if Ruby or I weren't with him. His clothes worn and hair matted. He didn't always smell very good. Kids made fun of him, but I knew better than those silly kids. So did Ruby. One time, Tim stayed with me when I scraped my knee falling off the slide. His arm, skinny and ashy, a comfort, and I leaned on him until Momma found us together several minutes later.

"Your dad was the one who suggested the army. He took me to the recruitment office. Helped me study. Don't you remember?"

I shake my head again.

But I do remember. My dad leaning over Tim, timing the practice tests for the ASVAB, or some other aptitude test with a lot of capital letters. The tests. Dad would go over the answers in a gentle way. The encouragement. It was like the spelling tests he'd help me study for. Dad has the same smile when he's proud. It takes over his whole face. And the hugs he'd give. Now Tim has me softening my resolve when all I want is to rant and be angry. When all I want is to dig and find answers to help Ruby and now I'm considering going back into that church and hugging Dad and asking if we can start over.

"Why don't you come to my place for a while? Cool off." Tim suggests, snapping me out of my thoughts.

I check my phone for any other texts, calls. "I can't. I gotta be somewhere."

"Ruby," Tim says answering a question that no one asked.

"I didn't say that."

"You didn't have to, Layla. Everything you want to say, even when you're not talking, is on your face."

I hear the loose gravel from the cracked concrete underneath Tim's feet shift as he makes his way down the stairs.

I catch up to him and look in Tim's eyes. He knew I was going to speak, but he did so first.

"I know he upsets you and I know he's not easy, but you're not either. Make the effort while he's here. If these past few days didn't teach you anything, learn that. Please."

The deep brown globes of his eyes show concern and something softer.

"I'll talk to you later," he says.

"So there'll be a later?"

Tim smiles, a sole dimple embedded in his right cheek. "You don't get rid of me that easy." The gravel shifts under his feet once again as he walks down the final few stairs, past the guys on the corner, and out of my sight.

CALVARY

April 22, 1971

Lebanon is a little older and my locks are a little weaker. He can easily find openings and enter without others knowing he walked my halls. It's nice to have unexpected company. I've always been happy to see him and he is happy to have a place where *Sara* isn't around. I am home when he can't stay with his best friend or doesn't want to be around all that happiness. Happiness is sometimes too much for him.

Lebanon tries to figure out the last of his math homework. He'll start on English next.

His birthday is tomorrow.

I feel from him dread instead of the happy anticipation that comes along with one's day of birth.

Looking inside him, I see *Sara* is always in a foul mood, but his birthday brings out something very bad. Lebanon can hear her in the bedroom. When the door is closed and she wails and drinks and then leaves to go meet more strangers.

There is a draft in the hall and he feels cool air and it's nice to feel something other than her hot breath, smoky with the cheap whiskey bought in the store downstairs from their dirty apartment, where burnt embers of old cigarettes and the musty smell of another man leaving her bed perfume the narrow hallway and empty living room.

The Strangers. Their gold teeth mouthing familiar pleasantries to which they are not entitled. Slapping him on the back, as they buckle their pants and drunkenly bellow, "Hey, little nigga!"

These wretched festivities always begin at least a week before his birthday. Lebanon doesn't know why.

I do.

I can't speak and if I could, I wouldn't tell him. Lebanon

wanted *Sara* to love him and now all he wants is to be left alone. Sometimes he goes to the bathroom and stares at himself in the dirty looking glass. To ponder, to brood, to covet white-picket-fenced lives—dads that smiled and played baseball on fake green grass and moms that made apple pies and didn't sleep with random men picked up in dark lounges at desperate hours, before daylight intruded on evil indulgences and thin mirages of humanity.

RUBY

The bell tinkles, but it isn't Layla. Not yet, but she'll come. She always does.

The dark scarlet peeling wallpaper in the coffee shop reminds me of Grandma Naomi's home. I trace it with my fingertips. There was a similar paisley pattern of thick teardrops floating from top to bottom on each strip in the living room. The white of the design yellowed with age, the wood floors creaked and groaned when you stepped on them, but her house was always clean and warm.

You could breathe there. And smile. And laugh. Smell the fresh sunflowers in the vase on the table. Lebanon, my father, wasn't watching and Mom wasn't hiding her tears by bowing her head lower than normal while washing dishes, her sorrow in salty droplets hitting the water while she washed plates and cups and forks and sharp knives. I taste something nasty on my tongue like bile or soap or blood when I think of my connection to Lebanon, not one of love or admiration. Lebanon isn't anything to love. He's something to be overcome.

But when I sink somewhere deep and dark in my memories, I pull out something golden and good. And I remember Mom and me leaving, in the night, like our ancestors searching for a North Star. And we'd end up on Grandma Naomi's doorstep, hundreds of miles away.

Sometimes God took pity and answered the prayer of a little black girl and it was peaceful when we'd leave the house with the apple blossom tree in the front yard. But Lebanon would come find us and stand on the porch, for hours or days. Three days was his record. He slept on the porch like a dog.

Then Mom would take pity. Then Lebanon would be nice and maybe make Mom smile or laugh. Lebanon might twirl her around and talk about how pretty she looked on their wedding day, or Lebanon might buy her gardenias and kiss her on her swollen cheek or blackened eye. And Mom would tell Grandma Naomi things were okay and we'd leave. Grandma Naomi would hold on to my arm, say, "Let me keep the girl until things settle." Or Grandma Naomi would say, "You foolish! He means you no good! Don't go, baby. Don't go!"

But Mom would pry my arm from her grip. She'd kiss her grandma Naomi and we'd leave.

Lebanon would be nice for a while. Then mean. Then Lebanon said, "Sorry." And then we'd all try to forget. Then something would happen. Like it always does. A bad day at work. Not enough money. Someone told him *No*.

When we stayed at Grandma Naomi's in Tennessee, when Lebanon didn't hunt us down right away, I liked to sit and absorb all the silence. There was no crying or fighting. No grabbing or bruising. I'd sit and my eyes would soak in all the details of Grandma Naomi's home. The feel of the pine floors. The notches on the fireplace, each one its own piece of natural, world-worn art. And on the mantel of Grandma Naomi's fireplace was one picture in a silver frame. There were three girls and they all smiled except for the girl in the middle. She seemed so familiar. I swear she even looked like me a little or maybe I recognized that same look of desolate sadness. I would make stories in my head about who these three girls were together.

Sunlight from windows bounced off the frame in sharp, naked pieces, and found the grim corners of each room filling them with life, enlarging the space of the tiny raised ranch house so much so that the small living room seemed comparable to a palace.

But I missed Layla. I'd talk to her on the phone. Mom would talk to Ms. Joanna. Mom and I enjoyed our time with Grandma Naomi, but we had our people.

We had our own friendships, and, in those friendships, we had our places, our pacts, our unspoken vows. We had our disagreements and reconciliations. We had each other and that was enough.

Mom had Ms. Joanna. I have Layla.

Layla is smart. People in church talked about that, still do. They remark on how smart Layla is and how pretty I am.

Smart. Pretty. Like no woman can be both. And I suspect church folk, in their own way, mean it as a compliment, but these are the only two attributes assigned to me and Layla.

One time when we were about twelve, in the basement of the church, Layla and I sat in her dad's office. This was before there were scars marring the skin of my arms. Elder Alma came in with paperwork for Reverend Potter to sign.

"Layla, your dad told me you made the honor roll again. I'm not surprised in the least," she beamed. "And, Ruby, you just growing up to be such a beautiful young lady. Mmm-hmm."

And she left and Layla and I laughed. I reached into the pocket of my blouse and handed her a dollar.

"You were right," I admitted. "Elder Alma just can't help herself."

"Or Sister Cullen or Sister Ellison," added Layla.

"Who knows? Most of the time they're gossiping anyway! Like we believe they're discussing Jesus. They barely look at those Bibles!"

But I remember Layla's face and how it drew down slowly, her smile disappearing. "You know," she said, "for once I'd like to be pretty."

"And I'd like to be smart," I replied.

So it went. People say things so much we believe them, and Layla is good with strategy, but I don't want her to scheme and plot and plan. I don't want her to tell me things are going to be okay. I just need her to do something small but hard at the same time.

I just need her to listen. Even if I don't talk much.

I just need my friend to look at me, be with me. Even if it's only for a short time.

The bell rings again shaking me from my thoughts and Layla walks through the door. My friend is here.

LEBANON

I used to wait for Alice here, at the top of the church stairs. She was always inside those walls helping with something. Fundraisers. Sunday School. Usher Board. Anniversary Committee. She didn't want to leave this place. I didn't much like to stay. It was always "God this" and "Faith that." I went from one woman who couldn't stand the inside of a church to one who couldn't stand to be outside of one.

Alice felt guilty all the time. Felt guilty she couldn't give more time to the church though she was here sunup to sundown. Felt guilty she didn't pray more or read the Bible more. Felt guilty she didn't change me or couldn't leave me. Alice wanted me in some kind of box, and it was a box I had to stay in. "You're a good person," she'd say. "God knows that. I know that, too. You need to learn that." She'd tell me, "You're better than what's at the bottom of a glass." How the hell would she know who I am? She had no right to think that. She wanted to fix people that liked being broken. Me. The girl. You can't make a triangle a square or a circle a rectangle.

You can't change the shape of things. Not with words or good thoughts. Not with love. Not with God.

There are some boys smoking on the corner. A mixture of cigarette and weed smoke singes my nostrils. They start sliding away from the church one by one. I suspect they feel as comfortable here as I do. A thing like a church can mess with your head if you let it. One of them still lingers finishing his cigarette by the time I make my way to the street.

"Let me get one of them squares," I say.

I'm polite enough about it, but the boy still looks at me like I'm crazy. His pants sagging too damn low like these young ones do nowadays, but there's a book in the left back pocket of his jeans. His hat is angled, low, to the left. There's something familiar in his face, but I can't place it right now.

"Thought people in church didn't smoke or drink," he says, throwing the smoldering butt of his cigarette in the street. Smoke hangs above him for a moment then disappears. His eyes don't hit mine. He glances past me down the block.

"You the expert on church folk?"

"Didn't say all that, but I—"

A car rumbles up from behind us, his hand grabs for his waist as he turns his head. It's just a Toyota with an old man behind the wheel. The boy takes a loose square behind his left ear and a lighter from his right pocket. He hands it to me. Letters in cheap green ink on his left hand spell out the name *Anne*. He takes a deep breath.

I say, "What's the verse in Saint Mark? 'Don't trouble your heart…'"

"Nah bruh, that's Saint John, fourteenth chapter and it's, 'Let not your heart be troubled…'"

Guess my face showed some kind of surprise before I could hide it. The boy smirks a little. "I can show you I'm right about that verse. Where's your Bible?"

"Don't got one on me right now."

"Damn, man, what kind of Christian is you?"

"Kind that don't like a lot of questions. And if you so smart, what the hell you doing hanging with those boys that left?" I ask.

He doesn't answer. His smirk leaves, his eyes narrow some, but he isn't challenging me. He's sizing up my intentions. Information, giving it to someone, is a heavy gamble especially in a gray place with high walls and thick bars or a holy place with red doors and stained glass. Ragged bits of gossip or knowledge can get you extra cigarettes or a knife in the belly. Church and jail ain't *that* different most times.

"You read a lot on the inside?" I take a drag.

"I read some," he finally answers. "You read a lot when you was in?"

Guess my nice suit and shoes don't always cover up things. One convict can most times recognize another. It's a brand we carry like scars or tattoos, but it's in our eyes, the stain of lost freedom. The stink of a jail doesn't leave you. It's a cross between sweat, shit, metal and the cheap cologne the guards would wear. You never quite get comfortable with the sun and the air, walking to the bathroom when you want to, eating when you want or doing anything you please without someone watching you.

"Obvious to you I spent time downstate?"

"Figured you spent time somewhere. Game recognize game, Old Man."

"Name's Lebanon, not Old Man."

"Yeah, I know. You live next door to my grandma."

"I thought you looked familiar. You Ms. Anne's grandson."

"LeTrell. Yeah, I come by and check on her time to time."

"She's a nice lady."

LeTrell nods while I take another drag from my cigarette. Strips of cloud cover the sun before it peaks out again from its momentary veil.

"So what're you reading?"

He takes out an old paperback edition of *Moby Dick*. "I prefer the classics, but Grandma's always trying to read to me from the 'Lord's Good Word.' That what she calls it. She goes to this church sometimes. I probably know the Bible better than the pastor."

"Doubt that."

"Yeah, Bibles didn't do me much good before or now. Places like this either," he says placing the book back in his left back pocket.

"The church?"

"Lotta churches, not a lotta anything else around here. Grandma just gives them her money. Nothing really changes. No matter how black you make Jesus, we blindly follow the adopted religion from our adopted country."

"Okay, Malcolm X, besides hanging on the corner, what you doing to make things better?"

"Opportunities ain't always easy to come by."

"So it's everyone else's fault, that it?"

"I didn't say that, but it's either our people being scared of us or white people being scared of us. Either way, none of it puts food in me or my brother's mouth."

"Yeah, we all got a pretty side and an ugly one."

"There's a lot ugly round this city."

"Suppose so. Maybe not always."

A dark sedan pulls up slowly. Two white faces peer through the dirty windshield. Detectives. Gotta be. No other reason for two white men to drive down a street in Bronzeville than to size up the people that live here. They're not looking for directions. They know *exactly* where they want to be. No smiles from them. We don't smile either. Why bother with niceties? We don't want them here and they think the boy is a statistic waiting to happen. It's just the matter of whose gun would take his life—theirs or a rival gang member's. He'd be dead just the same.

"What you do now to make it by? Support yourself?" I ask.

"Whatever it is I gotta do."

I know what that feels like, the inevitability of a lifestyle, trying to find some other way, but the streets and the schools and the damn government at times are pushing you toward those corners instead of away from them, but I made something of myself regardless. I have a business and a little money. But now I also got a dead wife and cops that wanna tear down everything I built. And I can't go back there, prison. The smells, the bodies, the guards. The piss and shit and sweat. The hopeless, endless feeling of nighttime. I don't care if I've done things that deserve to put me back there. I can't go back.

I won't.

This boy isn't cut out for whatever it is he thinks he's doing. None of them are, but not many here to show them different.

"You know, I'm a businessman."

"Like a pimp or some shit?"

"What? Hell no! I work at the bakery a couple blocks over. Gets pretty busy."

"You ain't got nobody else to help you over there?"

I stub out the last of my square. "Look you want a job or not? Better than waiting for someone to come put a bullet in your ass."

He shrugs.

"Come by tomorrow. I'll see if I can find something for you."

"Cool."

"I believe you mean, *Thank you*."

"Yeah. Thanks."

He offers his hand. He has a firm grip. Not too tight trying to challenge me, but strong. I like strong.

CHAPTER 7

LAYLA

The vanilla latte in my hands does nothing to warm me and even after taking two strong gulps, which burn my tongue, Ruby's eyes still cause me to shiver. Every word I try out in my head sounds forced and all I do is worry about my friend who won't look at me.

"I saw a couple of houses for sale around here."

Ruby's eyes leave the patterns on the wall and follow my voice. Her mouth turns slightly upward to a smile, thoughtful and sad. "Did you?"

"Yeah, one has a big front yard with an apple blossom tree and the other one looks like your grandma's house. The street was quiet."

My search for a parking spot took me a bit deeper than I planned, into the tree-lined blocks of the historic Beverly neighborhood, one of the few places seen as desirable to live on the South Side. Beverly or Hyde Park it seemed were the only two places subtly trendy enough to be livable by people other than blacks. This somehow gave those neighborhoods acclaim other

South Side boroughs like Bronzeville and Washington Heights didn't yet have, white acknowledgement, which always translates into positive attention and expensive real estate.

Small chic boutique shops and some recognizable chain restaurants nestled between the historic mansions on Longwood Drive and the well-kept lawns of the smaller Georgians, bungalows and raised ranch houses give the appearance of traditional American family living.

It is so strange that only a few blocks east, past Ashland Avenue, the homes and the schools and the streets are tougher, but more honest and real without the polish. I am proud of where I come from, but also, and I hate admitting this, I long for life those few blocks west.

Ruby and I talk about living here. Less now, but when we were younger, this neighborhood was movie picture-perfect in our minds, preserved like those insects in ancient amber tombs, a place to somehow distance ourselves from our fathers.

"You're biting your lip," says Ruby.

I let my lip go and find some Carmex in my bag and rub the menthol-smelling balm over the damaged portion of skin. Now I'm hot. Like my mind, my body temperature can't figure out what it wants to do, liquid beads cascade from my temples down my cheeks, but my hands are still cold. The coffee shop door opens and closes every few minutes, the brass bell ringing and fading, the harsh breeze disrupting the still air in the room.

I can't tell if the steam from the drinks being crafted a few feet away or if nervousness causes my forehead to remain damp. Finally, I decide to take off my coat.

"Aren't you hot with your coat on?"

She stretches her arms slightly and I can see the darker, serrated mark down her left wrist, an almost smile-like path of puckered skin. A thick turquoise bracelet falls back into place after a moment, but the long, crooked path is still so visible. I know it ends about another inch below the sleeve.

She says, "We're all just a collection of scars, you know."

"What are you talking about, Rue?"

"The mistakes our parents make, the mistakes we make. We're as much marked by the things we don't do as the things we accomplish. Jagged skin pulled over jagged skin."

"No, Ruby, I *am not* a scar. You *are not* a scar! You gotta stop thinking like that."

When Ruby gets like this, dark and deep in her thoughts, I have a very low tolerance. Wallowing in melancholy, it wastes energy. Find a solution instead. I can find a solution. *We* can find a solution.

"I didn't come here to listen to you feel sorry for yourself."

"You came here to feel better about yourself. You came here to try and save me, didn't you?" Ruby says, still not really looking at me.

"But you texted me, you're the one who asked to meet me!"

"I do want to see you, Layla."

She reaches for my hand, firmly wraps her fingers around my wrist. They are so cold.

"To pick a fight," I say, snatching my hand away.

"No." Ruby's lips purse and open like she wants to say something more but thinks better of it.

I try to let my anger recede, try to place myself in my friend's shoes, try to imagine the mix of sadness and freedom she probably feels now that she's experienced a tragedy, or rather a public tragedy, as she and her mom no doubt endured an abundance of private ones. Why try to make polite conversation while you're grieving?

"How are you doing since… It's a stupid question, but I want to know," I ask.

"I can't think of any answers you want to hear right now."

That damn bell chimes again. People walk in and out with cappuccinos, pastries. The wind cuts our exposed skin into buttery slices. I shudder and she looks past me, out the window. I don't say anything in response but keep looking at her.

"Well, Layla, I guess I'm as I always am."

"Which is what?"

"Surviving. I breathe in and out. You can't ask much more from me than that right now."

"I suppose not."

To do nothing right now. Drink my overly sweet coffee. Nod my head and smile and leave Ruby the exact same way I found her, without doing something to help, it feels like being ripped in two. Is this how Momma felt when she talked to Auntie Alice?

She looks down at her left wrist and then asks, "What do you think happens when you die?"

"You can't expect me to answer that."

"It's a question that deserves an honest answer. You're an honest person, or you try to be sometimes," Ruby presses.

"We go to Heaven."

Her eyes all but stop just shy of rolling themselves. "I said *an honest* answer, Layla."

"Fine! My honest answer is I don't know!"

"I think there's nothing," says Ruby. "Well, nothing for people who are bad. There's black and that's it. For good people, maybe there's something. Some light. Some peace. Anything's better than what I'm dealing with now."

My skin starts to break out and long skinny portions of my right arm raise and bump and turn red. There is a burning in my belly and some unsettling quiet emotion I don't want to own.

"I can't say I know about God like that or death, but I know about being a friend, showing up."

"Yes, you show up. After. Like everybody else, when there's nothing left to do but stare or gossip and say things are going to be okay when they're not going to be."

"So, you asked me to come here to put your shit on me, Rue? No. You don't get to do that. I know you're in pain. But we all have choices in this world. I made my choice to come here, and you're making a choice now, to do what? Do you want to stay with him, with Lebanon? Do you wanna come be with us for a while?"

Ruby remains silent.

"What do you want, Ruby?"

Is she going to try to kill herself again? Is she looking for some kind of subconscious approval from me? I don't have a response to her question.

Her eyes search mine for something deeper, something that resembles hope and I want more than anything to give that to her. I wonder if I'm coming up short. I probably am.

"We can find somewhere safe," I blurt out.

"I have less than five hundred dollars which won't get me far in this city. I have a job as an office assistant where I'm invisible and the people call me Rachel or Rosey instead of Ruby, because they can't remember my name and barely pay me a living wage."

"There are ways we can help. My dad—"

"Your dad helps my dad. Without thought. Without question. He's not gonna stand up to Lebanon. Your dad always caves to him."

Heat invades my face. I keep my tone low.

"Excuse me?" I counter. Ruby is right, but she doesn't know everything about my dad. Maybe he'll surprise her, surprise me. Grow a backbone and stand up. Even if he doesn't, Ruby talking about my father without respect I can't abide. Only I can do that. "What you won't do is talk about my dad like he's some kind of lap dog. That's what you're not gonna do!"

Ruby sighs. "Make up your mind, Layla. Either you're going to see Reverend Potter for everything he is or build a fantasy about the man you want him to be."

"Is that what your mom did? Build a fantasy about Lebanon. Is that why she stayed?"

"Don't have an answer to that question. I'd like to know myself." Ruby looks at the door, like she expects Lebanon or my dad to walk through any moment. "Look, I'm not… I don't want to fight with you."

"Fine, then let's figure this out, Rue. I can take you somewhere, not our house. Maybe someone at church will—"

"Lebanon will find me. You know that."

Ruby started referring to her father by his first name when we were about eleven. I always thought it strange she said his name and it sounded so right on her lips and the word *dad* or *father* so wrong.

"We can call the police."

"This conversation we're having, I've heard your mom saying the exact same words to my mom."

"I'll tell them what he's done."

"You have no idea what he's done."

"I know he killed your mom. You don't have to hide it."

Ruby's bottom lip trembles. She lays her head on the fake wood table and gazes at me, eyes puncturing me full of holes, like a voodoo doll.

"I know you're living with a monster," I continue.

"I am."

"So let me help you. I believe you can start over."

"You believe a lot of things." She said it to cut me a little, impress upon me some lesson she'd learned long ago: hope in too many things is as frivolous a luxury as a genuine Louis Vuitton bag.

"It's nice to wish for new things, but it's too late for new beginnings. We have now and we make the best of it," Ruby says and looks down at her arms. "Scars don't go back into not existing again. You have them. You live with them. You live with them like you live with monsters, or fathers."

"There's a difference between monsters and fathers, between their lives and the scars they pass along."

"You're preaching at me, like your dad."

I hate it when people compare me to him and though most mean it as a compliment, I rarely take it that way. She knows this.

My nails dig into the palm of my hand. The image of her blood lurks behind my eyes. The scene of her near-death projects itself in my mind. It's something only I can see. Her smile. She seemed so at peace on that bathroom floor. My eyes are blurring with tears, so I look up and to the left. The red pendant light above us could use some dusting. The table is wobbly and knocks against the floor when I pick up my coffee to sip it again. The temperature is just right, but it tastes like syrupy, vanilla-flavored dirt. I added too much sugar.

"How will you make the best of your scars then, Rue?"

"How will you make the best of yours?"

The mug feels like a ceramic rock. I look back in Ruby's eyes and see nothing, just pretty brown-jade glass.

"I know why you're talking about dying," I say.

"No. You don't."

"I worry about you."

"I know."

"Is that all you're gonna say?"

"What do you want me to say?"

"That you're not gonna hurt yourself."

"You want a happy ending and there are none. There are no resolutions. No happy endings. There's just a bunch of shit that's all fucked and I have to deal with it. Me."

"How?" I ask, my voice extending to the other side of the café. Two white ladies glance in our direction, their mouths slightly pursed and eyes narrowed.

"I have two weights in my hand, Layla. Both of them are really heavy and if I let one go, then I fall to one side, tip over and disappear."

"So be free. Let both weights go."

"Then what will I have to hold on to?"

I want to flip this table over. All she has are words and nonanswers. Dismal riddles and sad eyes. "You don't want to change. You don't want to have Lebanon arrested. You don't want to talk about that night! What's the point of—"

"I just want you to see I'm still here. I wanted you to listen for once instead of talk so… I could do something for you, for myself."

Ruby gazes again at me and past me. Like she can see our futures and where all the dirt lanes and forks in the road lead. I want her to promise she won't kill herself. I want her to give me that assurance because she owes me at least that!

"Protection. I'm trying to protect you," she answers.

"From what?"

No answer.

"From Lebanon? What are you going to do? Am I going to find you on the bathroom floor again?"

No answer.

The slivers of ice that pass for her fingers reach out again and squeeze my hand hard. She gets up from the table and walks out of the door and maybe out of my life. I am letting Ruby walk and I'm not running after her, tackling her to the ground. I'm just sitting in this coffee shop full of white people and watching her disappear. The odd, high tinkling of the bell above the wooden door summons in me a silent rage.

CALVARY

September 23, 1960

Sara wills her face to remain calm. She wills her stomach to as well, but the urge to vomit steadily rises when she sees her father's face as he shakes each hand, kisses each cheek, laughs like he is human, frowns like he is human. When he is not, he is the thing she must escape. Violet and Naomi will help her do this after Revival.

Ushers in crisply pressed burgundy-and-pink uniforms with snow-white-gloved hands and shining gold pins on lapels guide visitors and members alike to seats, quickly and efficiently. Down my three aisles on the main floor, each row can easily seat ten people, or for those who like more room, eight. Today, ushers try to seat ten to each row. Feet press into carpet and it cushions the weight on my floors. Reverend Saul wants as many bodies as can fit. "Pack them in," he orders. "All God's children need to be here for this occasion!" So, they place worshipers where they can as if it's their sole duty and one in which they take tremendous pride.

Reverend Saul King sits, a ruler amid the congregants in front of him on the floor and above him in the balcony. A midnight-black robe, complete with hand-stitched bright gold crosses flank his right and left sides. Two gold rings adorn his left hand and a pinkie ring with diamonds ornaments his right.

"Passa just looks so regal up there. Makes me proud I'm here. Got the best representin' us tonight," someone says from behind Sara. The lazy drawl of the word *Passa* instead of crisp enunciation of *Pastor* reminds Sara most of the older members are barely a decade or two removed from the South, from Florida and Mississippi and New Orleans, from Tennessee, where she'll find herself soon.

The Best. The church member's words rollick across her mind

as Sara claps to the music on this second night of celebration and redemption. Revival.

Under a dozen old robes, a turquoise suitcase is hidden in the back of the choir room closet. It holds a few dresses, pants, tops and shoes. Fifty dollars remains folded in Sara's purse. She places none of the money into the fake brass collection plate as it glides past her and she finds within herself the faintest glimmer of a smile.

Naomi passes Sara a scrap of paper. Carefully, unfolding it she sees the words scribbled in Violet's barely legible handwriting: "10:30, 42nd & State."

Glancing at Violet, she nods. Her friends are willing to do what few others, probably no others, would do for her and for this Sara is grateful. Clutching that piece of paper is like holding a bit of sunlight, some form of hope Sara can carry in the palm of her hand, and at that moment, she's humbled by Violet and Naomi, her best friends, her sisters. There is love. There is also jealousy and low tides of animosity, but mostly love because what is love without a little hate?

Naomi whispers in Sara's ear, but the music and praises of the people nearby make it almost impossible to hear. Sara presses her body closer, her left ear almost touching Naomi's lips. "Fake like you're sick. Violet's gonna tell her parents you're going home, that she'll take you. We'll all meet and get you out."

Sara nods her head in agreement. Naomi takes her hand and squeezes, a tentative half smile ending the conversation. After this service of celebration, Sara will leave on a bus to Tennessee, and she hopes to never see King Saul again.

Hands clap on beat. Tambourines keep tempo. Hymnals stay tucked in the backs of my pews for these songs aren't ones written down. These are the songs passed down from the elders and from their elders before them. The organ and piano find their root in the melodies of old spirituals, words whose origin isn't always clear, but the undertone of suffering is, and in this there is something sacred and ancient and timeless. A people, especially ones whose trajectory is set and reset by those in power, a people trying to break patterns of injustice through votes and protests, through marches and sit-ins, a people like this knows about suffering. Blacks in America are the modern-day Children of Israel. They walk through a seemingly endless desert where the sun beats down at its highest point in the sky.

Cool night air dissipates among the crowded bodies and heavy perfume. The penitent line up in front of the pulpit for a touch from the appointed one, from King Saul.

Coming down the stage, King Saul chooses a woman from the shuddering crowd of sinners, one who isn't a member of his church, but attends a church on the West Side of the city. "Sista, sista, tell me why you're here tonight?"

The young lady King Saul singles out is barely twenty, a round face, the color of melted chocolate. "My momma's sick. Doctor said she ain't got much time. She's down in Georgia and I can't get to her."

Saul shakes his head, putting his arm around the girl's shoulders. Sara shudders.

"What's your name, child?"

"Hattie. My name's Hattie Brown."

"Well, Hattie, we gonna pray in Jesus's name! Lord, we come to you bended knee and body bowed on behalf of dear Sister Hattie Brown and her mother..."

The deacons, like a flock of finely tailored birds, place their hands on King Saul's shoulders, the church nurses dressed in white surround Hattie Brown and put their hands on her shoulders, they steady her in case she is overcome with the Holy Spirit. Each group imbues whatever goodwill or faith they can muster; they in earnest pray for Hattie, for her mother, pray their prayers aren't superficial wishes, but instead powerful commands. Some of them imagine Hattie's mother arising from her hospital bed at that very moment, healed from whatever ailment currently afflicts her body.

Tears soak Hattie's face as King Saul bellows out to the Lord. Many in the congregation rise to their feet, yell out: "Help her, Lord!"

"Heal her, Jesus!"

"We bind Satan!"

In all directions, a rush of voices. Bodies sway from side to side, in communion, in plea to God, most never knowing if their prayers will be answered. There is freedom in their cries, there is desire for alignment with a force larger than them. There is oneness in these moments, however temporal they may be, and I am filled with something pure and radiant.

Could this be the presence of God?

Makeshift fans born from folded paper, attempt to circulate the heavy air in my balcony. Children snore softly in laps while their parents look up and over to the congregation below. Their bodies, hardened by manual labor and persistent indifference, are tucked up and away from others with slightly more money and more prestige. The grocery store owner, the elementary schoolteacher, those who could afford the celluloid fans with hand-painted decorations of the Bible or Christ's crucifixion, they perch in the plush pews on the floor, closer to the preacher, closer to salvation. But words spoken can rise, can climb and find ears up here just the same as on the floor.

Reverend Saul King steps to the pulpit from the altar, especially joyous as he knows the count from the two offerings collected thus far. After that performance, where the people felt as if the Lord himself touched them, he'll have one more offering right before the Benediction, the prayer and dismissal. A nice night indeed he reckons. He can soothe whatever ails their troubled souls. He's good with words. He's good with people, most of them. He's good at everything. That's why a few congregants are jealous of him, he tells himself. It's why they'll do anything, *any-damn-thing,* to steal away what he's worked so hard for. Like Assistant Pastor Andrew Morrison, Violet's father, who barely conceals his envy behind a flat voice and tepid grins and weak handshakes. Those people aren't meant to lead, not like him, he believes. This church, the trusting faces he brought through the door, the money in the collection plate are his! His alone! God help anyone who'd try to take it away!

He'll revel in his victory, in his belief of wholeness. He'll speak of Jesus on the cross and get each congregant to see themselves. He'll get them to see him as holy as God, as righteous, damn near as perfect! He's good at that.

Looking out at the crowd, he sees Sara is smiling. He *swears* she is, and this makes King Saul happy. There is no one to question his power, nothing to usurp his rule, over this church and his home he shall reign forever. And ever.

Amen!

JACKSON

I am making yet another trek to yet another church to deliver yet another sermon about spiritual characteristics of which I'm in deeply short supply. Roscoe Alman asked me to speak at his church's anniversary service a month ago. And I agreed because a month ago everything was fine; rather everything had the illusion of appearing fine and that was good enough for me. Alice wasn't dead. Lebanon wasn't hustling me for more money and a politician wasn't trying to bribe me for an advantage.

The tension in the car makes it hard for me to focus on my next sermon. From Joanna's silence and the rigid fold of her crossed arms, I can tell she's upset about the conversation I had with Layla earlier today. I saw my mom speak to Joanna before she got in the car. I know Mom relayed the information in absolute detail, from the timbre of our voices to the exact position of each dust particle in the air.

"Are you going to say anything?" I say, looking peripherally at the grim set of Joanna's mouth.

"I'm measuring my words, because anything I say now could be out of anger and hurtful."

"You know I'm not always the one to blame."

"No one said anything about blame. You blame yourself enough for things that can't be changed."

I shake my head. "I thought you said you were going to measure your words."

Joanna continues, "You need to learn how to talk to Layla. Not lecture her. Not overestimate your authority with her."

"You just took everything Mom said for fact. You weren't there!"

"I don't have to be there because I deal with you both all the time! I referee and pass messages between the two of you because you don't talk to each other. And your son, J.P., dismisses you altogether."

I feel like I'm trying to breathe underwater.

In the middle of the street, I stop our black Hyundai Sonata in front of a sturdy three-story gray stone apartment building on Garfield Boulevard. The metallic rush of cars on the nearby Dan Ryan fills my ears. I turn to Joanna. Sun refracts the light causing bursts of rainbow patterns in the car covering our hands.

"Let's lay it out. You say you don't blame me, but you blame me for not being there when they were younger."

"Jackson, that was your choice. Yours. And I did what I've always done, which is whatever I have to do."

"God is important. We must place Him above all else. I want Layla and J.P. to see that by how I live and I don't think they get that. If they ever will."

"Baby, you placed *church* above your family. Not God."

"So you do resent me. For being gone. What else are you holding against me? For introducing Alice to Lebanon? I could have never known it would turn out likes this."

"She was a grown woman and made her own decisions. I made my decisions, too. I could have offered her a place to stay the first time Lebanon hit her."

"He wasn't always that way."

"You're holding on to a person who isn't there anymore."

"You don't understand."

"Try me."

My hands are gripping the steering wheel so firmly my fingers are numb. The loud, booming voice I've used to deliver so many charismatic sermons can't even whisper now. Not about a winter night in a hotel room, how Lebanon took the blame for a sin I committed while I sat safe and away and he sat in a prison cell. I can't tell my wife what is shared between me and a man who stopped being a friend long ago and became an anchor around my neck. I can't tell her about Syrus Myllstone.

Joanna's brown eyes look at me, celestially twinkling. They could unlock the mysteries of God's universe if she looked at the heavens the right way, but she can't comprehend why I'm so deeply rooted in my own anguish.

"Jackson, talk to me. *Please.*"

"There was a guy. Me and Lebanon... I mean I—"

A car horn blares behind us interrupting my confession, taking me away from this moment, and I'm slammed back into my shame.

"I have to make a quick stop."

Starting the car again, I drive east. Joanna's perfume wafts throughout the car and I don't dare turn toward her again. She glances at me out of the corner of her eye, then stares out the window as the landscape blurs until I stop near 37th and State Street. The small, nondescript storefront buildings on the block vary in size and shape. Across the street, newly constructed apartment buildings with giant windows line the block. The wind pummels my back, urging me to move faster. Behind me the Green Line train chugs past on the elevated tracks. The Chicago Bee Library is on my right side, and though I'm pressed for time, though I have a wife who's not happy with me and though I must deliver a check that might bankrupt my church, I still stop.

The structure housed a black newspaper, the *Chicago Bee*, and I always imagined what went on there. What injustices were reported, how words nicked and chipped away at wrongs endured by an oppressed part of America. My father would bring me and Lebanon by here when the building held a cosmetics firm and tell us about the history. The *Chicago Bee*, the *Chicago Defender*, were *only two* of the black-owned papers in America, but they ran in this city. This wasn't in our hand-me-down history books. It was told orally by my father to me, and I brought Layla and J.P. when they were little, and I told them what I remembered from my father about these papers, about our people's time here. Maybe they'll visit the same block with their children and repeat the story, our collective history, that unless told remains buried in this city.

"Still a nice building. Remember when your dad would bring us here?"

I turn around to find Lebanon with a dirty wrinkled brown bag in his hand. I give him the envelope. And he smirks, easy and arrogant. I suppress the desire to punch him. "Joanna not too thrilled with you giving me this, I suppose. What did she say?"

"What do you care about the conversations between me and my wife?"

"Watch your tone, Jackson. I'm just trying to make sure she won't make things complicated. She has a talent for that you know. Can't tell you how many times she almost got Alice to leave me."

The wind picks up even more, lifting the tails of our coats, the few remaining dead leaves on the street carelessly roll down the block. "You almost sound impressed someone could go against you."

"I respect it in a way. Someone's got to have the balls in your family."

I take a step closer to Lebanon. "That's nice. Now, leave Joanna's name out of your mouth and take the last of the money I'm *ever* going to give to you."

"Did you practice that line, like you do one of your sermons?"

I glance down the block. I could still hit him. Punch him and leave him on the street hurt and bleeding, and it'd feel so good to do it. But I have a church to speak at in half an hour, and I can't explain away bruised knuckles and blood on my suit.

"You could try it, Jackson. You could try and hit me if you want, but don't think I'm an easy win. Besides, Joanna is waiting for you."

"I didn't—"

"Yeah, you want to hit me. I know that look well when it comes to me."

He could always do that, say what I'm thinking before I said a word. It pissed me off and fascinated me at the same time. When we were younger, that made him a great friend. Now, his ability to reach into my being and cypher my thoughts is a violation, one I can't prevent.

"I was jealous of you when we were younger," Lebanon continues. "You had a nice life, and I figured if we hung out enough, your life would be my life. If we were friends. Your mom would be mine. Pastor Thomas, too. Even dead your father was better than the one I never had."

I meet his gaze, but it's unfocused. The beat of his voice reminds me of someone telling a story to people round a campfire.

"You know what it was like with her. The drinking, the hitting, the men in and out. Being with you and Ms. Violet, I was good for just a little while. I used that to get me through everything else."

There's no response needed for these ancient memories so I don't interrupt.

"I ached to be with y'all, but I know I couldn't stay too long, be happy too long. There's always a sad part to being happy."

When we play as little boys, I am a king and Lebanon is a knight. Sometimes Lebanon wants to be the king, but he is just happy to be in a place where he can breathe and where shadows don't overrun the light. In the backyard of my home, we slay dragons and save princesses and defeat an evil witch. We wear robes of gold and red, old bedsheets Momma ties around our necks. In our urban kingdom, the difference between good and evil is simple, a line drawn in the dirt. And, after a night or two or three, Sara always comes for Lebanon, takes him back to the apartment. She doesn't want her son but can't let him be free from whatever ghosts torment her mind.

Just like that I feel sorry for him. I don't know how he can reach into my mind and influence me this way.

"Look, I won't bother you anymore, if you do this one last thing for me," says Lebanon.

"To never have to see you again, deal with your favors, I'll do anything you want."

Lebanon smirks again, the easy, arrogant one from before. He shoves the dirty brown paper bag into my hand. "Be careful what you say, Jackson. Get rid of what's in this bag, and you won't see me again. Ever."

Without another word, Lebanon turns and walks way.

I open the bag, the dirt from it staining my fingers. I close my eyes, take a deep breath and look again hoping to see something different and not a gun, the one I'm sure killed Alice.

CHAPTER 8

RUBY

TWELVE DAYS BEFORE ALICE KING'S DEATH

Before I open the door I listen behind it, the low and steady music of sewing machine whir, of cutting fabric and snapping thread, the rhythm of the pedal and the dull knock of the chair against the floor as Mom twists and turns to adjust a hem or stitch. I've never seen her nick or cut herself when she sews. And she smiles this smile, like everything is rightly placed in the world along with the seams on a quilt. This is her happy or some version of it when she is alone and apart from me or Lebanon. It's nice she has something she loves that doesn't hurt her.

Mom sings the same song each time she closes herself in this room.

Ask the Savior to help you. Comfort, strengthen and keep you; He is willing to aid you; He will carry you through.

It's a pretty song, and I wish I could believe the words. It brings me a memory associated with hope or love or some other good feeling. When I hear this song, I reach back into my mind.

I remember the creak of the porch in Tennessee as Grandma Naomi rocked back and forth in her wicker chair. Billowy wisps of white dandelion fluff float by, tickle my nose, and fall back down on the tops of the grass. I can *almost* feel the sun on my knees and the split board of the top stair slightly digging into my thigh. I don't move though. I'm tasting the sweetness of the tea as it slips sweet and cold to the back of my throat. I hear laughter. My laughter. Grandma smiles at me, and I'm happy and free in the Tennessee sunlight, hidden in its indigo dreams.

Ask the Savior to help you. Comfort, strengthen and keep you; He is willing to aid you; He will carry you through.

Light floods the hall from the sewing room, and I stand face-to-face with Mom; the wrinkles around her mouth pulling down her lips into a tight smile.

"You realize you were singing, Ruby?"

"No."

"Your singing is just like Mom's. So pretty. You're such a pretty girl." She caresses my face. The faraway sound in her voice lingers in my ears and burrows its way into my heart, cracking it just a little bit more. "Wanna come sit down and keep me company for a minute or two?"

I move a stray hair from her forehead and she flinches, then smiles wide. I can never really say no to Momma. She asks for so little. When it comes to everything, even people loving her, she asks for so little. She should ask for more. We both should ask for more, believe we deserve more.

"So how's work, baby girl?"

"The same. Not much to report. Not a lot of overtime, but I'll be able to help with the mortgage."

"No, no. Just wanted to make sure you were good there. Happy."

"Happy?"

"Yeah. That's important."

I lean forward and Mom scoots her chair away, at a slightly

different angle, so that if I were to try to touch her, I'd be just out of reach.

"Why'd you move?"

"It's just these stitches are giving me the blues and my back is acting up."

Grabbing a dark green pillow from the small chair next to her, I stand behind her. "Move forward," I say. Mom does what I ask. Her movements are stiff, ready for anything I suppose. She can't switch that off, the constant awareness. He's not even in the room, and she's prepared to hurt at every turn. How can she think I'm happy when I see this, when I see her live like this?

She leans back. "Hmm. That is better."

"Well, I do have a good idea occasionally. I'm not just a pretty face."

"Now where did that come from? I just said thank you."

I feel the muscles of my cheeks snatch back in some kind of way. "You don't have to look like that. You remind me of your father when you make that face," Mom says.

"I can't see how I look," I reply, folding my arms across my chest.

"Oh, baby, come on, come on. Don't be like that. I didn't mean anything by it, okay?" She scoots her chair near to me and reaches out to take my hand. Her fingers are warm and firm and they grip mine.

"Now, tell me about something nice today," she says.

I'm trying to think of something, *anything* to put a smile on her face and mine. I hate my job. I hate my father. But I want to tell her something nice.

"They have dance classes starting up at the new community center, in a month or so," I offer.

"That's nice. How much are they?"

"Ummm, I'm not sure."

"Okay, well I mean we can figure it out. If you can still help around here, I don't see why you can't go. We'll of course have to ask your father."

"Why does it matter what Lebanon thinks?"

"Don't refer to your father by his first name!"

"He's not a father! He's not a husband! He's the thing that makes everything ugly like him."

"We're all he has, do you know that? You don't walk away from that, from the responsibility of someone needing you. People have hurt him and let him down his whole life. Even his mother...she...she..." Mom searches for words, some improbable sentence that'll help her explain why Lebanon is the way he is, and why she stays, and because of her, why I stay.

Mom sighs. "I know your father in a way no one else does, and somewhere deep down he loved me once, he still does. What he does is...it's more than bones and bruises, and the world can be so unkind to people, relentless, especially to men like him, to people like us. And those few times when it gets to be too much, he loses himself a little. But I find him, and he comes back or at least he used to, and maybe I can do that again. One more time."

"And...what if you can't, Momma? What if he kills you? You want to live like this forever? You want me to stay in this house, at a job I hate, and help you pay bills he can't? Never do anything with my life?"

"He's not a perfect person, but you can't blame him for everything wrong with you."

"You're right. I can blame you, too."

There is a silence now, one held in the walls and floorboards. A silence that screams. Water spills from Mom's eyes and I'm being pulled further and further from her. I have this sticky feeling of being both right and cruel. I become *Him*, Lebanon, my father. The lashes of my words and the soft pleasure I find in my mother's tears bind me to him. In this fractured moment, I resemble the person I hate the most—yes, this is a sticky feeling. Guilt and vindication and fear cling to me.

Mom hugs me hard, like Grandma Naomi. She and I are in this together; us against him, and I don't want Mom thinking I really blame her for everything that's happened in my life. I do own some part of my situation. I can leave, but I can't leave her with him. I couldn't be happy like that. So, if I can't be happy as a party of one, I'll be miserable as a party of two.

"Look, I'm not good at talking. Why don't I watch you work on this quilt? After, I can make us some blackened catfish. You like that, right?"

"Okay, baby." Mom dabs away the last of the tears leaking from her eyes, then sniffs, the phlegmy sound filling the quiet around the rest of my choked-on words, the ones I will never share with her.

"You know I love you, Ruby."

"I know."

Watching her work on the quilt, the metallic melody of the sewing machine fills the still air. The white bench in her room looks out onto the street. It digs into my flesh like the top stair of Grandma Naomi's porch. I don't move or adjust my position. I stay with the pain, and Mom begins humming the song once more.

Ask the Savior to help you. Comfort, strengthen and keep you; He is willing to aid you; He will carry you through.

LAYLA

My mind constantly replays Ruby walking out of the café door. The tinkling of the bell. And me still sitting with a cup of coffee in front of me. A cup of coffee and no friend.

Pulsing beats greet my ears as I open the door leading into the vestibule of the house. Two overstuffed ivory couches, dark cherry end tables and a longer cocktail table expertly arranged by my mom who has a knack for complementary colors.

As I walk past the kitchen, J.P. stands in his room ironing a blue-collared shirt and black jeans. I know why his shirts are so wrinkly all the time. The iron barely touches them. His full lips are too busy mouthing a song. The complexion of a melted Hershey bar and a baritone voice that fills a room much the way my father's does, but without the pretention or ceremony. His toothpick legs bounce up and down to the beat somehow supporting his almost seven-foot frame and muscles hardened by manual labor during night shifts at the post office.

"I thought you were gonna be asleep," I shout over the music.

J.P. turns down the volume. "Grandma Violet called from the church. I'm picking her up and bringing her back to the house. You're early though. Thought you'd be home later," he says.

"I had some stuff to do so I didn't go to the other service."

J.P. turns his head and looks at me. His eyes, a darker shade of cinnamon than my father's, make some unspoken judgment about my words.

He makes a sound between a chuckle and a snort, "How'd that go over with the old man?"

"It didn't. But I don't care."

"You do. You're just frontin' with me right now. You care."

Unlike me, J.P. isn't fooling himself. He's not trying to shield his emotions like I am. He really doesn't give a shit about dad being angry at him. J.P.'s free enough to let things fall off him like a set of oversized clothes. I move to leave. But before I leave his doorway, J.P. says, "You went to see Ruby, didn't you?"

I say nothing. I don't want to break a confidence, but when I turn around, I don't look him in the eyes which is as good as saying yes and confessing every detail of my uneasy conversation in the coffee shop.

"You always look—" he pauses to find the right words "—a little less after you see her."

"A little less what?"

"Everything. You look tired. Defeated. Sad. You look sad as hell, sis."

I feel how my shoulders slump forward and all I want to do right now is sleep, but at this point I'm afraid I'll have dreams of what I fear for Ruby.

"When will you be finished working on the painting?"

J.P. smiles and points to the corner. "I'm gonna work on the detailing of the background before I move on to finish the rest. It should take me a few more days."

An easel next to his bed holds an incomplete landscape, a waterfall and a dense meadow, wildflower carpets and birds circling the sky. There is a man in the middle of the painting and he gazes at the unfinished horizon of the canvas.

"It looks good so far," I say.

"How much do you think I'll get for it?"

"I'm my brother's keeper, not my brother's art dealer."

J.P. laughs and claps his massive black paws two times. Another rapper comes on the radio with a new song, a serenade on the world's beauty, a caution about its seductive, harsh nature on a disenfranchised people. A million lyrical metaphors say the same thing, again and again.

I walk into my small room with one window facing a timeworn tree. Did I make a mistake letting Ruby leave that coffee shop without me? Is Ruby going to hurt herself? What do I do?

When I crave peace, I go into my closet. Really, that's what I do. I place a folded towel at the bottom of the door to block out the remaining strip of light. I pray.

God, there are a lot of things I can't see. I don't know how I'm supposed to fix this or if I'm sticking my nose where it doesn't belong, but I have to help Ruby so please Lord, help me do that. Please.

I wait. Not for a hand on a wall or a burning bush that talks. If I saw those things, I'd freak the hell out and run yelling from my home. But I need a sign, something to tell me what to do.

It's been at least ten minutes and nothing. Leaning against the wall, I slide down and my bottom hits the floor. Part of a heel wedges itself uncomfortably underneath my backside. I place it to the side and yawn.

Not to rush you, God, but what am I supposed to do? I kinda need an answer now.

I wait some more.

J.P.'s music no longer plays. I hear the front door close. I feel foolish. Maybe I just need to rest.

I hear murmurs at first. I can't make out the words. They break and crash on the edges of my consciousness. I open my eyes. I'm lying in a valley of downy grass. I look to my left and behold three rolling hills of lilies and gardenias and sunflowers, and blossoms that have no business being in the same place but are so pretty bunched and mingled together. The valley is green and blue and bright. The sun softens in saffron shades and golden light warms my skin. I'm dressed in a long white calico dress, but it's not any shade of white with which I'm familiar. It's pure and pretty and I'm happy. Grass rises up to meet my fingers and I walk up the second hill to a tall oak tree. Branches twist and bend. All the leaves are alive and a light, not coming from the sun, surrounds the tree and I see Three Women. There is such peace on their faces. One of them takes my hand and whispers. I try to hear her but can't. I want to hold on to her hand longer, but her fingers loosen from mine and her hand gently pulls away. She caresses my face and walks back to the other two women and stands in the middle. I focus on their beauty. It's not the kind of beauty on which one gauges attractiveness. It's a beauty beyond physical features and proportions. I feel I know all of them but they have no names. I want to ask who they are but can't form words. The Three Women look to the right, the day's glow is swallowed by slate skies, and I hear thunder and see hot, pulsing curtains of lightning slamming into the ground in restless and violent intervals. The wind whips my white calico dress around my knees. I see the woman in the middle mouth a word once more. I reach out...

The walls of the closet surround me again and my arm is still extended in the darkness of my space. My eyes are adjusting again, but I don't feel comforted by the stillness. The light musty smell of worn shoes lingers. I'm left with my thoughts, the sound of my breathing and the one word the woman in the middle repeated to me in the green valley over and over: *Go!*

I race outside to the Black Stallion and it won't start. I take deep breaths, meditate, pray, beg, turn the key in the ignition. Metal grinds against metal, a stuttering, piercing whir murders the quiet of the neighborhood on a Sunday afternoon. It just sits, a rusting piece of motorized aluminum. Smoke seeps from under the hood; a toxic smell of burnt rubber and motor oil float in the atmosphere and now in addition to letting down my friend, I'm also contributing to global warming.

Damn it!

If this were a movie, after a couple of tries, the car would magically come to life and I'd drive off into a rust-colored sunset to save Ruby. But in this life, I now have to abandon my smoking car, pump my mighty thighs and run three blocks to the bus stop.

In that closet, in that vision, once I heard the word *Go!* I knew it was God.

Ruby is too precious and we're too close for me to do nothing. I'll make her see what I see. I'll make her see how she can have a life, a new life away from Lebanon.

Not on a bathroom floor. Not with me saying goodbye to a friend in a casket like Momma had to. This story is ending a different way. With her and me. With marriages. With our kids getting on our damn nerves. This ends with phone calls and laughter and barbeques. Maybe even with our families coming back together. With grandkids and us complaining about how everything is too expensive now. This ends for us as old women rocking in porch chairs, hot days with cold sweet tea.

But for a happy ending, I need to find Ruby. I need her to see our future, the possibility of it.

I need Ruby to see how this, *our story* ends.

With both of us. Together.

CALVARY

September 23, 1960

Sara tries to make no sound as she enters her father's office. Where would he hide her doll, Louisa? So busy figuring out her plan to escape, she almost forgot the one thing she loves most. Blue-black shadows hover in parts of the room where the luminescent fingers of streetlamps do not reach.

Light suddenly floods the office and Sara racks her brain of any and all plausible lies to tell her father why she's in his office. Turning around she finds only Naomi.

If she's here, King Saul can't be far behind; she's already taken up too much time. Seeing her panic, Naomi tries to put her friend at ease. "He was in the back of the church locking up. He didn't see you."

Sara exhales, but that doesn't stop the nausea making waves in her belly. "How didn't he see you?"

"I'm small. No one ever sees me. It's a blessing now, I guess. You're supposed to be gone already," scolds Naomi.

"I left Louisa. I have to get her." She walks to the bookshelf across from his desk. There's a wooden box on the second row where King Saul hides a small bottle of whiskey among the books. Sometimes Sara takes a small sip or two of the whiskey. It helps her with memories, making them less defined and sharp.

"It's just a doll. This is your life. Please let's just go. He hasn't locked the back door yet." Naomi's voice barely whispering, afraid of her words, afraid they might somehow reach King Saul.

"It's all I have from my mom, the only thing he can't touch, the only thing that's truly mine."

The stark brown-black of Sara's eyes betray her desperation and pierce Naomi. Naomi knows she will help her friend. She always has. She always will.

Forever and to the end.

God will give them the strength to get through this. God will protect them.

Sara blindly grabs at the air under her father's desk and her hands grasp a few strands of yarn and smiling she grabs Louisa. If she concentrates, she can smell her mom, Sophia, remember her pretty golden-brown eyes, and find a small bit of happiness. Rising, Sara's shoulder bumps the leg of the desk and a key taped underneath falls to the floor.

"We gotta go, now!" Naomi pleads.

Sara picks up the key, staring at the locked drawer right in her line of sight. Unlocking the drawer, she finds an envelope, thick with what is no doubt money, neatly tucked, lying on top of papers and pens and other junk. The proceeds of the offerings taken earlier that evening. King Saul wasn't good at hiding things from her. You can't hide things from someone who knows all the ugly of you. She can't hide things from Violet and Naomi, and King Saul can't hide things from her.

Naomi widens her eyes as Sara removes the money from the envelope, a little more than $380, enough to at least get a better footing in Tennessee, but not enough to pay for those nights and her tears and her fear, not enough to sweep away the detritus or mend her life until this point.

Sara steadies herself and carefully steps from behind the desk to grab her purse on the worn emerald green couch against the opposite wall next to a cheap pine table, a pane of glass sporting a crack which spreads diagonally from one end to the other.

Sara hears the creak of the old door before watching her father walk through it.

Full lips in a tight straight line, his husky voice behind clenched teeth. "What the fuck you think you doing, little girl?"

People look so hard on Saul's appearance, no one sees the monster underneath. She thinks her mother, Sophia, saw the monster, and protected her even when she was dying. Sophia was the prettiest woman Sara had ever seen even when she was sick. Sara swore her Mom had golden eyes, such a bright brown they shined and shimmered when happy. Sophia kept Sara close, read books in funny voices, until she was so weak, Sara began reading to her. If Sara didn't know how to pronounce the complicated syllables, she'd make it up as she went along, sometimes creating a whole new story. Those were the best books, where you came up with your own ending, no matter what the words on the pages said. Eventually the adults didn't let Sara read to her mom anymore. They spoke in hushed whispers about the illness, though no one said *cancer* out loud, as if the disease would spread if they spoke its name.

Naomi steps forward. "Reverend, Sara and I just wanted…"

"Shut the hell up!" he says.

He turns to Sara. "I say again, whatchu doing, little girl?" His tone is suddenly calmer, more sinister, a rhythm to the question.

Clutching Louisa and the envelope tight to her chest, Sara fibs, "I just needed my doll to make me feel better. That's all, Daddy. That's all."

"You needed *my money* to do that?"

"I was going to put it back. I just wanted to double-count it to make sure it was all there for you."

"So sick as you supposed to be, you felt the need to find that key and count my money?"

It was a stupid lie. Stupid. *Stupid.* She shouldn't have lied.

King Saul looms over Sara who stands only two inches shorter, but her lithe frame seems diminished compared to his strong stature.

"Daddy," she begins.

"What do we say about liars, Sara?"

Sara's eyes dart behind King Saul and find Naomi. She motions her friend to leave, but Naomi stays.

His finger sharply snapping her chin to meet his eyes, King Saul says again, "What do we say about liars?"

"All liars shall have their part in the Lake of Fire," Sara whispers.

Sara knows this verse. It's in Revelation. It's about the End Times. Saul makes her repeat it often. The way he makes her say this verse isn't word for word like the Bible. He whittled it down to a simple action and a compelling consequence.

Sara steps back until she feels the desk behind her.

"Please, Reverend Saul, we didn't mean any harm…" Naomi says, trying to diffuse a situation over which they have no control.

Sara moves slightly aside and tries to dodge Saul's hand, but it quickly grabs her and throws her across the floor near Naomi's feet.

Reaching for her friend, Naomi meets Sara's gaze, a trickle of blood ornamenting her full lips as she mouths the word "No."

Viciously hauling Sara up by her shoulders, Saul shakes her. "You leavin' me girl? You leavin' me?"

There's a low moan from Sara, somewhere deep within, an unfixable place. Naomi listens for footsteps, voices, any sign of deliverance, but she hears only the thud of her friend's body hitting the floor and the smack of hand across skin as Saul strikes Sara again.

Naomi feels her fists hitting Saul's back before her brain tells her she can't help her friend like this. They do no more damage than a mosquito does with an elephant; Saul tosses her off just as easily as the insect. Naomi crashes to the ground, toppling over the pine table, the air in her lungs hovering somewhere above her body for the moment. Sharp knives of glass from the overturned table glisten in her blurred vision.

It always amazes Sara how soft Saul's fingers are, even as they are squeezing her throat, ten velvety light brown digits bruising and crushing her fragile windpipe. He shouldn't have beautiful hands.

Sara stops struggling. What good does fighting do anyone? Let go. She'd see her mom, Sophia. She misses her mom. She misses looking at her calming, golden-brown eyes. She misses reading to someone she loves.

But she's not dying. She's breathing, easier. King Saul's grip loosens. His eyes, green as spring grass, go wide, close and he falls forward. A heap of dead muscle and bone that she pushes off her.

Behind him, Sara sees Naomi, a large shard of glass in her hands baptized in blood.

CHAPTER 9

JACKSON

FIVE DAYS BEFORE ALICE KING'S DEATH

These walls close in on me after church ends, when the Benediction is delivered, hands are shaken, hugs and parting words spoken. As the congregation slowly filters outside, I gather myself alone in an office once occupied by my grandfather, Andrew Morrison, and for a very brief time, my father, Thomas Potter. The books and shelves, framed pictures and degrees, I find it suffocating. Its history and expectation alone could be crushing. The unyielding guilt inside of my heart at my inability to stop it. I never wanted this office, this title *Pastor*.

I know the weight of it. I saw how it aged my father in the short time he stood behind the pulpit where I now plant my feet Sunday after Sunday.

Mom knew how to carefully navigate the city, its invisible rules, and somehow keep her dignity. I remember going with her once to the Chicago Theatre. The ticket taker was smiling, handing each ticket to each white patron, but flung it at Mom when it was our turn. She promptly turned around and left the tickets. She took us for ice cream instead.

Mom and Dad witnessed Chicago at it's very worst, boiling with hate. Malcolm X and Martin Luther King Jr. were assassinated. Our hopes for self-sustaining pride or peaceful resolution bled out on the wood floors of the Audubon Ballroom and the concrete balcony of the Lorraine Motel. Civil rights leaders, a president and his brother were bloodied and murdered before television screens. America was on fire.

I asked Dad once, it happened to be the week before he died, why he did any of it. Why serve when it doesn't make a difference, to congregants who'll constantly let you down, who don't see the burdens you bear on their behalf day in and day out? And, my dad, deep thought creasing his skin of burnt umber, answered, "God does it all the time for us, son. And I guess it's about courage, too. The courage to love despite loss of any kind. If you can't see anything good in yourself or the world right now, see that part. See courage. That will guide you like it guides me."

Knocking on the door interrupts my thoughts. Alice King rushes past the threshold, a manila folder clutched in her hands. She normally waits for permission to enter. She normally waits for permission to do most everything.

"Pastor, I know I'm disturbing you and I greatly apologize, but it's important. It's Lebanon."

"Yes?"

"You know, I've been doing the accounting for the church. Making sure everything is correct, orderly, honest."

"You do a wonderful job, Alice. Couldn't ask—"

"No. No I don't."

Alice sits down across from me, wringing her hands. "I've stolen, from the church, for Lebanon…so he could keep up payments for the bakery, to pay it off. The mortgage payment is due on Thursday."

The folder now meekly lies on my desk, thick with papers, ones and zeroes, facts and figures, ripe with the possibility of sending Lebanon, and Alice, to jail for God knows how long. Is she intentionally wanting to ruin her life? Does she want me to escort her to the police station? The church would never forgive me for not taking action. If I'd manage to keep it quiet, Lebanon still would know I'd helped Alice and he'd take the opportunity to make me pay for doing so. Even from a jail, he could do damage. He could talk, get others gossiping. He could still turn the church against me. Just an accusation, true or not, has devastating consequences. A small crack in trust becomes a gigantic fissure, decimating a once rock-solid foundation.

"What are you asking me to do?"

"I was hoping you'd have an idea," she says, her eyes wide in anticipation; she's waiting for an answer to it all, a way to leave Lebanon for good, to give Ruby and herself some hope. Freedom. She wants me to come to her aid by taking action against Lebanon. She's waiting for an answer to her freedom.

"You should go home. On Sunday, I'll announce to the church board you're stepping down from the treasurer position, for personal reasons. Maybe I can use my savings or something to cover the missing money." Walking over to the desk, I take the folder and place it in the top drawer. My hands are shaking. "I'll figure some way to put the money back. Don't worry. I won't tell Lebanon you came here with this."

She bows her head low, takes deep breaths. "You weren't gonna help me. Part of me knew that, but I hoped, I *prayed* I was wrong."

"He's my friend, Alice. What good would locking him up do?"

"He's no more a friend to you now than he ever was a husband to me or a father to Ruby."

"So, this is worth you going to jail, too? Because that's what would happen. You wouldn't last a day there, Alice. You're not strong enough to—"

"Twenty years with Lebanon King. I'm stronger than you'll *ever* know, Jackson. If those files put me in jail, so be it. But he'd be put away too, and at least Ruby would be safe!"

She seems to be talking to herself more than having a conversation with me. "I tried. I prayed for him. Did what God asked, what my vows demanded. I loved him. Some broken part of me still does, but he can't be saved. You made me believe once he could be, but he can't."

Walking quickly back to the door, Alice opens it and adds, "You choosing him this last time over me and Ruby, maybe you can't be saved either." The suddenness of her departure is punctuated by the dull thump of the door closing behind her.

If you can't see anything good in yourself... See courage.

I wait for a few minutes making sure Alice has left the church. Then I turn off the lights and head home.

LAYLA

My thighs are still burning as I leave the bus and run down-stairs to catch the train at the 95th Red Line Station. Signs boasting a new station coming soon have been here for months and they haven't so much as put a new tile down yet.

A man peddling from one train car to the other offers candy, headphones, bootleg DVDs and tube socks. Body oils are fastened in bandolier-type belts crisscross on his chest. A younger man enters the opposite way, proclaiming, "Got dem squares. Eight-dollar packs. Got dat loud."

A hustler sits in the middle of the aisle and tries enticing us to play a shell game, already rigged in his favor. The train is a mobile market, squeezing together the good, the needy, the savage and the gullible.

There is a man on the train who keeps looking for something in his bag. He takes out coins and old newspapers and used tissues. He mumbles to himself and I can't really make out any of the words. He can't find what he's looking for so he keeps searching.

I call Ruby's phone. Straight to voice mail. Damn it.

After Ruby tried to kill herself, she had a copy made of her house key and gave it to me. You know, just in case, she said. After the hospital, Ruby stayed with me. Becoming as much of a fixture at our house as the leaking faucet, the cracked third stair, the buckled roof tiles where the squirrels would get in and scurry about.

I hated her. I loved her. I love her. I'm angry with her, for not doing more, the ways she harms herself. I'm scared of Ruby's pain and how that pain consumes everything, how it consumes me.

Memories and regrets and hopes are the annoying song on repeat in my head. The train flies down the tracks. I rock side to side and look through the graffiti-decorated window. This place, these gatherings of neighborhoods and streets and people are so easily dismissed by others and sometimes myself. The South Side. It is still magic. Troubled, but still magnificent. Dark and light and loud mingle, and I wish we could see our purpose, our gathered meaning. I wish I knew myself with some kind of certainty. I want to help her better. I want so badly to help Ruby.

A bright voice declares my stop, 79th Street, is next. I don't move from my seat. I still sit. I don't want to leave, but the voice of the Three Women tell me to *Go!*

The train stops. Doors open. Young men beat on upside-down ten-gallon buckets in the station, and a primal beat pulses through me, from the top of my head to the soles of my feet. The Bucket Boys move back and forth, twirl the sticks through their nimble, ebony fingers and wooden knocking provides a *rat-tat-pop-boom* over and over on those buckets. The blocks on this side of the city might stay this way forever, this violent and this beautiful and this hopeful and this tortured.

Each street leading to her house shows some sort of contradiction of wealth and class. Broken beer bottles and plastic containers for cheap wine litter some properties. Other streets are pristine with perfectly cut grass and landscaping.

There are boarded-up buildings and cellular stores boasting they accept Link cards. Through the asphalt canals of brick homes, side-by-side storefront churches, barbershops, hair salons and fast-food parlors that make up rowdy 'hoods, I see glimpses of a past imperfect and distant. I weave a familiar path of blocks as I make it to Ruby's house.

It's so pretty. The nicest house on the block in fact. That's what gets me every time I stand in front of it. One of the many brick bungalows, this is the only one on this stretch made of red brick. Shy buds of the apple blossom tree in the front yard yield tiny bursts of green.

When Ruby and I were girls, we ran around the lawn and

J.P. would watch us and sketch on blank pieces of paper. When you're a kid there are details that are going to stick with you, but you don't know the significance. You just remember silly games, the feeling of wet grass under your feet.

As an adult, the things I remember now: we didn't really go into the house. Momma and Auntie Alice sat on the front steps. Auntie Alice would wear long-sleeved sweaters even in the summer and I could see sweat on her forehead. Momma always held her hand. And they watched us. Then Momma and J.P. and I went home.

Ruby looked sad and Auntie Alice looked even sadder when we left, but I didn't understand. I didn't know. When I did know, I still didn't feel like I could do anything. If my father didn't get involved, if he was seen as powerful in our community, but he felt powerless, what the hell could I do?

That was the way I kept myself in denial. The easiest thing to do is nothing and we were all guilty of it. My parents. People in church. Our community. We sang our songs and prayed our prayers and talked in pleasantries, but very few of us really knew the business of the other. Though gossip would flow, secrecy also flourished. All the evil we find and leave be, we can't be surprised when it visits, shows up all sharp teeth and vileness.

The lock to this door doesn't stick and seize up. I can easily fit in the key and I walk right in. Uninvited, just like that night when I found Ruby. I pray I won't find her the same way.

Go!

"Ruby! Rue, you here?"

No answer.

The wind from the door feels like it's pushing me farther into the house. I know where her room is and I move toward it. I see the portion of the floor where Auntie Alice lay dead a week ago.

Crimson, in muted shades, still binds itself to the wood. There was an Oriental carpet there, but they probably had to throw it out or maybe it is evidence in her murder and locked up in a dusty lab. I don't know the procedure. Most of my criminal or legal knowledge comes from movies and television shows.

My legs work where my heart falters. I try to make no sound. No one seems to be home, but this house is watching. These walls know things I don't know; things that would make a lesser person turn and leave.

There are two breakfast bar stools knocked over in the kitchen and a sink full of dishes. A pearl necklace lies on the table.

Auntie Alice's craft room is the first door I come to. I enter. Gardenias. It smells like gardenias. A half-finished blanket, folded in thirds, lies across a wood chair. I know Auntie Alice loved to sew. She put tattered things back together in this little room. I close the door.

Lebanon and Auntie Alice's room is on the other side of the house beyond the bathroom where the door is open. I step quickly, lightly. The bed is unmade and Auntie Alice's clothes hang in the closet. Limp ghosts of cotton and silk and chiffon in dull colors lightly billow from a weak draft in the floor. Long sleeves and even longer skirts, low heels. She didn't like to be dressy, said it was vanity and being showy displeased God.

She liked quiet things, flying under the radar. Everything Auntie Alice did was to avoid notice. Attention brought Lebanon and if he was in a mood, pain and trouble would follow. That trouble brought phone calls to my home in the middle of the night or early in the morning.

Momma would answer those calls. Always. Dad stayed in their bedroom, but I know he was awake. I heard the floors creak as he paced back and forth. What are you supposed to say when a friend says her husband beats her? What do you do when you know your friend suffers? There are no rules, there is only listening. That's what Mom did, that's what I tried to do, but I can leave my ears open for only so long before my brain churns, makes plans.

The room is humid and dense with an odor of musky, rotting leaves and incense. There's a picture of Auntie Alice in a bronze frame smiling with Lebanon. I didn't know she could do that. Smile. Normally the roundness of her face perpetually sagged, and it seemed her mouth could never turn upward. She was always crying or about to cry. The whites of her eyes, slightly yellowed like old lace, held water; a never-ending flow of tears just waiting to free themselves.

I have all these bad memories of her.

Memories, the good ones, are the ones Mom told me about when they were young, before Auntie Alice met Lebanon. Auntie Alice was witty and wanted to be a doctor and was a really good dancer. But that changed, not all of a sudden and at once, but gradually and irreversibly.

Between the bedpost and the wall near the window something dully glints in the fading sunlight. My brain tells me what it is, my heart just doesn't want to acknowledge the stiff, cold thing I hold in my hand. A bullet. But I can't change what I see. Bend the shape of it into something pretty. A small thing causing such destruction, and it's in *his* room. Which means Lebanon has or had a gun. Which means he very likely killed Auntie Alice. He certainly had the means to. Jesus, I knew it!

And even telling this to my father, saying I found a damn bullet in Lebanon's bedroom perhaps won't be enough to convince him that Lebanon is someone beyond his reach.

Out of Lebanon and Auntie Alice's room, a smaller bedroom lies across the hall—and that room, that tiny box of a world, is Ruby's.

I open her door with the bullet still in my hand. There's nothing on the walls but old pink paint. To the right is her small, creaky bed and a Bible in the middle partially covered by her grandma's blanket. An ugly purple lamp. Her laptop. No Ruby.

I want to wait for something, some clue as to where she is, but I also want to get the hell out of here before Lebanon comes back. I quickly pull open drawers and rummage superficially. A slightly open window allows a small breeze to animate the room. The hum of the laptop pulls my attention and I open it. Greyhound bus schedules from Chicago to Memphis, one way. The next one leaves in four hours. I scribble the bus number and time on a scrap piece of paper I pull from my pocket.

My hand accidentally brushes a piece of paper on the nightstand that falls and floats under the bed. As I try to reach for it, I hear him laugh. I stuff the bullet and my scrap paper into my coat pocket.

My bones melt and I start to tremble. I know my friend's terror.

CALVARY

September 23, 1960

Saul looks asleep on the floor. Sara stole the large yellow blanket from the desk of the church secretary, Sister Coates. Sister Coates kept it on hand as she always got "god-awful cold" in the building. Sara covered Saul, and she did so delicately. Crimson calmly soaks the wool shroud, a macabre sunset. She hates herself, for keeping some tattered remains of love for someone who did what he did to her. She still somehow loved the man who lied and beat and stole and raped and was her father.

A voice from behind shakily says, "Tell me this is how you found him, Sara."

"You know I can't do that Violet."

"What happened?"

Sara turns around and faces her friend. "He tried to kill me. He knew I was leaving. I found his money in the desk. I took it. He owed me that much, I guess."

The envelope almost bursting with cash, smeared with blood, is now clutched in Sara's hand. Violet shakes her head. "I knew something was wrong. You both didn't show up, and I knew I had to come back, but…"

Sara walks to the bookshelf across from the desk, a few feet away from King Saul's body; she opens a small wooden box and pulls out a small bottle of whiskey and takes two strong sips.

Wide-eyed sitting on the floor, Naomi repeats the same thing: "What could I do?"

Violet closes her eyes, trying to remove what she's seen, praying perhaps when she opens them, it'll be a bad dream. But when Violet opens her eyes again, King Saul is still dead, Naomi remains on the floor clutching a bloody piece of glass, and Sara stands before her in a blue dress slightly torn at the shoulder.

There are scrapes on her arms, knees, marks on her throat and a small bottle of whiskey in her hand.

There is a line Violet crosses in her mind and heart, one presenting options, ugly choices. It might be over soon. Their lives, the circumstances planned and unplanned, light and shadow, leave them stifled and still in a dim church office. Yes, there is a line Violet must cross, and on the road of her mind much of what she picks up along the way are Old Testament stories, times when vengeance was warranted, justified and even celebrated.

Naomi did what needed to be done. King Saul was a bad man and bad men deserve what they get, even if it's death on a dirty floor. It was right and it is well with God. Violet knows this. That man was already in Hell. Violet knows this, too.

Crouching down to Naomi who gently rocks herself still asking that one question, Violet brushes hair away from her light yellow, angular face. She removes the wine-stained shard of glass, fiercely gripped in delicate hands.

"Did anyone see you and Sara come here?"

Words sound far away to Naomi. There are things still frozen in her mind. Shock clings to her, sweaty clothes on a muggy summer day. Only the whoosh of blood cycling through her trembling frame signals she still exists in the land of the living.

She still exists. King Saul does not.

"No," Sara finally answers from behind her. "I don't think so."

With everything quiet, Violet further clears the fog in her mind and reasons it's important to take care of things step by step, contain one crisis at a time. If she didn't keep moving, she'd surely stop and collapse on the floor, joining Naomi, both of them held captive by inaction.

"Put that bottle back and help me," she orders Sara.

Sara returns the bottle to the wooden box but remains in front of the bookshelf.

Violet removes the blanket. Blood, an unholy glue, initially resistant to Violet's pull, finally loosens its grip. A few stray fibers cling to the wound.

Sara just watches. Offers no help. Cries no tears. Her eyes vacantly follow movement.

Naomi still rocks to and fro.

Violet continues to pray and acts fast.

The scene will be more convincing as a robbery so she'll make it look like that as much as she can. She takes a few bills from the envelope and scatters them around the body.

She removes Saul's wallet from his back pocket, a subtle lump of black leather embossed with his initials, taking the $42 and stuffing it in her bra. He has his rings, including a plain gold ring on his left pinkie finger and the one with diamonds on his right pinkie finger. She confiscates those as well, placing them in her pocket. They'll fetch a few more dollars to help Sara on her journey to Tennessee. Plenty of shops in the city are willing to take jewelry with blood on it. They'll wipe it off and sell it just the same.

As best as she can, Violet rubs fingerprints from the glass that killed Saul and gathers it up along with the blanket to take with her to discard in a dumpster a few blocks away.

"Get Naomi," Violet orders Sara.

Violet looks on the street from the window. People linger in front of the building so they'll escape out the back.

"We're gonna take you home, Naomi, and you're gonna go to sleep because this is a bad dream. Nothing but a bad dream," says Violet.

Naomi leaves the office and waits for Sara and Violet in Sister Coates's chair.

Sara closes the door after her. "She's not strong like we are," says Sara.

"Strong? You went to get a doll. She saved your ass and you want to talk about strength now?"

"I'm just saying she's gonna break. Tell someone. Then it's all done. It's over."

"All you had to do was follow directions! We should already be at the train station."

Sara's eyes even in the dim light grow darker, her lips curl. She looks like Saul. The streetlights bounce shapes and shadows, ghostly witnesses to fresh secrets.

"I needed to get Louisa. It's the only thing I have left from her."

"This ring was your mom's." Violet pulls the cheap wedding band from her pocket. "You didn't even flinch when I took it."

"What would I want it for? He gave it to her and it kept her chained to him. She gave Louisa to me. She was mine!"

"You almost died to get a damn doll! Naomi almost died to save you!"

"Y'all got involved. I didn't ask for your help. You see me like some charity case. You always need to be the hero. The good girl. You need someone to save all the damn time! You need to feel like you Jesus or some shit."

Violet's head cocks to her left much as it did before she was about to say something she'd later regret. Her lips hot and ready to burn.

"No. I'm not Jesus. I'm the one who is keeping a bitch like you from going to jail with a bastard in your belly. I'm the one who can tell you the truth. And I can tell you this—without Naomi doing what she did, you'd be dead. And yeah, we'd be sad. But we'd eventually move on with our lives just the same, and you'd be in the ground. So yeah, I'm Jesus, fine. Act like you don't want my help and find yourself in Hell just the same."

"Fuck you!" shouts Sara, reaching for Violet's neck much the same as Saul did to her earlier. The angry tangling of limbs, muffled yelps. The girls tussle on in anger and fear, all the hidden competitions and jealousies on display, the abundance of emotion without an easy release.

Each girl loses momentum and breath, hate drains from their limbs and fingers. They're left sore and scratched and winded. Nothing has been alleviated, nothing has been gained, but with the broken love left between them, Violet and Sara trudge out of the office and gather Naomi. They leave my halls with a bloody blanket, a blade of glass and a new burden to shoulder.

More than hate binds them now. Secrets and blood can fortify the shakiest of bonds.

Forever and to the end.

CHAPTER 10

LAYLA

"You looking for the girl?"

This is why Ruby can't leave. He's terrifying. He imposes himself; a monarch, a pharaoh, a vengeful god of all around him. He circles me like prey. His smile, even and iceberg white, one that charms so many, seems more of a snarl. He might kill me. "What are you doing here?" he asks.

The bravery I thought I had. The Three Women and the faith I thought guided me into Ruby's small room begins to abandon me.

He takes only two steps and we're inches apart.

"It doesn't matter. I'm leaving."

I try to step around him but he matches my stride. Dancing with an unwanted partner.

"Again, I ask what you're doing here? You collecting her belongings? She leaving?"

"If she is gone, what the hell are you gonna do about it?"

He laughs and I think the devil must laugh this way. He's

a shuddering bag of yellow-brown bones. His green eyes slice into me.

"That little bitch thinks she can go?"

I flinch when I hear what he calls Ruby. I remember the bruises on her neck. I remember the black eyes that Auntie Alice so expertly learned to cover up and the lies she knew how to tell and how people believed her because they didn't want to believe anything else. All that pain, hate, anger, wasted time, wasted lives. And I can't let him intimidate me. I can't give him my power. I breathe deep. I remember again the Three Women. I'm not alone. I have my faith and that's going to give me courage. Something has to.

"You're the reason she left."

"She better get her ass back here before the sun goes down."

"You don't own her. She's not property."

"That girl owes me."

"That's your problem. You think everyone owes you."

"Little girl, you better stop talking before you say something that's gonna get you hurt."

"Like what? Like you're a shitty father. Like you were a terrible husband to one of the sweetest women in the world. Like you're *nothing* and I know you're *nothing*! You're a bully. You're a coward. A scared, little boy."

It feels so good to say all of this. I am burning with righteous anger and my mouth is firing out everything I've wanted to say to Lebanon, maybe to my father, too. All the hate and the rage, the sadness and the loathing I've let myself feel, I get to free it, put it on someone else. I get to breathe!

"I'm going to tell everyone, any person who'll listen, at the church, on the street that you're the reason a woman is dead. You're the reason my friend is broken. You are *everything* that is wrong."

"Shut up," he whispers, trembling like someone experiencing an earthquake only they can feel.

"Or what? You're gonna shoot me like you shot Auntie Alice?"

Fingers grip my face and squeeze. He tightens enough to

make the muscles throb instantly. He can break my jaw. He can bloody me. I think he might kill me. I think of Mom and J.P.

I think of Dad. What would he do if Lebanon killed me? Would that break the spell, destroy their connection? If Lebanon killed me right now, would it be enough to free my father? And I want to believe it will.

Looking into Lebanon's eyes my stray thoughts flicker like those bugs in the summertime.

"You know, your dad tried to play the hero, even when we were younger. You should ask him how playing the hero turned out."

It's a few seconds, a minute at the most, and he lets me go. "Tell her to get her ass back here and you get your ass out of my house. If I see you in here again, you'll get worse than Ruby or Alice ever got."

He doesn't yell or scream. His voice isn't raised. It is so even and soft, his words spoken don't sound like threats, but they are.

"I'm not scared of you, Lebanon." My left arm begins to break out in small bumps again.

"You should be scared of your daddy. So busy looking for me, you don't realize monsters live in all families. Not just mine."

I walk out of the bedroom and try not to look back at him. He utters one final question as I make my way to the front door: "Who's the coward now?" There is an unmistakable smile in his voice.

My face still pulses like it remains in Lebanon's grip. I almost run out of that place.

Ruby wasn't there, but bad memories and sadness and violence still reside in the cute bungalow with an apple blossom tree in the front yard. Worse, Lebanon still lives there and none of us are safe.

Who's the coward now?

Fear is such a warm blanket and I feel it fold over me, but I still hear this:

Go!

RUBY

I felt bad leaving Layla the way I did, the empty ringing of a bell my final goodbye. She wanted me to talk. I wanted to say something, but I want her to be free of me. I want to be free of me, too.

Longwood Drive is a few beautiful blocks lined with old houses and even older trees on small hilltops that look like mountains to me. It lies only about three or four miles from where I live, on the southwestern tip of Chicago.

There are distinct boundaries here like there are with all communities, certain streets cordoning off where this neighborhood is from that neighborhood. Beverly is no different. Eighty Seventh Street kisses the north border, then Vincennes Road lies east; Francisco Avenue and Western Avenue lie west and 107th Street holds up the southern tip. Potawatomi Indians used to live here until white people came and kicked them out, like every other scrap of land in this country.

What sets this place apart is that white people in this area of the city never left, didn't flee and scatter to the North Side or the suburbs. The white flight of the '60s, '70s, '80s didn't totally affect this area. I mean we moved in, but they stayed. It's one of the few places white flight didn't hold its power.

It was also one of the few places I felt happy with Layla. Reverend Potter would take us to this neighborhood for Halloween and we'd get full-size candy bars, none of the fun-size stuff. Reverend Potter would take our hands, I'd be on his right and Layla on his left and we'd go house to house. And everyone, white, black, didn't matter would smile at us and ask if we were sisters. I'd say yes. One time we were ketchup and mustard. Another time we both dressed up as Princess Leia and got in a fight about it, but we reconciled after we ate candy.

In Beverly I imagined I was a Potter, Ruby Naomi Potter.

Reverend Potter was my dad. Auntie Joanna was my mom. J.P. was my little brother. Layla, she was my sister. Finally.

And now there's no place where I can go in this city, where he can't find me. No place where I can disappear in the streets and homes with boutique shops and pubs and rolling hills and big trees.

He will find me like he found Mom. You can't dream when you're not safe so I can't stay in Beverly, in Chicago, have the life I dreamed about running up and down the streets with Layla holding bags of candy, pretending I belonged to a family that loved me and made me feel safe.

"Save yourself, baby."

There are two white women talking on the corner across the street. Both are stick figures with golden hair cut in perfect layers and enshrined in designer clothes I've likely never ever heard of and can't afford. Their lips part and collapse in strange ways, their faces take on distorted shapes. I think they must have wonderful lives and tiny inconveniences. Maybe I'm wrong and these rich girls have a million problems I'd never want to have. But I don't want their lives and I have my own problems. So what do I want?

To leave and never, ever come back.

LEBANON

TWO YEARS BEFORE ALICE KING'S DEATH

Alice is waiting on the porch for me. She has some kinda look on her face soon as I come up the stairs with a mostly empty beer bottle in my hand. It's just my third, maybe fourth, I think. The nighttime, this particular brand of it, right before one day turns into the next, makes her look small, like she needs protecting, but that isn't a job I've ever been good at.

"You're late," she says, but she puts her arms around me.

"I'm tired."

"I know. I know. Did you have a good day at work?"

I take her hands and unwrap them from my waist. She steps back, her lips downturned and trembling. "What you want, woman? Told you I'm tired. Don't wanna be bothered with no nonsense. Got enough of that at work."

"What happened?" Alice's voice, it's always light, never angry. Maybe there's love there. She grabs for my hand. I let her hold it and I squeeze back the tiniest bit. Streetlamp glow through the bare tree branches in our front yard covers our hands in striped light, like tigers.

"Just tell me what happened. It'll make you feel better. Talking always makes me feel better."

"Talk about it, huh?"

"Nonnie, please…just try," she begs. She's the only one I let call me "Nonnie" or anything other than Lebanon and she calls me "Nonnie" only when she wants to get something out of me. Nothing material, just my feelings or some such shit that won't make a bit of difference though she believes it will.

"Deliveries were all late. Mr. Wright kept getting lost, giving customers the wrong orders. I had to go back out and fix everything!"

"Well, is he okay?"

"Hell if I know, but it's been going on for too damn long. His family is thinking about selling the place. They might shut it down. I mean if he can't run it, then someone needs to."

Her eyes sparkle even in the deep blue black of night. "Why not you?"

"Why not me what? Buy the bakery? You must be crazy!"

"You're smart, Nonnie, and talented. Everyone at church asks about that pineapple upside-down cake you make, the cookies, that sweet potato pie. You could do it!"

Buying the place means money, means more responsibility, too. Means more eyes, but if Mr. Wright's family let me make payments, if I could find another source of income, if someone took care of the numbers, it's possible. Alice is good with numbers. Best with a needle and thread, but pretty good with numbers, too. And she really believes it, that I could be good at managing the bakery. The shadow of her hand as it caresses my face startles me, just a bit. The skin of her palm is warm on my cheek. I could run the bakery. Like she said, people love my food. Enough people come, I get enough money together, I could open another bakery maybe, and another after that. All I need is opportunity.

"I do this, you're doing the books, Alice. If I can get enough money together, maybe we could use some of the money from the church. Enough comes in, Jackson might not notice a few hundred here and there. I mean he has about two or three services on Sunday alone!"

"Well, I was thinking maybe we could get a loan, Nonnie."

"No one's gonna give me a damn loan! You either! Two broke-ass black people on the South Side of Chicago is not some banker's idea of the American Dream to throw money at. We're not the kind of people white people loan money to!"

"Well, we can't steal from the church, from the people, from *Jackson*! No one deserves that."

"What about what *I deserve*!"

She shrinks back. "Oh, Nonnie, I'm just saying I don't know if I'm good enough to do bookkeeping. I just took a few classes at Daley. I'm not good enough for what you need. That's all."

"You've been able to do numbers in your head since I met you, like some kind of genius and now all of a sudden you don't know if you can move a few decimals?"

She gets my head all full up with what-if's and possibilities, and now she has qualms about putting some numbers on a book! Grabbing her arm, I twist. Something between a yelp and a groan escapes her mouth. "You a dream killer, that it? You wanna lift someone up, then smack them down 'cause it's a game to you? You think this shit is funny?"

I lose my grip on the bottle, the smooth edge slips from my fingers and shatters on the stairs. "Look what you made me do! Damn it! You're more trouble than you're worth! I'm asking you to do one goddamn thing for me! You can't even do that? You're worthless, fucking worthless."

Alice shakes her head, tears spill down her cheeks. "I just want to help you, Nonnie. That's all I ever want to do." I scared her. I'm scaring myself, too. I can't see my face, but I know I look like Sara. I'm no better than her, but one time, long ago I wanted to be. I still want to be. The bakery, it can help me do that... be better. I just need Alice to see how much this means to me.

I let her arm go and tilt her face to mine. Tears stream from her eyes, those big brown eyes that still hold forgiveness and love, and I feel bad. I didn't mean to say those things or grab her, but I didn't hit her. I haven't done that in a while. So we're okay. We'll be okay. "Look, come on now. Stop crying. I just got upset. That's all. You're just so smart and I need you to do this for me. Can you help me? You're the only one I got, Alice. The only one I trust. You know that, don't you?"

Her breath is shaky. "I know, Nonnie. I know."

I kiss her and I try to think about the day we got married. Smiling on those courthouse steps. Alice covering her growing belly with a bouquet of gardenias. I try opening up some place inside me where I convince myself I love her, and I find…nothing. And somehow, I'm relieved. Loving her, despite how long we've been together, isn't something I'm built for. Love is a liability. It's a way for people to control you.

"Give me a little smile then, Alice. We're gonna get everything *you* wanted. This was *your idea*, wasn't it?"

"Yes. You're right. I can help you. I'm happy to do it." A car glides past the house. From a driver's side window, we could've been a couple having a nice conversation. People never look too close at the things around them.

"Good. Now, I'm going to bed. You gonna clean up that glass?"

Her face, those doe eyes of hers, worse than Bambi's. "Yes."

"Good girl."

She cries behind me as I close the screen door. She's always trying to live up to something impossible. Be what you are. Not what society expects. Not what a wife wants. Not what the preacher says. You're a doctor, fix bodies. You're a janitor, sweep floors. You're a dealer, make sure you got a steady plug and a foolproof place you hide your shit. But don't try and be something you're not 'cause that's how you fuck things up.

LAYLA

I turn my head to make sure Lebanon isn't following me out of the house, making sure an outstretched hand isn't trying to pull me back inside.

"You bolted out of there pretty fast, young lady. Are you okay?" a voice comes from behind.

Whipping around, two white men stand in front of me. One smiling and one not. "I'm fine."

"Oh okay, 'cause you looked scared is all I'm saying," says the man with buzz-cut red hair.

I'm terrified of what happened with Lebanon and what he probably did to Auntie Alice. I'm terrified by the fact I can't find Ruby. But even though these men inquire about my welfare, they don't make me feel any safer than if I remained in the house with Lebanon. Two white men in this neighborhood, who aren't real estate agents or Jehovah's Witnesses looking for their latest converts, must be cops. They're detectives, the ones from the night of Auntie Alice's murder. I remember the non-smiling one. Graying hair, fat face and mean eyes.

"Um, I'm going to go catch my train, you gentlemen have a good day."

"Listen, I'm not sure you remember us, but I recognize you from the night Mrs. King was murdered. I'm Detective Cantor and this is Detective Jurgensen. We just want to ask you some questions."

He still smiles when he says the word *murdered*. I take a step back. "Look, I have to go. My family is waiting for me. I just came by to pay my condolences again to the family."

Jurgensen steps forward, dwarfing his partner by his girth. If I ran right now, he'd have a heart attack before catching me, but if he grabbed me, he could do serious damage.

It doesn't matter I'm educated, that I volunteer at church. It doesn't matter I have a family that loves me, or that I don't have so much as a speeding ticket to my name, I'm black. That's what matters. Cops cover for cops. Blue covers blue. Blue doesn't cover black. And there'd be no one to speak for me. I have a bullet in my pocket right now and that'd probably be enough for them to take me into a police station where they could keep me for however long they want. My education doesn't protect me. My father can't protect me. In this moment, I question if even God can.

I scan the street and find not a soul around. If the Rapture just happened, this was the most inconvenient moment.

"You're the pastor's daughter, Layla, right?" asks Jurgensen.

"Yeah."

"Well, we just have a few more questions about that night."

"I'm not sure I can help you and like I said I have to go home."

Jurgensen steps closer to me and I step back again.

"A woman was murdered, and you're fine to let the guy roam these streets and call us when he inevitably kills again. I don't understand you people."

My left fist balls up and I wonder how much bail money I'd need if I punch him square in his face. Instead of stepping back, I step forward and am face-to-face with my second bully in less than five minutes. "Really, you're going to 'you people' me? It must be nice to look down your nose on a race of people you can shoot down in the street with no consequence."

"Hey, hey, let's all calm down." Cantor squeezes himself between me and Jurgensen. "We're just trying to get some answers, and we're sure your friend's dad has something to hide. We need you to help us out." He places his hand on my arm and I jerk back without thought.

They do a better version of good cop–bad cop on *Law & Order*.

"Do you want us to protect your friend? She might be living with a murderer—you know that don't you? Do you want something bad to happen to her? We don't. Me and my partner want to save her. Just tell us what's going on. Nothing bad will happen to you or your friend," Cantor promises.

I have a hard time believing he wants to protect her, to actually protect Ruby. She's a number, a case file and Lebanon would be another black man in jail. If it makes sense for them to somehow blame Ruby, say that she was involved, then they'd back that up, and Ruby would truly be lost.

Bad things already happened to her and Auntie Alice. Where were they then? Where were my parents or the church? Where was I? What could I have done? What should I do now?

Go!

"Well, I'm so glad we have you here to protect us from bad things happening," I say dryly.

The smile melts from Cantor's face. I turn from him and his partner and walk away. I half expect hands to pull me back and shove me in a car. I walk calmly toward the bus stop on 79th Street that'll take me to the Red Line Station a couple of miles away.

On the train, I see very few bodies, except those of the homeless who make this their temporary apartment during much of the weekend. I dig in my pocket and touch the bullet. Sharp edges of paper poke my sensitive skin. I pull it out and unwrap the scrap paper I wrote on. The bus number. Ruby is going to Tennessee. Naomi, her grandmother, lived there before she died. Ruby was happy there.

So is she going to Tennessee to escape Lebanon or to take her life? It would be just like Ruby to want some kind of closure with her mom and grandma before doing something she can never, ever take back.

What do you think happens when you die?

It's too late for new beginnings.

We're all just a collection of scars.

Ruby said all of this at the coffee shop. Ending it in the place she was happiest instead of the place she was miserable. Leaving Lebanon alone. That has its own vengeance. Would she really do that? Take her life? Is she that desperate? Or is she going to start over in a new place? Disappear into a city where Lebanon doesn't have a strong foothold? Auntie Alice may have shielded her from most of Lebanon's blows, but she also kept Ruby captive.

If she's on this bus, she'll be in Tennessee soon enough and I have to be there. I don't know what she's planning. I just need Ruby to know she's not alone, that someone cares for her, loves her. I care for her. I love her.

Go!

The only problem is I have no idea exactly where Ms. Naomi's house is and of the people who can tell me: one is dead, one probably wants to kill me and the other is on a bus bound for the same state. I'm giving myself two minutes to panic, then I must figure out a solution. I'll let my fear drown me only for a little bit.

My body jars, jolts and stops, and I realize the train is already at 95th Street, the end of the line. I rise and step off and climb the stairs. Standing in the T-shaped corridor of the terminal, I know getting home requires one bus, the one to my left. I turn right. There's only one person to whom I can turn, one person who can help that I can trust. One person. A soldier.

Go!

The thirty minutes it took to get here seemed like thirty years. More than I hear it, I feel the vibration of the doorbell through my index finger as I ring the doorbell. Static-filled, barely audible words come through the cheap intercom and I assume make up the phrase "Come in." As there is a hissing buzz that signals the unlocking of the main door, I walk past the threshold. Even with the rude electronic interference, hearing Timothy's voice is soothing, and I feel better.

Nestled on a tree-lined block, with an occasional empty lot

giving the appearance of much larger plots of land, the other two apartment buildings, like Tim's, rest near the end of Green Street right off the busy street of 117th. These blocks are known, for better or worse, as the "Wild Hundreds"—as much a call of pride as it is a warning. Rows of houses and apartments are clustered with small mom-and-pop barbershops, urban boutiques, fast food restaurants and liquor stores.

As I walk into the carpeted vestibule, I hear his shoes galloping down the stairs. I can go to Tim for help, not just because he's my boyfriend, not because I know he'll agree to whatever I ask him. I go to him because he's tactical, he can see a way out sometimes when I can't. I know his courage. I know his loyalty. I know that deep wisdom, which I'm sometimes jealous of, but yearn for when I have no answers of my own. Most of all, I know he can keep a secret, and I don't know if I can trust Christy to keep a secret like this.

From the first-floor apartment, comforting smells of chicken and greens and God knows what other savory goodness waft throughout the narrow hallway.

Normally smooth as chocolate brown marble, Tim's brow is furrowed with concern and I let go of it all. I unburden. I tell him about the phone call, Ruby and our talk in the coffee shop, my argument with Lebanon, my run-in with the detectives.

I don't remember walking up the stairs. I'm just somehow magically transported to his place and there I sit in his favorite chair with a cup of strong coffee in my hands. The part about Lebanon got to Tim more than he'd care to show. He keeps clenching and unclenching his fists. The rigid stance of his figure above mine gives him an oddly menacing look. Perhaps he's imaging his hands around Lebanon's neck. And I can't help but wonder if this is how he was on his tour of duty? Has he killed people? I wonder what kinds of violence he witnessed or participated in.

Bending down to investigate any possible bruising, Tim gently turns my face left, then right. His fingers are soft, and with apprehension in his eyes, he says, "We gotta go and talk to your dad."

"No, the hell we don't!"

I stand up and gulp down the last bit of coffee like a shot of whiskey. I burn my tongue.

He replies, "We need to find Ruby. We need to figure out what Lebanon is up to. If he killed Alice, he's going to want to keep that secret. If he thinks Ruby is an obstacle to that, he'll kill her, too."

I hesitate to show him the small piece of lead in my pocket, but I do and set the bullet down on his table. "He might also kill me."

"Where did you get that?"

"I found it in Lebanon's room. It was near his bed."

"Why didn't you tell those detectives?"

"Those men could twist anything. They'd probably try to say I murdered Auntie Alice. Besides, those cops just want to close a case. And the bullet now has my prints on it. I can't believe I just picked it up. That was so stupid of me. They like Lebanon for Auntie Alice's murder, but a bullet with my prints on it might make me a suspect. Everyone with our skin is a suspect to them. You know that."

"Like I said, we need to talk to your dad."

"Talking to my father is going to make it worse."

"Why?"

"Because it always does, Tim. I came to you. I need your help to find Ruby and protect her. Not his."

Tim clenches and unclenches his fists again and takes a deep breath.

The stress. Damn it. Asking him to help me and he's still adjusting to civilian life and trying to find his own way and I have to drag him into this mess.

"What's your plan then, Layla?"

"She's going to Tennessee. I don't know if it's to start over or do something…more drastic. She might want to—"

I can't bring myself to finish my sentence. My tongue has a numbing, tingling sensation and my eyes are watering. I'm going to cry. I don't want to in front of Timothy, but I'm going to break down and probably blubber like a baby. I just have no more strength or pride or ideas.

I'm empty. I'm empty. I'm empty.

Tim hugs me. I'm not a pretty crier. I want to fold into myself until I'm nothing, and, while Tim holds me, I wonder if this is how Ruby feels every day of her life.

"We'll figure all this out. We're gonna find Ruby and it'll be okay," Tim tells me.

"You can't promise that."

"I know whatever it is we find, whatever happens, we'll learn to live with it. And, by learning to live with things, even the bad things of this world, we'll be okay. That's what I can promise, Layla."

I look at Timothy and his calming smile and locate whatever goodness, whatever trust is still left in my spirit, and I make my way toward the door.

Go!

"Let's talk to my dad."

CHAPTER 11

LEBANON

Dear Lebanon,

I hope I'm long gone by the time you read this, because it's a goodbye letter and you don't deserve a goodbye, but Mom would want me to say something to you. So I have a request, and seeing as how I never asked you for anything, I figured you can give me this one thing: let me go. I just want to be left alone, with my thoughts of Mom and Grandma and be in a place where I am happy. I don't want to see you or hear from you. You live your life. I'll live mine. Goodbye.

Ruby

I read the letter again and search for clues because people always leave them, even when they don't want to. I knew Layla was reaching for something but didn't get a chance to grab it before I found her. That girl was speaking on things when she didn't have any idea of what's going on, of what I've done for her family. And for mine, too! If anyone is scared, it's her daddy. Not me. Never me. I have courage.

I might've even made a good cop when I was younger. I always wanted to help people, even though they didn't help me. But then I went to jail. My body took more pain than I thought possible, and in those moments where darkness swallowed me and fists beat me, I thanked Sara.

She bred me to this and for this. I survived prison because she gifted me pain while Jackson was gifted with love by his parents. Desolation ruled my life and hope ruled his. We grew, two sides to a coin always landing in Jackson's favor.

So, I make my luck and find my opportunities and search out my clues. And the girl is part of that. It's nothing to do with love between us. There is none. It's about legacy.

A man's legacy is a difficult thing to build, but very easy to destroy. When building a legacy, don't start off big. Don't think you're going be president of the United States, a billionaire, a movie star. Start off small. If you want to create a legacy, just stay alive.

Go from there.

I learned this walking around yards built of concrete and circled by barbed wire, in cells so small your hands touch both sides without stretching them far.

Now, the problem with having a legacy is you need someone to hand it down to, even if they hate you. Sara would sometimes give me something after she was really bad to me. She made me pineapple upside-down cake once. It was damn good. Maybe that's why I'm good at baking. This other time, she bought me a fire truck with a working siren. Couldn't play with it much on account my left arm was broke thanks to her. Soon enough, the noise got on her nerves and she eventually threw it out the window. It broke into pieces of sharp red-and-white plastic on the street. Another time, she took me out to a nice restaurant. It had linen tablecloths and a lotta white people. One of them was our server, and he didn't seem too thrilled about tending to us, but brought our food just the same.

I didn't look at her during that dinner. Mostly paid attention to my steak. I didn't know the next time I was getting a meal like that—hell, I didn't know the next time I was putting food in my belly. She felt bad after she did things. I knew that, but gifts didn't take away from what she did and it didn't never stop her from losing her temper and hurting me again. But it was all she knew. It's what I know now. I guess she and I got the same type of anger.

You sacrifice a part of yourself when you hurt someone and maybe you barter your way back if you show someone you didn't want to do what you did. You can't take back that hit or slap, punch or kick. The bruise or blackened eye or broken bone still taunts you, still lingers for a time.

A gift if you mean it, really mean it, can heal that wound, take over that memory, make you feel generous if only for a moment. Just one moment.

A toy. A steak dinner. A pearl necklace. A bakery.

One time I had this dream and Alice said I was crying, crying for *her*, for Sara. Couldn't have been true. Alice probably just said it to give my dream some meaning. She always wanted everything to have a purpose to it. A logic behind why something happens. I think it gave her peace or at least a reason to not try and end it all in the bathroom like that selfish little girl did years ago.

Took me forever to clean that blood off the bathroom floor. Blood's fickle. Sometimes it stains, wants you to know it was there. Other times that shit will wipe away as if the world's willing to forget you in the blink of an eye.

If I can get the girl to see the potential, what I'm trying to build, she can see what her Mom never got a chance to witness. A success. Me as a success. This family not biting or scratching or clawing to survive. Jackson and his meddling daughter have never known hunger or despair. Not like I have. I just need them to stay out of my way. I just need to find the clues and she left them. Yes, she did. She almost spelled it out by bringing up her Grandma. Tennessee. The girl is going to Tennessee. But first things first, I'm going to talk to Jackson about his daughter. Then, I'm going to bring my girl back. And if she doesn't want to come, well, I'll make her see where she belongs.

RUBY

When I was nine years old, Mom and Lebanon bought me a pink-and-white bike. It also had pink-and-white streamers and a pink basket in the front. I wanted this bike for months, so my parents scrimped and saved. And, the morning of my birthday, at the edge of my bed stood my new bike. Oh, I was so happy. I rode it all day. When I thought my parents were asleep, I rode it in the alley behind my house that night. But, when I tried to do this really cool trick, I fell off and broke my left arm. Lebanon found me and my parents took me to the hospital. When Lebanon went back to the alley to retrieve the bike later that evening, it was gone, stolen. I wore a cast for six weeks.

I've told this story dozens of times to Grandma Naomi, teachers, adults at church, my mom's friends. The story of my youthful exuberance, eventual disobedience and my punishment: the fall, my arm, the stolen bike.

That was about the time when I started losing faith in God. People, losing faith in them, happened before that. I knew way before most kids there was no Santa Claus, Easter Bunny, Tooth Fairy. I wasn't a jerk. I didn't ruin the make-believe for the other kids. I just thought they were stupid to believe in those things. I had bigger issues living in the house with the apple blossom tree in the front yard.

He would come in drunk, after working at the bakery or after Bible study where he pretended being some pious believer. You gotta admire the dysfunctional hypocrisy in that kind of act. Mom would always try to calm him down by being as perfect as possible: a neat house, his favorite foods cooked to his liking. Sometimes it worked, sometimes it didn't. So they would go down to the basement and that's when I'd hear the thumps, the breaking of glass or, if he was in a particularly foul mood, a piece of furniture. Mom learned to cry softly, to not wail or scream.

She didn't want the police at the house. How would that look to others? Someone at the church could find out. What would people think about her, that she wasn't a good enough wife for her husband not to beat her?

I learned the consequences of calling for help that day with my bike. If you ask for help, you'll be hurt by the person who's supposed to protect you. If you call for help, your Mom can't help you because two of her ribs are cracked and no matter how much she begs and pleads, she can't do anything. But you need a way to explain away the broken bone, the scrapes and bruises, so we blamed it on my bike, which never existed. Because the truth was far uglier.

Lebanon was beating Mom. I tried to stop him, and he threw me against a wall, breaking my arm. But we couldn't tell that story. So, in an emergency room sitting next to Mom, she made up one to tell the doctor and we told that story to Grandma Naomi and people at church. If you repeat something untrue over and over, you can start to believe it.

That's where Mom found her comfort. That's where Lebanon discovered his power.

If Mom couldn't tell the truth, if not acknowledging it made her feel better, how could she stand up to the man who hurt her child? If she couldn't see a way out, how could I raise my voice? I did what I was taught. I lied about my pain. To cover Lebanon's abuse. To maintain my family's image. And I sat with a broken arm in a noisy hospital, collateral damage of shame and shadow.

Save yourself, baby.

I make it a point never to come to this neighborhood. If you're not known by others, you're not safe, but someone here has what I need. Night rushes to consume the pale blue-gray light of the fading afternoon. The two or three boarded-up homes on this block aren't abandoned. They look that way for the sole purpose of avoiding attention. I walk around the back. The overgrown shrubs and weeds would make Mom itch. The white back door bares black scuff marks, different sizes and shapes. The dents mark the edges. I knock twice, wait five seconds and knock three more times.

"You crazy you know that, doing all that coded knockin' shit. I got a peephole. I can see it's you."

"I try to be careful, LeTrell."

His chestnut-tinged skin looks even darker in the stingy evening light. His head barely clears the top of the door frame. "What happened this morning? I waited outside of church like you asked."

I rub my left wrist. "Sorry about that. Change of plans. I got caught up. Family situation, you know."

"Yeah, heard about your mom. Grandma Anne told me when I came by to see her yesterday. Sorry for your loss."

"Thanks."

LeTrell moves into the living room, the glow from the streetlamps and a television guide his way. The wideness of his shoulders and his height smother the remaining light in the hall. He cranes his neck back at me and says, "It's cool though. I caught up with a few people from the block. You know I saw your friend today, Layla, and your dad. Offered me a job in his bakery. Seems like a cool dude."

I let my silence speak for itself.

"Oh so you ain't close with your pops? It's cool. I ain't close with mine either. Don't even know if he's dead or alive or what."

"Better off not knowing," I respond.

"Guess so." He flops down on his couch and lights a cigarette, taking a long slow drag. He places a dog-eared copy of *Moby Dick* on the table in front of him, a tattoo on his left hand spelling his grandmother's name, Anne, is etched in evergreen-colored ink.

"You have it?"

"Yeah." LeTrell exhales the smoke billowing out of his broad nostrils like some lazy dragon. He bends down. His fingers pry open a small slat of wood in the floor. Before he hands me the purse, black leather with a gold buckle on the front, he asks, "You sure you want this?"

I snatch the purse from his hand, stuff two hundred dollars in its place and leave the house. I quickly walk north two blocks then one block east. The corner is deserted except for me and an old man waiting for the last bus headed east to the Lakefront. The purse is pretty. I could take this on a date or to church if I ever bothered to go anymore. My fingers trace the slightly raised pattern of the purse and when I open it, I'm hopeful again.

I know what needs to be done.

JACKSON

Joanna hasn't said more than a few words to me since we drove down Garfield Boulevard, barely acknowledged my existence since we left Roscoe Alman's church an hour ago. Layla's car is in front of the house, but she's not here. I can't find my pipe wrench. I know where the gun is though. The pipe under the kitchen faucet is leaking. Joanna asked me to fix it three weeks ago. Now is as good a time as any. A good time to get my mind off other pressing matters like murder and the disintegration of my family and jail time.

I really need to clean the basement, too. You can't find anything down here; I can't find my damn pipe wrench anywhere. It's not in my tool box. I think I might have placed it upstairs, so I go back into the kitchen, and then the living room and Mom patiently waits.

Footsteps and a voice behind me. I hear Joanna say, "Violet, thank you so much for being here. I know it wasn't the kind of trip you had in mind, but at least you're here for another few days. We can do something nice. I can make you breakfast tomorrow. How does that sound?"

"Fine, baby, fine. Right now, I'm gonna sit here and talk to my son for a bit."

Joanna hugs my mother. She turns to me. "I'm tired." She leaves the living room.

That's about four words now. Maybe five.

Mom turns to me. "Sit down, Jackson."

The damn wrench has got to be up here, because I was supposed to fix something else, but Sister Austen called about her husband in the hospital, so I had to go to them and I didn't get a chance to finish whatever it was I was doing.

I need to paint soon, too. I don't like this brown color on the walls. Where is the damn wrench?

"Jackson! Sit down! You're restless."

"No, I'm not."

My mom's face is calm and not tense with argument because, as always, she knows she's right. She needs no one else's affirmation of what she knows to be true.

"Whenever you're doing everything else but what you're supposed to be doing, you have no peace."

I just need to find my wrench. I need to fix that faucet. Joanna just needs me to do one thing. I just need to do this one thing.

Her hands, warm and firm, grip my wrist and barely encircle it. I see the difference in our tones, hers the color of ocean-kissed sand, and mine, darker like my father's. She always said one of the things she liked most about Daddy was his color. She complained she was too light and though it was more popular and attractive, she believed the opposite—that her skin color dictated how black she really was.

I want to tell Mom everything, share with her who I thought I was and who I should be, but am not. I can't speak and tears sting the backs of my pupils, their wet weight pressing forward and I try to take a deep breath. I try to think about something happy and there is only hot, blank white space where something happy should be.

"I'm fine."

Chuckling, she replies, "You're no more fine than I am white and rich and hell, that's always been the best thing to be."

My mom can see. She can see I'm hiding. She can't see what it is, but she can see the pressure of it is breaking me. God, help me. I need to close these doors. I need to be free of secrets. I need to be free of guilt. I need to be free of Lebanon King, our hatred and my regret.

"Look, you're not gonna get anything done like this. Take me to see Sara. I wanna sit with her for a bit."

"I don't know about the visiting hours."

"Boy, I know you don't like Sara, but we both know the visiting hours at that place. So just take me 'cause I'm not asking you again."

I put on my coat and help Mom into hers. In the car, as I turn the ignition, I remember what is still in the trunk. I don't turn to look Mom in her eyes. "I forgot my wallet," I lie.

I pop the trunk and exit the car. Her stare burns a hole in my back. "I'll be right back."

Jogging to the trunk, I open it and dig behind the boring contents. My fingers find the paper bag tucked in the crevice behind the spare wheel hidden by the twenty-four pack of bottled water Joanna's asked me three times now to bring into the house.

Mom rolls down the window and yells, "You forgot your wallet in the trunk, son?"

"I'll be right back," I repeat.

Grimly clutching the bag to my side, I walk to the garage. I worry about fingerprints, mine and Lebanon's. Did he find out Alice wanted to leave him? That she was willing to put him in jail and possibly go to prison herself to be rid of him? Her eyes were wide when she begged me to help her, when she confessed her sins. And I did what I always did. I protected him to protect me, saved myself instead of someone else.

Scanning the shelves above my worktable, a large cookie jar sporting the title #1 Dad (And Cookie Eater) is the best temporary spot to hide this sin. I'm again covering for Lebanon like he did for me all those years go. Will this finally repay my debt to him? I send up a silent prayer that Joanna or J.P. or Layla don't find this weapon.

Damn. There's the wrench! Sitting plain as day on the work table. I grab it and move toward the car.

Before I take a few steps, I see Lebanon standing on my walkway in front me and he says, "We need to talk about Layla."

CHAPTER 12

CALVARY

September 27, 1963

Sara sits in the same pew she did a few years ago, when she begged God to not carry the life now sitting beside her. Her prayers weren't answered then and she doubts they'll be answered now. The little boy with her squirms. He doesn't want to be held, and she doesn't want to hold him, but he makes too much noise when he roams free. Making noise that strips away the last of her patience. All the little boy is good for is getting on her few good nerves and noise. Then he looks at her and smiles, and for the briefest moment, she smiles back. Then she remembers how he came to be and she stops smiling. Happiness isn't normal for her. Pain is normal, heartache is normal. A black hole of regret and loss is normal.

Not happy.

Sara found it once, found happy, in the last place she thought it'd be—Tennessee. Sara hated Memphis at first and then she met Jonas and he was good and kind, but good and kind people always die before their time.

It was true for her Mom. It was true for Jonas.

She ached for him. Jonas made her see love was possible, to be free was a choice and to love her son was so much easier than she believed. Sara found the things she suffered in Chicago floated away. She cooked at Ms. Lennie Mae's boardinghouse, and people loved her pineapple upside-down cake! She found her laugh was high-pitched and she would snort if Jonas did a silly little dance. Her boy would mimic Jonas and try to dance too, and she'd double over in laughter, so happy. Jonas said her laugh was contagious.

And in the deep black of the Tennessee night where the moon hung in the sky big and wide with alabaster glow, and the stars shimmered, she and Jonas would sit on the porch. He'd speak on all the injustices he saw blacks suffer not just in the South, but all over, and how he would help with the latest voting drive, how education would be the key equal to treatment in the world. Sara would listen, but she knew suffering, and being on a quiet porch with someone she loved was the furthest thing from suffering she knew.

But happy doesn't last, and good and kind people die before their time. First her mother. Then Jonas.

Not Sara.

She wasn't good or kind. She reaches into her bag and pulls out a bottle of cheap whiskey and takes two strong sips, and she holds the boy tight, but he's stopped squirming. He's asleep.

Sara knows she isn't worth loving. People who love her die. She won't let that happen to the boy. She'll make sure he doesn't love her. Her love is poison. She'll make him hate her. That's the only way she knows how to love him, to prepare him for the life he'll lead which will be hard and bad and if they're both lucky, brief.

LEBANON

Jackson rummages in his garage looking lost on his own property. Turning off the light, he moves toward the driveway with a wrench in his hand and freezes soon as he sees me.

"We need to talk about Layla."

"What are you doing here?"

"Layla was at my house."

Jackson's face is blank. The grip on the pipe wrench tightens. "Where is my daughter?"

"Why was she at my house?"

He searches my face for clues, my clothes, my nice suit for blood.

"Where is she?"

"I can't be responsible for every little thing. If something happened to Layla, I'm not—"

His hand firms around the wrench and he swings it at my head. I duck low and swing my fist and miss him.

We're both too old for this shit, but it doesn't stop us from trying to fight like we're twenty years younger than our bodies perform. He manages to grab the right lapel of my suit, raising the wrench.

"Where the hell is Layla? If you hurt her I'll kill—"

"Calm the hell down! I didn't do anything to her. She was fine when she left my house. Kinda fine," I manage to choke out.

"What do you mean 'kinda fine'?"

"Has everybody lost their damn mind!" a voice calls out from behind. Auntie Violet. She's all of five feet, but about as big and bad as any man I'd met in prison. She's the only woman I know that seems to carry no fear.

She marches up to Jackson and me. "Jackson Blaisdell Potter, let him go *right now*!"

His hands release me. I forgot how strong he is. Most of the time that strength is cloaked in some turn-the-other-cheek-type bullshit he can preach to other people who don't know what I know about him.

"Hey, Auntie Vi. Me and Jackson was just messing around is all."

She crosses her arms. Much like she did when me and Jackson were kids, before she was gonna let us have it for whatever rule we broke. "Lebanon, do you take me for a fool?"

"No, ma'am, I don't. Tensions are running high is all. It was just a misunderstanding."

"About what? I heard you talking about Layla when I got out the car. The whole neighborhood could probably hear the both of you." She expects an honest answer, and that, though I love her, I can't give her.

"Auntie, me and Jackson is gonna get it squared away. We'll figure it out like we always do, right?"

I turn and look at Jackson, and hope he understands my look, that all I need him to do is agree and shut the hell up about what's going on…about the girls and about us.

"Momma, really, things got heated. We weren't going to do any harm. Not really. Can you go back in the house and wait for me? I'll come back in a few minutes and we'll go visit Sara."

Auntie Violet uncrosses her arms and looks at me. I already know the question forming in her mind.

"Lebanon, baby, you want to come? See Sara, talk to her?"

"I already did."

"Well, why don't you come up with us again. I'm sure Sara still wants to see you no matter what time of day or night. Maybe she—"

"Just…just don't. Please. She ain't you, Auntie Vi. She's always gonna be the way she is, so stop hoping for different. I did a long time ago."

Auntie Violet comes up to me, takes my face in her hands. For a moment, I bask in that warmth, the same kind when I was a kid, it was like she could reach this deep part of me I didn't even know existed. Her touch and those eyes were what I always expected love to feel and look like. And the only reason I don't try to start back up with Jackson is because of this woman here. If there's anything good in me, anything at all, it was Auntie Violet who planted that seed. It might have fallen on hard ground, but at least she saw something in me enough to try and nurture whatever it was.

Behind me Jackson pleads, "Momma, go inside. I'll be there soon to take you to see Sara. Lebanon and I have to finish talking."

"Y'all weren't talking. Y'all were fighting."

"Mom, we got that out of our system."

"We're good, Auntie Vi. I promise."

She lets go of my face and steps back and proceeds into the house. She turns around one last time, and I see her face search mine and I plaster on the most peaceful look I can muster. "I love you, Auntie."

"Love you, too," she replies. "Love you both." And she disappears into the house.

Turning to face Jackson, I resume the line of questioning before our fight. "Why the hell was your daughter at my house?"

"I don't know. She didn't tell me what she was doing after church. She was probably looking for Ruby," he mutters.

"You need to learn to keep her in check."

"Yeah, I see how well that's worked out for you."

"Watch it before you find yourself having to explain for past sins. I could go right into that house and tell Auntie Violet everything. Remember, none of us ever gets away from what we do. We might get by, but we never get away."

"Believe me. I don't want Layla doing what she's doing, but Ruby is like her sister. She's concerned for her like I was for you. Like when you'd come to my house after Sara had a go at you."

"I remember that, but I remember other things, too." I think about Jackson and how he was my brother, how the girl thinks of his daughter as her sister. These thoughts and this night, it's too much. Alice is gone and my girl has run away. I just need it all to stop. I need his daughter to mind her own business. I need the girl to come back and she won't do that unless it's me and her, and only me and her.

"Just tell your girl to stay away from mine."

"You know she won't do that."

"Make her, Jackson! Find a way to get Layla to listen to you."

"You can't even get Ruby to listen to you!"

"My family. My business."

"It's your business when it's convenient, but it's my problem when you come to me with your hand out, asking for another check."

Jackson has this air about him when he feels justified. Standing tall, chest all puffed out, arrogant as hell and it makes me want to take the wrench in his hand and smash in that self-righteous face. Just hit him over and over and—

"This is done, Lebanon, this protecting you. The money, the lies, the gun. All of it! It's been too long, and I'm done."

All I do is laugh. It hurts like hell to do it, but I laugh.

"You protecting me? How soon we forget."

"That was a long time ago." His voice is softer.

That grip on the wrench is still tight, but Jackson won't do anything. He's probably mad he doesn't have the courage to follow through on what he really wants to do. Not like I do.

"A long time ago, huh? That was fucking yesterday for me! I protect you, Jackson. Remember that. Those years I spent in that damn cell. That was to protect you. As far as what's on paper, I'm the one who killed Syrus Myllstone. I'm the one who spent five years in a fucking cell! I'm the one who cops beat on over and over, and I never said your name. I remember the smell of my flesh burning with their cigarettes. I remember you not being able to look at me in that courtroom. Auntie Violet crying. Sara not coming at all. I protected you from all of that. So for the fucking love of Almighty God, do what I ask and keep your girl away from mine. I got plans too. May not be as big as the pastor of a church who people think pisses ginger ale, but I can carve out my own little stretch of the world. And you or Layla or anyone better not get in my way again."

His fingers loosen on that wrench and his dark face is all screwed up, wrinkled in the wrong places.

"That's right. I'm your savior. You never were tough. Not like me, so I saved you. Remember that and we won't have to have any more of these conversations."

I straighten my suit and my tie. "I'm gonna go home and get some sleep, then get the girl. She thinks she's gonna make some kinda life for herself in Tennessee, get her happily-ever-after."

"You can leave her be. Give her a chance to—"

Holding up my hand to stop any more of this spouting off of nonsense, I continue, "Now you know I hate repeating myself, but, because we're friends, I'll do it for you. Tell Layla to stop minding business that ain't hers. Stay away from my house. Stay away from Ruby."

I turn around and stroll away. I hear nothing from him. All I hear is the wind, just the wind.

LAYLA

I'm still in that house with Lebanon standing in front of me, a warped grin and green eyes. I'm still on the sidewalk standing in front of two white detectives with guns, badges and veiled threats. Physically, my body has just arrived back at home in the kitchen with Timothy, but my mind hasn't caught up. Tim still holds this belief Dad will do the right thing. I'm not so sure. I know whatever this connection is between him and Lebanon, it will cause Dad to do the exact opposite of the right thing. Tim believes in the good of people. I'm more of the James Baldwin school: "I can't believe what you say, because I see what you do."

Grandma Violet sits at the small table off to the side of the kitchen in her coat, a rare grimace creasing the edges of her soft face. When I asked her what's wrong, all that came out of her mouth was "Grown folks' business." Code for: Mind your business, Layla.

But now this is something I can't do. Minding our business got us in the mess we're in, and I plan to clean it up: the secrets, lies, shame. It's got to end if anyone in Ruby's family or mine has a chance at some semblance of being free from whatever's haunted our families generation after generation.

The back door of the house slams shut and within seconds my father's hulking frame storms through the kitchen with a wrench in his hand. He stops short when he sees me. I'm expecting a lecture, some scripture, a why couldn't you be a better daughter look in his eye, but instead his arms scoop me up and hold me. He just says "Layla" over and over again. My arms encircle his massive waist and I hug my dad back. The world melts away and we're like we once were, when I was small and I'd run up to him after church and he'd pick me up and put me on his shoulders. I'd laugh and he'd laugh. I believed I could see the whole world when he did that and I knew, *I knew* my father loved me.

Dad lets me go and I want to hold him tighter, but I don't.

"Where were you?"

I look at Tim and he nods. "I went to meet Ruby after church. I think something bad is gonna happen. I think Lebanon really killed Auntie Alice. I think Ruby is next. I don't think she can take much more of him now that Auntie Alice isn't here. I think she'd rather hurt herself than live with Lebanon."

Dad's light brown eyes darken and narrow. He shakes his head. "You don't know that."

"I know I found a bullet in his bedroom. I know there are two detectives who think he did it, too! Why are you still protecting him? He's a monster, and if you keep taking up for him, you're no better than he is!"

"Leave it alone, Layla."

I turn to Tim and say the four words I knew I'd say when we left his apartment: "I told you so."

The small patter of footsteps I hear behind me and Grandma Violet stands between me and Dad for the second time today.

"I told you both this fighting nonsense has got to stop."

"We're going to find Ruby, Grandma. I'll let you know when we do."

Dad grabs for my arm, but I snatch it away just before he manages to get me. "You will do no such thing, Layla."

"Yes, because forbidding me to do things always works out so well for you."

Mom opens her bedroom door and comes out to see, and possibly to play peacekeeper between me and my father. Tim touches my arm, a signal to calm down.

Grandma Violet takes my hands in hers. "Baby, there's some more to this than you know, you and your dad. You can't keep trying to fix what's broken."

"You do it all the time." I look from Grandma Violet to my father.

"Child, be better than me! Be better than your daddy."

"I'm trying to be, which is why I'm going to find Ruby."

"I've had about enough of your insolent attitude, Layla. You will obey me!" I can't remember a time he looked more angry.

"You can't control me," I shoot back. "You order me to obey, talk about God and love. You don't do any of it. You're a fraud! You're not a pastor. You're a fake."

Grandma's and Mom's eyes sharply turn in my direction. I poured tons of gasoline on this situation and just lit the match. My father's eyes grow wide.

"Reverend Potter, we just want to make sure—"

"I'm not asking for your permission," I say cutting off Tim's predictably diplomatic response. "I'm telling you we're going so no one is wondering where I am."

"Honey, let her go do this. Ruby needs help. Let Layla help her," Momma pleads.

"I'm not debating this, Joanna. I've made my decision."

"She doesn't need your approval to make a decision, Jackson. She's already made it. She just needs you to respect it. That's all."

"I'm not a child," I add echoing my Mom's sentiment. "I'm not under your thumb. I'm not going to let you hold me back from saving Ruby."

His meaty hand curls into a fist. He might hit me. I might push him just that far. Yet while it's all hot under my skin and I know I should be calm, I'm not because it feels good to let go of this anger, and to hurt my father while doing it.

"I'm trying to protect you."

"You don't want to protect me. You couldn't give a damn about anyone but yourself—just like always."

"I care about—"

"About your reputation, *Pastor*, but not about me or Ruby or what I'm trying to do!"

"So you're just going to go off in the middle of the night with him?" He gestures at Tim. "You know people talk about the two of you already. Do you know how that looks to others in the congregation?"

"I don't give a good damn how it looks to anybody!"

"You don't care about how your actions affect this family," he accuses.

"That's all I care about. Everything I do, I wonder how it looks. What you'd do. What you'd think. I'm so mixed-up because I barely have time for my own thoughts. I'm done with it! I'm done with you!"

We are less than two feet apart and my eyes match his—our color, our stubbornness, our pride; all of it crackles and pops like cooking oil over a high fire.

Tim wedges himself between the two of us and says, "Reverend, Ruby and Layla grew up together. Layla just wants to be a good friend, a good person, like you raised her to be. Haven't you needed to be a good friend before?"

Something snaps across those light brown eyes, but my father quickly regains his anger.

I haven't lost mine.

"If you leave, Layla, you're not welcome back in this house. The church. You're not welcome with me. You're a disgrace and no better than a whore if you leave."

Momma yells, "Jackson!"

"He doesn't mean that, baby. He's just angry," Grandma Violet consoles.

I laugh. I am mad as hell and I laugh. It is a weird and slightly unhinged sound. Tim looks at me with a measure of what I assume is concern as I cock my head and spout, "Better his whore than your daughter!"

I turn and stalk out of the kitchen. I don't look at Grandma Violet's face or Momma's. I know they're sad and hurt, for my father and me.

Timothy's hard footsteps follow mine out the door, and into the night. The rotting pile of aluminum, metal and rubber that is the Black Stallion slumbers in front of the house.

"He's not as bad as you make him out to be...Reverend Potter. There's something to be said for protection," Tim offered.

"He protected me by calling me a whore. That's what passes for protection with you?" I fume.

"You said your words, too."

Frigid gusts of wind chafe my lips and I believe it some appropriate penance by nature.

"My dad said a lot of messed-up stuff when he was drunk," Tim confesses, "but none of it was to keep me from anything." He doesn't meet my eyes as he speaks, but peers through threadbare tree branches to a somber black sky. "His drinking never served a purpose, never covered up how broken he was."

"Your dad used liquor. Mine uses God and self-righteousness."

"I'm not thinking about whiskey or Bibles or God, Layla. I'm thinking about actions," Tim says and, though his tone is sharper than I've heard, an earnest plea belies his frustration.

I grab Tim's hand. He stops looking at the sky and his eyes bore into mine. "There's something going on, and whatever it is, your dad's afraid for you, for himself," he cautions.

The rumbling of J.P.'s blue-and-white Mustang pulling up to the curb interrupts our conversation. I let go of Tim's hand. Stepping out of his car, J.P. plants his legs on the grass and he stands, but he keeps going up and up and up.

"Lala!"

Holding a paper bag with light streaks of grease and the aroma of something deliciously grilled, he gives Tim a quick punch on the shoulder. J.P. goes to hug me, but stops short when he sees my face. "What's wrong?"

"Dad." All this word implies, all prior fights, history, the general knowledge of who Jackson Blaisdell Potter Sr. is and how who he is affects us, is wrapped up in our sibling understanding when I just say "Dad" to J.P.

"Alright then," J.P. says. "So where you off to?"

"Going to find Ruby before Lebanon finds her."

"You need my help?"

"The less people involved, J.P., the better."

"You sure you got this, sis?"

"Honestly, I don't know. I don't know if I can do this. I want to, but so much can go wrong. So much has gone wrong already."

"All this shit, with you, with Ruby, with Dad, you looking at your problems like they bigger than you. You looking at your situation like it's a wall. It's not. It's a hurdle. Jump the hell over it."

I hug J.P. I squeeze him for all it's worth and he lets out this big whoosh of air when I let go.

"Thanks for the kick in the ass."

He laughs, it's more like a yuck-howl, then smiles.

"He's in a bad mood so if you can, try and steer clear," my last and only parting words of wisdom to my baby brother.

"Unlike you, sis, the old man can't get to me. All that melancholy, spiritual bullshit he puts himself through, hell, that's on him."

I want to be like him in that moment. To give not one good damn.

I suddenly feel Tim's hand grip mine. "We have to go to the church," I say.

"The church? You wanna pray for Ruby?"

"No. Buy plane tickets."

Tim looks at me puzzled, waiting for the punch line.

Grabbing his muscular arm, I lightly tug as my feet move through the grass toward his dark blue Ford F-150.

"If it makes you feel better, we can also pray for Ruby and cheap seats while I'm buying the tickets from Dad's office."

Go!

JACKSON

The door is slammed so hard it shakes the house. It is the exclamation point on the end of her rebellious sentence. Lebanon threatened to kill her in so many words, but I couldn't tell her that. She would ask questions. She always asks questions. She wouldn't cower like Alice. Go into her shell like Ruby. She would ask everything she could and there are answers that I'm not giving her. If she knew them, the risk of having her contempt for me grow into hatred becomes a certainty.

"I don't know what to do with you both!" Joanna fumes beside me.

Moments of sorrow like this, the weariness in her eyes, the desperation of trying to pull two people together when both haven't the will or heart to connect, cause me anguish. I see what Joanna gave up for me, what she continues to sacrifice. And I will continue to hold on to my secret. Joanna can be angry with me, be exasperated with me, but she can't hate me if she doesn't know. For her to hate me means she's given up on me. And if she does this, I'm truly lost.

As I reach for her hand, she pulls it away, but I grab it. Not as a sign of aggression or dominance, but simply as an oath I mean to keep to her, though I have broken so many.

"I'll make this right, Joanna. I will."

No change in her face, in that beautiful caramel face. She only whispers, "I'm going to pray, Jackson. I'm going to pray and then I'm going to bed."

The reassurance I seek I'll not find from her tonight. Dulling thuds of water droplets continue to hit the inside of the cabinet coming from the leaking pipe. The gentle closing of the door and the hard squeak of the floor herald the entrance of J.P. and he just nods at me, goes to his room.

I follow him the few steps and ask, "You got something for dinner?"

A simple, "Mmm-hmm," is the only response I receive.

"A burger?"

"Mmm-hmm."

He turns on his music, some rapper whose lyrics I can't begin to decipher. Keeping the volume low, he then sits and begins laying out the materials to finish his portrait for a member our church, Minister Fitzgerald who commissioned it as a present for his brother's eightieth birthday. Wilderness, a view of trees and grass and sky.

"Nice composition of the scene," I say.

"Mmm-hmm."

Dear God, is everyone in this house against me?

Layla, Joanna and J.P., we are family, but they are a close-knit tribe and I'm an interloper. That's how it is and that's my fault, but I want to change. I just don't know how to talk to them, how to break through that wall.

I don't know how to be a part of my family.

Effortlessly J.P. weaves the brush on the canvas and what was once bright white is green or blue or red or brown. And I envy him, because I think this is as close as one can possibly get to feeling like God did those first six days of the Earth's genesis.

The lightest scratching of paint over the canvas is the only conversation inhabiting the room while I ponder another way to get more than one-word answers from my son.

"Your sister and I had a disagreement."

He stops painting. "Dad, is there something you want?"

"I was wondering if you saw her before she left?"

"Yeah, she was pissed off. Y'all both have that thing where you squint really hard when you're upset."

"We do?"

"Mmm-hmm. You're doing it now," he points out. His smirk

still manages to remain humble. He and Joanna both have *that* in common.

He continues, "Y'all are so much alike, which is why you're at each other's throats all the time."

"Did she tell you where she was going, what she was doing?"

"Yes." He continues to paint.

"Are you going to tell me?"

"No."

Unlike his sister, there is no defiance in his voice, no disdain. There is simply the calm, honest conviction of the answers he will and will not give me.

"J.P., I'm going to figure out what that girl is up to, and she may get herself hurt while trying to find Ruby. We both don't want that to happen."

"If you're talking about Lebanon, he isn't going to do anything. He's an old man."

"We're the same age, son."

J.P. looks at me as if my statement failed to change his mind of what he considers old to be.

I'll see what he says about this in thirty years.

"Lebanon is more dangerous than you think. He might try to hurt your sister to get to Ruby."

"Isn't he your friend?"

"Yes, he is."

"My friends wouldn't try to hurt someone I love."

"He wasn't—"

"Always like this," J.P. finishes the sentence. "Yeah, I've heard you say that a lot. Thing is, me and Layla don't know him like you used to. We only know him now."

"He was kind—give you the shirt off his back."

"You're missing my point. I'm trying to say this holding on you're doing, convincing yourself he's still the same guy somewhere deep down, it isn't serving anyone. Well, it's not serving anyone that should really matter to you."

"You do matter to me. You all do!"

"Mmm-hmm."

The wood floor sings a creaky ballad as I move toward my son and his painting.

"I just want to protect her. Bring her home and keep her safe."

"She wants to do the same thing for Ruby. Let her work this out."

"I can't do that, son."

"Why not?"

I can't provide him with an answer so I have nothing to offer, but silence.

"Tim is going with Layla and I trust he won't let anything happen to her."

"You don't know that," I say.

"Layla isn't stupid. She has a plan and she'll bring Ruby back, make her safe, get her away from Lebanon."

"It's not that simple."

"Life for us in this world, especially in this city, is never simple, but that doesn't mean we don't try and make it better."

J.P. looks at me for some response, some affirmation to the truth of his statement, one that was wise beyond his almost twenty-one years, but I have nothing and my only reply before I walk out the door of his room is, "Mmm-hmm."

CALVARY

September 27, 1960

King Saul lies inside a silver-and-brass casket; a plush ivory-colored lining cradles his corpse. It's a handsome corpse missing King Saul's signature rings that fetched Violet three hundred dollars at the pawnshop downtown yesterday.

She gave the money to Sara.

Mourners file past. "He look like he sleepin'."

"They did him right," says another.

"What world we livin' in where they do this to a man of God? The Lord's Chosen are surely living in the last days!" sobs Sister Wilson, throwing herself onto the coffin, her theatrics barely causing a raised head for she's known to be dramatic, in need of great amounts of attention. Ushers rush to the front guiding her back to the pews and fan her with the cheap paper of an abandoned funeral program.

Chaos swirls inside those passing by his casket, the ones who mourned him. Did someone kill him because he had money? Because he was powerful? Because he was black? All of those things? Was he just in the wrong place at the wrong time?

Many of the church members loved King Saul but didn't know much about him. He was private about his home life, about his daughter, Sara. They often wondered how he could afford his tailored suits or fancy rings on a part-time construction worker's salary. Did it matter though? They adored his looks, reveled in his smooth words; others who harbored suspicions looked the other way because it wasn't their business, and he was bringing enough bodies through the doors and money in the coffers to keep most satisfied. If he had failings, they were overlooked.

What goes on in your house, stays in your house.

Violet remains straight-backed in the first row. She recalls

Gwendolyn Brooks's poem "We Real Cool." Thinking about rebellion and untimely death. But this time, it was necessary.

There isn't anything to feel guilty about, Violet tells herself. Naomi merely did what was necessary, brought something ugly to an inevitable conclusion. Heroes kill ogres and dragons and bad men. King Saul was a bad man. They were heroes. Violet repeats this in her mind, over and over…and over still. All of us were responsible for this monster, and someone had to slay him, someone had to end this dark fairy tale.

No gaze of suspicion floats in their direction. Sara's face remains as detached and beautiful as the marble cherubs posted on gravestones at Restvale Cemetery, where they'll lay King Saul to rest in an hour. Naomi's sullen appearance is the same as the faces gathering in the worship hall. She hasn't spoken a word since that night four days prior.

"Sweetheart." Violet's father gently touches her arm. No longer Assistant Pastor Andrew Morrison, but now Senior Pastor Andrew Morrison, he bleakly smiles at his child. "Everyone's fittin' to leave after the last look at the body."

"Good eulogy, Daddy. King—Pastor Saul would've loved what you said."

Pastor Andrew Morrison glances at the casket. "I hope so." He sits down, putting his arm around Violet, crushing her to him, a fierce embrace, something people tend to do at funerals. When it comes to death, there's an unsettling awakening in the human spirit. Holding the people they love closer, wary something unfortunate or evil can befall them, causes such elevated affection, I assume.

Pastor Morrison whispers in Violet's ear, "Thank you for your kind words, baby. Honestly, I don't know if he'd like what I said. Saul was private, quiet about his faith, his life and such, but he was magic at that pulpit. I guess that's what was important. God uses everyone. Even if we don't always understand." He glances again at the casket and kisses Violet on the cheek.

"I also wanted to say thank you for being such a good friend to Sara. She's been through a lot. I'm glad she's going to Tennessee for a while. Isn't that awful to say? Happy she's going South? Lord knows what she might find there."

"No. It isn't awful to say that at all. Whatever she finds can't be any worse than what she found here."

Violet's father cocks his head, looks at his daughter for some answer he won't be able to retrieve from the depths of her dark gaze. "Hmph" is the only sound that escapes his lips.

King Saul's body wasn't discovered until the next morning by Sister Coates, the church secretary. The girls weren't seen near the church as far as she could tell. The police questioned Sara later that day. Pants and a long-sleeved blouse covered any possible markings left by King Saul. They didn't pay attention to the slight bruising near Sara's neck, a possible clue left among the shattered glass. The detectives focused on a recent spate of robberies a few blocks north, figured King Saul surprised the thieves, fought them and was killed in the process. A tragedy.

Rising from the pew, Pastor Morrison walks over to Sara. "Pastor Saul's godliness, his charity, all of the good things and the good times, that's what people will remember. Not how he died, but that he was a righteous person, a righteous man. I pray you'll take hold of the blessed fact your daddy's in the loving arms of our Lord, rejoicing with Him, watching over you forever."

All Sara can do is not scream at Pastor Morrison, at all of them. Congregants and pastors and ministers, everyone said nice things during the homegoing. The choir sang all King Saul's favorite songs. They talked about a man who never existed: someone who was good and loved his poor, dead wife, Sophia, a pretty soul with golden eyes; how he never got over her passing; a man who cherished his daughter; a man who feared the Lord God with all his being until unexpectedly God called him Home.

No one speaks on King Saul's most memorable traits for Sara: how hard he hit or slapped, how a very special look from him made you feel worthless, how his touch in the dark of night made your skin crawl.

Pastor Morrison hands Sara an envelope, which she opens to find fifty dollars. "Thank you," Sara mumbles.

"Okay," Pastor Morrison looks over the three girls. "We're going to leave for Restvale in a few minutes. Lord knows how long it'll take to get Sister Wilson to come to after all that whoopin' and hollerin'." Pastor Morrison makes his way past the girls and out of the main worship hall with the last batch of church members conversing in the back. Sara peaks over at Sister Wilson who seems to finally be regaining consciousness from whatever fake piety caused her to pass out in the first place. The ushers are escorting her away.

Now that the funeral is finally over, Violet smiles.

No one knows. No one knows.

The three girls remain while others wander off to their cars, sated from grief and graveside theatrics.

"The sun refused to shine today. Even it knew he was a piece of shit," Sara says, first to break the long silence.

"It's not Providence, Sara. It's just the damn weather," Naomi says.

Violet stares at Naomi's mouth making sure she's talking, her words almost suffocated by sudden and violent rumbles of thunder.

"Don't look at me like that, Violet!"

"It's just, you haven't really said anything, since that night."

"I'm just...still getting my head around what happened. I still see his blood. Feel it on my hands. I'm so scared of doing something wrong, saying something wrong. I don't know how to be normal right now, speak normal. Everything I know about myself is gone. The only thing I do know is I'm damned," says Naomi.

"No! You did what needed to be done to save yourself, to save Sara. King Saul could've been doing things to other girls. You're not damned. You're a hero. You're a damn hero," says Violet.

"I don't think God sees me as a hero. God sees me as—" whispers Naomi.

"This time we leave God out of it," says Sara. "If he had anything to do with creating Saul King, I'm leaving God out of what happened and what I'll be doing with the rest of my life from now on. I suggest you both do the same."

Errant drops of rain smack my windows. Sara walks to the casket. Long slender fingers caress the cold brass handles. "He's gonna be buried next to Momma." Sara closes her eyes and raises her head. "I'm sorry they're burying him next to you."

"We should go," says Violet, extending her hand.

Sara lingers at the casket a bit longer. Bad people can do good things. Good people can say bad things. The world is mixed-up and when people do for you what Violet and Naomi did for her, then you cling to those people. No matter what.

"I died a lot of different ways these past few years, but I'd have been here—" she motions at the casket "—without y'all. There's no thanking you, not enough words in the world to do that." Sara turns to her friends. She repeats their promise, the phrase that holds all the gratitude and love she feels for her friends. "Forever and to the end," Sara whispers.

"Forever and to the end," Violet agrees.

Naomi gazes far off into the empty pews. She thinks about the cemetery, all the various stones representing lives once occupying the same world. She wonders how many of them were murdered. Feeling cold hands grip her shoulder, she thinks it's Death, but finds only Sara's face.

"You're gonna be fine because you have to be," Sara says firmly. "You can become okay with the bad things. If anyone can, it's you. I used to think I was stronger than you, but I'm not. You're stronger than me. You always will be."

This is as close to hope Naomi has ever heard in Sara's voice. More tears escape her eyes. Violet embraces them both. Six of the deacons, pallbearers, in blazing white gloves trudge to the front, ready to escort the casket to the hearse waiting outside. Even as the drops on my windows become a torrent, a cascade of miniature rivers saturating my bricks, the three girls remain.

They are made to stand together.

JACKSON

Mom sits with Sara who still sleeps deeply and softly hums a song I don't know. The air holds the fragrance of dying roses. The time in this room seems a never-ending compilation of milliseconds, which gather into actual seconds and those seconds into minutes and those minutes into this last half hour. There are beeps from various expensive machines I can't name. There's a smell like someone tried to get the room cleaned, but whatever nastiness was there wouldn't be removed by chemicals. I stand downwind from Mom so her magnolia perfume relieves my nostrils every few seconds.

"You need to fix this with Layla," Mom whispers. The first words she's uttered since the fight at the house.

"You're gonna lecture me about my child?"

Mom gives me that look, the one that crinkles the skin around her mouth. Her eyes transform into icy black lakes. "Yes, because *you* are *my* child!"

Sara wheezes, uneven and raspy. Her body struggles for one breath, then another, then another. Her body jerks and moves at irregular intervals. She can't even get peace when she closes her eyes.

"I raised you better than this, Jackson Blaisdell Potter. Much better. The things you said to her, it was beneath you."

Layla's words echo in my ears, *better his whore than your daughter.* I swear the girl split me clean in half. King Solomon couldn't have done a better job.

"Why does everyone take her side?"

"Because the one person who should, doesn't."

It would've been better for Mom to just take a knife and stab me in the heart than for me to see the disappointment lingering in her eyes.

"Damn, can y'all find somewhere else to fight?" Sara groggily croaks.

"We're sorry, sweetheart. Just go back to sleep," Mom croons.

"Naw. I'm awake now." Sara shakily pulls herself up in the bed, small and shrunken.

"How are you feeling?"

"Like shit."

Mom purses her lips but doesn't respond. She smooths the edges of the bed and stands up to fluff Sara's pillow like a parent dealing with a cranky child. Their friendship makes even less sense than mine and Lebanon's. Though we haven't had anything resembling a friendship in decades. But more things than love bind people together, secrets and lies make just as hearty a bond as love. Perhaps it's the wonder of having an unlikely companion, someone who mirrors your opposite in every way. All the places in which we feel we lack—perhaps we're drawn to someone who has what we crave in abundance. Sara is hard. Mom is softer. Sara is quiet. Mom speaks her mind. There are ways in which Sara seems resigned to the atrocities of the world; Mom rebels against them. And as I sit in this room smelling of disinfectant and dying flowers, I see Layla and Ruby in fifty years. The terrifying wonder of friendship and family embodied by the two women in this room who hold vast secrets I doubt we'll ever know.

"Close the door," Sara orders. I walk over and do her bidding. Sara reaches across Mom and opens a drawer. She grabs a tin decorated in roses, opens it, and pulls out a small plastic bottle of Jim Beam hidden under a stack of yellowed papers. She paws and twists until Mom gently takes the bottle, opens it and passes it back to Sara.

After taking a couple of gulps, she looks at Mom. "What y'all goin' on about anyway?"

"Nothing you need concern yourself with," I answer.

"I wasn't talkin' to you. This is grown folks' business, boy."

She takes another swig and looks at Mom. "You was always too easy on him."

"Yeah, guess she should've been more like you as a parent," I retort.

Her face twists into an ugly smile. Stale, tawny light in the room gives her eyes a hellish look. "Oh, so you're here about the boy or something about him. That's what you were arguing about? I swear, he's been a pain in my ass since he came on this earth." She takes another drink. Half of the bottle is already empty.

"Sara, settle yourself," Mom orders.

"Ain't no point in hidin' anythin' now. I'm dyin'. You ain't gonna be on this earth a lot longer either. Secrets, all this shit. It eats you up till you nothin' but bones. I'm just bones now. Just bones."

"Don't pay attention to her," Mom says as she tries to take the liquor away from Sara, who tries to valiantly tussle, to keep her good friend Jim. After a minute, Mom manages to snatch the bottle away and stuff it in her purse.

"I hate you," Sara slurs her words and unsuccessfully grabs for Mom's purse.

"No. You don't. Forever and to the end."

Sara's face softens for the briefest moment and a thin sheen of tears shimmers behind her brown-black eyes. "I should've stayed in Tennessee. I found someone there. Jonas loved me, but don't nothing last for me. I can't ever be happy."

Rocking back and forth, she murmurs, "He was there and he loved me and we was a family."

"Was Jonas Lebanon's father?" I ask Sara.

She shrinks back into bed.

"Jackson...leave this be," Mom cautions.

"Better off he knows, that someone knows—" says Sara.

"Sara, answer the question. Was it this Jonas guy?" I ask again, pressing for answers to secrets concealed in whispers and knowing glances among our mothers.

"Sara, we keep this to ourselves. For the good of everyone, you owe Naomi that. You owe yourself. You owe me!" pleads Mom, the earnest fear in her voice rattles something deep in me, but the need for the truth, closure for Lebanon, pushes me to know. Maybe that'll help him. Knowing his father could free him in a way my friendship, my protection and my fear have been unable to do.

"Sara, you need to tell someone. Your son needs to know about his father. Even now, it's not too late. It's okay. Maybe you're not clear on who it is, maybe you need to backtrack, think hard about who you were with at that time. We all have secrets. We all have shame."

I speak to Sara like a member of my church who needs to unburden but doesn't know where to begin. Someone who believes what they're holding in could destroy them if they revealed what it is they're hiding.

Sara's lip quivers. She closes her eyes and her mouth moves but utters no sound. Is she praying? I've never seen her do anything resembling prayer, but could this be it? Could this be her breaking point?

I press on, "Was Jonas Lebanon's father? Can you tell me that?"

Sara's mouth ceases to move and her eyes open. Tears leak from them. "No, foolish boy. My father was his father!"

Those five words don't register with me at first, or rather the horrific gravity of what was said doesn't register. I glance at Mom. There is no look of shock on her face.

"You knew this? You knew about Lebanon's father?"

"Why did you say anything, Sara?" Mom hisses.

"I deserve some peace. I do," she answers.

Mom looks past me. She smooths her dress and folds her hands in her lap. "I didn't want you to know about this. About the hard things, son. About things I had to do or things that happened long ago. Things I never even told your daddy."

My chest thumps with the regularity of a poorly dribbled basketball. Insane heat burrows its way to my stomach.

"Sara's father was… He did things to her," explains Mom. "So, myself and Naomi set out to get Sara settled in Tennessee, but Saul, Sara's father, found out. And we protected our friend."

"He was a bad man. He was gonna kill me. He was a bad man so got what he got."

Sara looks as far gone as Mom. Like they've both been sucked back in the past.

"What does that mean? Got what he got?"

Mom finally meets my eyes and I know the answer. To save a friend, a sister, Ms. Naomi, Sara and Momma killed a man. They killed Sara's father.

The friendship between Sara and Mom never made sense, but it does now. And though Mom tried to spare Lebanon the pain of his true parentage, though Sara in her own toxic way tried to drown her memories in liquor, though Ms. Naomi remained the sweetest soul somehow, all their children wound up continuing their dysfunction, reliving their sins. And now too their grandchildren are paying the price.

Mom's arms encircle my waist and hug me. "I'm so sorry. I never wanted to hurt you or Lebanon."

"John 15:13, Mom. 'Greater love hath no man than this, that a man lay down his life for his friends.'"

Sara tugs at Mom's dress. Wiping away tears, Mom sits on her bed and hugs her. It started low at first, like a gurgling murmur, then sobbing, then wailing, forceful and relieving. A nurse opens the door to check on the commotion. Mom is rocking Sara, comforting her. "It'll be okay. Hush now. It's over and it'll be okay. God's got you. Got us."

With easy and experienced grace, the nurse closes the door to allow us the private moment, the one forty years in the making, the one where Sara's hard shell cracks and shatters and perhaps something human is left for the small time she has remaining on this earth. The sobbing turns into moaning and deep uneven breathing as Sara falls back asleep.

Holding Mom close to me as we exit the room, I hear my name softly called from behind and turn around to find Dr. Savoie near Sara's hospital room door.

"I thought that was you," she says triumphantly. "I have someone asking for you and here you are. Isn't that something?"

"We were just finishing up a visit. It's so good to see you, Dr. Savoie, but I should be getting Mom home. It's getting pretty late," I respond trying to extract myself. All the knowledge I have, all the things I must fix and say and do, I can't shoulder another burden right now.

Not today.

"Oh, well this shouldn't take long. I'd consider it a personal favor, give you half off your next flu shot."

Dr. Savoie chuckles, then smiles, hopeful and genuine. I'd be a horrible pastor saying no to someone like that, someone who can heal the people who come to her. I guess it'll take only a few minutes. I can give someone who needs me, who still believes I have something to offer, a bit of my time. I turn to Mom.

"Don't worry about me, Jackson. I'm just gonna sit here. Me and the Good Lord have much to discuss."

I kiss her damp cheek, salt from her tears mixes with her magnolia perfume.

Two minutes down the hallway, Dr. Savoie and I walk through the glass-encased bridge connecting the hospital to the next building. I seek out the tops of skyscrapers miles away, eyes full of electric light. I know exactly the path we're taking.

I could do it blindfolded.

"I know you were getting ready to leave. That's not lost on me, Pastor, but we have a new resident and she was insistent on talking to you."

"I understand," I say and try to smile easy and calming.

The front station, painted in a cheerful light blue, holds two nurses, both of whom glance up at us and quickly return to the paperwork piled up on their respective desks. Walking past the large, ornate, gold lettering of The Lazarus House, pictures of the smiling residents decorate the walls surrounding the sign. Centered below it, a bigger framed picture of myself, the hospital CEO, the mayor and other politicians. All of us smiling, all of us looking like we're good people, and all of us with secrets we'd love to bury underneath the dirt we ceremoniously dug up with silver shovels. Perhaps we thought building a wing on the hospital as a haven for the elderly would help us barter our way into Heaven and make up for our other shortcomings.

As we come to a room, a woman with dark brown skin and soft wrinkles sits in a chair rocking back and forth. Her face is familiar and in my head. I try to place her: a member from my congregation, one of the people I've served meals to at Pacific Garden Mission, someone from the neighborhood.

Who *is* she?

The radio plays Mahalia Jackson who reverently sings "Lord, Don't Move the Mountain." Her voice baptizes the dusty air. Few know this song now. Mom used to sing this when she cooked meals for my dad before he came home from work. The song she hummed the night after the police came to tell her my father, her husband was dead. I still remember the pristine voices of the choir at Calvary Hope Christian Church singing it at his funeral as I bawled on the front row, Lebanon's arm around my quaking shoulders.

The woman in the chair grins at me like an old friend and I easily reciprocate. I feel at ease in this room with this woman and I don't know why, but now I want to help her, do whatever it is she asks.

"Pastor Potter, this is Thorolese Myllstone. She said she knows you."

CHAPTER 13

LAYLA

We're not going to be at my father's office long so I don't turn on the heat. Brown icicles that are my fingers turn on the computer. Elder Alma was here. Dad's office is only ever this tidy when she cleans it. Otherwise, it's a manageable disaster. Papers, books and dust.

Tim stands near the door and listens for what I assume is anything unusual. This old place always makes groaning noises, but I'm used to every one. I know every crevice and turn. I don't even need the lamp to know my way around, but the light is a comfort.

It takes about ten minutes to buy two tickets to Memphis for a morning flight leaving in a few hours from Midway Airport. It takes even less time to email my boss and explain why I need a few days off work for a family emergency. I said I'd need only three days; that I'd be back by Thursday. Take the time you need, Layla, my boss, Veronica, emails me right back.

I pray I'll be back by Thursday, that Ruby will be okay, that Lebanon will back off and let her be in peace. Me and Ruby could get an apartment together in Beverly or Hyde Park. Argue over which paint goes best on the walls, which couch fits the space. Take walks. Argue some more. Get coffee. Live our lives. Together.

I knew taking time off from work wouldn't be a challenge. In the nine months I've been at Myers & Solomon, I've signed new accounts, impressed clients. I'm the first one there, the last one to leave. I prove myself constantly. I have to. What's the saying? You have to be twice as good to get half as much. I don't know if that's even true. I just started working with that mentality and never let up. I swallow the backhanded compliments about how articulate I am, because in the end, most of them mean well, they're just not experienced with black people, like the people I went to college with, like Christy.

It takes longer for our tickets to Memphis to eke out of the printer than it did for me to purchase them. It's funny, but I've never been in my father's office without him in it. I never roam around or touch his things. This room is his sacred space, hallowed. I don't feel completely at ease here, but it's the only place with a computer and working printer so my options are limited. I sure as hell wasn't going to buy these at home with Dad breathing down my neck. Next to the computer there's a yellow pad that has only three lines written on it. He wasn't "touching up" like he said this morning. He barely started on the damn sermon! My suspicion about Dad is once again correct.

His old Bible, the one in tattered shambles, fastened with duct tape and prayers, sits in the middle of his desk. He's the only one who touches the ancient, ratty thing. He treats it as part of him. It doesn't stop me from picking it up and holding it over the garbage can, but my hand still grips it tight and refuses to let it fall.

Tim has that look again, the one he had in the kitchen as I argued with my father, as we exploded at one another.

"I was just kidding."

"No, you weren't," he says.

I put the Bible down just as a piece of paper falls out and onto the ground. An old newspaper clipping along with the paper lie at my feet. Grabbing them, I glance at the dog-eared piece of paper first, and then I focus on the words.

Good Morning Church,

I want to talk to you about two things this morning: Grace and Mercy. How the Lord uses those things to mold us, if we let them.

I've spoken about this before. I've taken you from the Old Testament to the New. But in all that back and forth, I didn't want to admit things to myself, didn't want to disclose things to you all. If you knew me, saints, really knew me, you wouldn't think me fit to stand up here. You wouldn't welcome me into your homes; give me your trust like each and every one of you do.

God's mercy is such that it covers the sins we cannot even speak of, the things we've done which we've never told our families, things we can't admit to ourselves. And in that mercy, in the deep and dark, we reach for God and He extends His hand back and pulls us up. God's mercy and grace sustain us even through our own shortcomings, through this life, and the one that is to come.

Saints, God's mercy is sufficient as to cover a multitude of sins: lying, bearing false witness, murder. And, I'm ashamed to say I've committed each one of these sins. I've lied to my church family, but most horrific of all, I've lied to my wife and children.

On a cold night in January, there was a boy named Syrus Myllstone.

My eyes blur over the rest of the page.

"...killed Syrus Myllstone"
"...let Lebanon King take the blame"
"...stepping down as Pastor of Calvary Hope immediately"

"I beg forgiveness from not only you, but my loving wife, Joanna, and my children, Layla and Jackson Jr...."

The clipping folded within the paper confirms my father's confession. The words *murder, guilty,* and the names *Lebanon King, Syrus Myllstone* and *Holden Walters* stab the backs of my eyes.

The discovery of this horrid information sets my hands trembling. Tears escape, salty atomic bombs that streak the old ink. Words, once seen, cannot be unseen, and the idea of my father seems as disfigured as the smudged ink of the article.

"What is it?" Tim asks. I pass him the sermon and the article and he reads them.

"Tell me it's going to be okay!"

"Layla, I—"

"How can I leave now? What am I supposed to do? Turn him in?"

There are no words that will make it alright. There is nothing real and permanent. I poked and prodded and ended up finding out something about Dad, something I could've never imagined. If I tell someone, if I speak to the cops, like the ones outside of Ruby's home, they'll haul Dad away, from mom and J.P., from Grandma Violet, from me. There'll be television reports and newspaper articles. Our church would probably never recover from that kind of scandal. My father, the murderer.

Everything is in a thousand pieces and those pieces are shattered into a thousand more.

RUBY

An old man keeps staring at me across the aisle. He's not dangerous. After living with Lebanon, I know dangerous. This man is just curious—and lonely. We're making our way out of Illinois. Deep, deep into a rabbit hole to the country and I'm Alice. The one in the book. Not my mother. I'm never her. Not a victim. Not a martyr.

White and green, a highway sign declares the bus has reached Effingham, Illinois. Miles down, on the right shoulder of the highway, a big white cross stands among brown grass, barren trees, concrete and asphalt. It's one bright thing among dead things.

Three or four people linger below the cross, capturing pictures, instant flashes of light dance around their bodies. An old finger the color of a tree root grazes my shoulder. "It's a tourist attraction," the old man offers. "The Effingham Cross, they call it. Supposed to be the biggest cross in the US, I think. Maybe people feel some way bein' round something so big and godly. Maybe they feel blessed."

"Blessed?" I can feel myself frowning. Mom always got on me about that. She said it made me look like Lebanon, like I didn't want to talk to anybody.

"You don't think you blessed, child?"

He smiles, his teeth are nice, even and white. It's a warm smile, not a pretend action of the mouth.

I want to return his smile. I can't.

"So where you headed, child?"

"Away from here."

"Visiting family?"

I'm still frowning. Because of the questions, the tightness in my forehead spreads to my mouth.

The stranger's face softens even more, brown and liquid like chocolate pudding. He says, "I'm sorry. I don't mean no harm. Not trying to be nosy."

But he is being nosy. He wants answers to his questions and, truth is, maybe I want to talk. Maybe Mom sent someone to me, a stranger, someone to talk to me, keep my words, like a living diary. Besides, a stranger can't really do any harm.

Family can.

"I'm heading to Tennessee. Just need a change is all."

I need a new life. I need to stop thinking about nights I can't take back, the people I won't see again. I've never been outside Chicago except for those hot summers in Tennessee with grandma.

The old man moves in his seat a bit to face me. His eyes are a pale blue, the result of age, the pigmentation of once earth-brown eyes now gone and replaced with two circles the color of the morning sky.

Dirty snow clings to the edges of the asphalt roads, most of them barren, ground frozen. Staring at nothing, focusing my eyes on a horizon far off; it's calming.

"Change. That's exciting depending on what you lookin' for. So what are you lookin' for, child?"

"Peace."

Ghostly golds and blues and pinks of early evening paint the sky, the warmth, the roll and bump of the highway. Far away I go. Down the rabbit hole. Like Alice.

"Peace. Still trying to find that myself. Old as I am, I ain't got much longer to find it." He laughs, it's high-pitched, but soft and his body trembles. "But I think peace is something we gotta fight ourselves for. God gives it to us, but we always find some way to kill it. Human nature, I'm guessing."

"So, it's my fault I'm not at peace." I see my reflection in the window across the aisle. It's smashed and misshapen. Everything is always my fault. From this stranger to Lebanon to my mom, everyone and everything is my fault. Hearing the same things from multiple people at multiple times, I think church folk call this *Confirmation.*

It's been confirmed, I am the problem. The Mistake.

"Well don't get ready to bite my head off just yet, child." He chuckles again. What the hell is so damn funny? "I just mean there are situations we come from, and we can't control what happens, but we can control how we allow God to help us through it. Giving up that control, that's peace."

"Are you trying to be a Bible study teacher? I didn't ask for your opinion." I know my tone is less than respectful. I feel the disapproving look of Mom from beyond.

"Not at all, but I know some part of you is listening. I don't have peace yet, child, but I do have faith."

"I don't have peace or much faith, but I have a plan."

"And what's that?"

I say nothing and he grins. I touch my black-and-gold purse. I search for the envelope in my jacket pocket. Again, I want to return his smile, but I can't.

LEBANON

If you don't have hope no more, you remember the time you gave up on it, the moment where you knew you weren't like a lot of other people, because you weren't still a fool like a lot of other people.

I lost hope about a week before Syrus.

Hell, I even remember where I was when I let that feeling forever abandon me.

There was this part of the kitchen in the old apartment where, if the light hit just right, everything's made to look beautiful. Stand right over the sink when the sun is coming up, and the prettiest diamond don't sparkle like the person standing in that light.

Only our place had this gift.

This one morning Sara was standing in the light.

She looked like what she probably did before I came along. Eyes not so full of hate and obligation. Could've even swore I saw a smile lingering on her lips. She was pretty to me in that moment. Looked like what I thought a mom could've looked like. Maybe she found some kind of peace or maybe she had a good meal. Maybe one of the men she brought home saw her as more than temporary entertainment, more than something to greedily grope at in the dark. I don't know, but I wanted to hug her. Never really felt that way before, but I did that time. And before I could stop myself, I threw my skinny arms around her ample body, holding on to her with any part of my heart I might've had left.

I held on tight. Tighter than anything. Nothing happened. No tears. No struggle. Just a slab of meat sparkling in the window. Pretty and dense and rigid.

And I waited. I waited for something. For love, I guess. I thought maybe if I tried really hard one more time, something would happen like magic, and she'd love me. Fuckin' stupid idea but it didn't stop me from trying.

I let go. Didn't even look at her. I walked out of the kitchen, out of the apartment. Went to Jackson's house. The spare key was under a green flower pot. Auntie Vi told me where it was in case of an emergency. I had a lot of those when I was younger.

Their house always was tidy. It smelled like magnolias and whatever she was cooking. There Jackson sat with Auntie Vi and they were laughing about some such nonsense. Even though he didn't have a dad no more, he had her. I didn't know my dad, didn't have a mom.

Killing someone might not be a sin if you want what they got bad enough. I wanted what was at that table even if it was half of what other people had. Still better than nothing.

JACKSON

I sit staring at Thorolese Myllstone in her sparsely decorated room. Most of her belongings are still in boxes piled against the wall behind me. The walls are painted a cheery yellow; a window behind her reveals the tops of budding tree branches made bare by the harsh winter. The architect said bright colors and lots of natural light were good for seniors, said there were studies done proving this. On a small maple shelf, a picture of Syrus, smiling wide and happy, a look so completely foreign to the boy I knew, the boy I killed that night in the snow.

"He only smiled like that for me," she brags like so many mothers, undeniably proud of their child and completely blind in the moment to their faults. She picks up the framed picture and hands it to me.

My hands tremble holding it. "He looks like a nice kid," I manage to say. I hand her back the picture.

"My niece is gonna help unpack the rest of this stuff an' finally get me nice an' settled. Patrice is a good girl. Takes care of me like she my own child," she boasts.

Thorolese smiles, the same as Syrus, and pats my hand. "Patrice the reason I sought you out. She took me to your church this morning. That was a mighty powerful sermon today. Mighty powerful indeed."

"I'm so happy you think so."

"Mmm-hmm. Sat right up in front." Her eyes glimmer searching mine for some recognition of her face. I don't remember her. I don't remember the face of the woman whose son I murdered. I saw her only once standing outside of the church where they held Syrus's funeral. Six men carried his oak casket down the stairs. She followed it, hunched over, face covered by a handkerchief while she bawled and wept and mourned her son, mourned Syrus.

Thorolese gets up and pours a cup of tea and serves it to me without request. I don't like tea, but I drink. The cup is small and delicate. I think about the tea parties Layla made me have with her when she was three or four years old. The cups and plates seemed tiny in my hands and so did she. Small and fragile, something to be protected and cherished. I failed at keeping her safe. I've failed at her loving me. Now God has delivered me to the hands of the woman whose life I've irreparably destroyed.

Words escape me, so I sip my tea and watch Thorolese do the same. She puts her cup down and tightens the scarf around her head, blue with white lilies.

"I know you got places to be, Reverend Potter."

"Call me Jackson, Mrs. Myllstone."

"I will do no such thing! That's disrespectful the way I was raised," she gasps. "And it's *Ms.* 'cause I was never married."

Fluorescent lighting emits this annoying buzz-hiss. "I asked you here 'cause what you said this morning when you was preaching about letting go of the people who've hurt you. I wanna do that for the man who took my baby, my Syrus. I know you know him. That y'all are friends. I saw him at your church today. I'd never forget his face, but I couldn't bring myself to say anything to that man." She sighs. "Thought I forgave him, but when I saw him, it all came back. Maybe I ain't as over everything as I think."

I almost drop my cup so I set it down on the small brown table. "Ms. Myllstone, to forgive someone who took from you what was taken, your child, some would say that's practically impossible."

"Pastor, you know better than anyone else with God all things are possible."

Would she believe all things possible if she knew the real murderer of her son is sitting across from her? That she served him a cup of tea?

"I do know Lebanon King. We are friends, but I'm not sure what you want from me, how you think I can be of service."

"I don't know. I was hoping you'd pray with me, for me, for my son, that he found peace away from this earth since he never found peace on it."

"You don't think he was at peace? Do you believe he is now?"

She rises again and shuffles behind me to refill her cup of tea. "I don't know, Pastor Jackson. I know he was, how you say it? Troubled. He could be downright mean, a bully, and he had the ability to hurt others. He's hurt me." Thorolese puts down her cup and softly pulls down the collar of her blouse, four small dark dots are embedded beneath her collarbone. "Syrus did this when he was twelve. Took the fork he was eatin' with and stabbed me with it. His daddy said he was comin' to visit him and never showed up. It hardened my boy, being disappointed like that, and I couldn't make it better. I tried though. But he still took his disappointment, his anger out on me."

Thorolese raised her sleeve where a scar, shaped like a crescent moon, was etched on her forearm. "Syrus did this when I didn't want him to go out that night, the night he was killed. He pushed me out the way and I cut myself on a broken door frame. I just knew something bad was gonna happen that night, but he didn't listen." She sniffles and wipes her eyes with the back of her hand. "He was still my child. I birthed him. I knew the bad, but I knew the good. He helped me with rent. Never forgot my birthday, and, if he was havin' a real good day, he gave the best hugs in the world, like a warm mountain of love surrounding you. My Syrus was hurt so he hurt other people. Maybe this was always gonna happen. Too many wounded out there. And maybe, well, I can't help but think to do what that boy did to my baby, that he was hurtin' somethin' awful, too."

"I'm sure he was Ms. Myllstone. I'm so sure he was."

She stirs honey into her tea and slowly nods, affirming there was enough pain in this world that plenty can be brought to any and all doorsteps, from a janitor to a president or even a pretend holy man like myself.

"Maybe then I can tell him, I can forgive him or learn to at least. Maybe I can look on his face and give him some peace and find some myself."

"Do you want me to bring him to you?"

She smiles wide, her gaze is far away, like Mom's and Sara's in the hospital room. "Well, Pastor, I think you can help me so when I get ready to see him, I can bear it. And then, maybe I'll get some peace for myself. Like I said, I know me and I knew Syrus. He wasn't a good boy, but he was *my boy*, and he didn't deserve what happened to him, that boy hittin' him all those times, but maybe I can find out why he did what he did."

Of all the wisdom Thorolese has shared, one fragment rings loud as a bell in my ears. Syrus was hit *all those times*. I hit Syrus once and I ran. One time.

"Ms. Myllstone, what do you mean all those times? From what I remember about—what Lebanon told me, I thought Syrus was hit once and died."

"Naw, baby. I saw my Syrus's body. I saw it." She shudders. "The doctor told me, what was the term? Blunt trauma."

"Blunt force trauma," I correct.

"Yes! That's what he said. Multiple blows. The first hit hurt him. Didn't kill him. He got hit at least seven times. Seven. Can you imagine what it took to do that?"

She finishes the rest of her tea and sets the cup down in front of her. "We had a closed casket. Couldn't let people see him like that."

Only from the edges of my vision do I see Thorolese make her way around the table to sit down next to me. "You okay, Pastor Jackson? You ill?"

"Where's your bathroom?"

"Just down the hall, first door on the right."

The bathroom is compact and smells like lavender. I vomit

into the sink. And now the bathroom smells like lavender and rancid meatloaf.

Thirty years! I've wasted thirty years. And I'm raging at myself, but even more than I want to yell and shout and scream, I just cry in sorrow and relief. I use a fancy rose-colored lace towel to muffle my sobs.

I'm not a murderer. I've spent what feels like an eternity believing I was! Lebanon was the only one there after I hit Syrus *once* and ran off. Lebanon was the one who hit Syrus over and over again. *He* was responsible for Syrus's death and held it over my head. And I've spent decades loathing and hiding and hating myself, keeping everyone around me far away and it was for nothing. Nothing!

All this time. *All this damn time!*

Ms. Myllstone might not get the closure she craves because I might kill him.

I might kill Lebanon.

CHAPTER 14

LEBANON

I hate packing, even for small trips. I always forget something simple: a toothbrush, belts, underwear. Alice did it best. Knew what I needed before I did. That was useful. I guess I miss that. I limit myself to just one or two more beers before I hit the road to find the girl.

I just need one day's worth of things so hopefully I don't mess that up. Sitting in the same pair of boxers for two days going back and forth to Tennessee is not my idea of fun. Losing a day of business isn't fun either, but the check I got from Jackson will help. I'll give whatever's leftover to the hospital and hopefully that'll shut them up for a while until Sara dies.

Pounding on the front door interrupts my process. Damn it. I'm gonna forget the underwear. I just know it.

Jackson stands on my porch. I let him in, and I close the door. Turning to ask him why he's here this time of night, he shoves me against the living room wall with the whole force of his body, a cinder-block wall of muscle and pressure suffocating me. A picture of Alice, the girl and me clatters to the floor.

"Sonofabitch!" he yells.

He puts his forearm against my windpipe and pushes into me harder and harder. I can't breathe. I try pushing his elbow up. It doesn't budge. The muscles in my face pulse and throb. My eyes meet his and witness his dark joy at my pain. I almost want to congratulate him. Jackson finally found the balls to do something he's wanted to do, in this case it's probably to kill me, but at least he seems to be going for it with gusto.

I don't quite plan on going to meet my Maker today. I kick his right knee and he buckles; his arm gives a little and I dodge to my left.

"This is the second time today you've tried to kick my ass," I accuse, but I'm laughing at him.

Hunched over, taking in deep breaths. Jackson mumbles something.

"What?"

"Thorolese Myllstone! I met Syrus's mother and she had an interesting story. Turns out Syrus was hit seven times, not once. I didn't kill him, you did!"

What does he want me to do? What does he want me to say? It's not like he didn't hurt the boy, too. So he didn't deal the death blow, but I wouldn't have had to if he just kept it together. Now he comes at me with this? When I need to find the girl? When I need to make sure my legacy is kept intact?

"I finished the job you were too chickenshit to finish, you self-righteous asshole!"

He lunges again, but his wounded knee prevents him from reaching me.

"You want me to cry for you? If I didn't take him out, he would've gone back and told everyone what you did…and then what? You would've gone to jail. I went instead of both of us going. My story was already told. Sara saw to that. And what's another black man behind bars? At least I gave you the chance to make something of yourself. You should thank me. I killed him *for you*, for the people who looked up to you—right or wrong. So all this whining about your damn conscience, your wasted potential, you can take that somewhere else."

"It only happened 'cause I was taking up for you that night. He called Sara a drunk, called you a piece of shit."

"So the hell what? Sara *was* a drunk, still is! I got called a piece of shit all the time. That day wasn't any different. I didn't ask for your help, but you gotta come out all big and bad trying to prove you're a hero, the church boy your daddy would've been proud of."

Jackson's breath slows, and he finally stands upright. "Thirty years, man. I lived with this for thirty years," he growls.

"And you still managed to get a family and a church and everybody acting like you the damn king. You're welcome."

"You don't feel bad about anything you've done? None of it?"

"Yeah, I feel bad. I feel bad you got all this shit handed to you. You had a mom who didn't beat your ass for just existing. You knew your daddy. You had a nice home, food in your belly and you *still* managed to almost fuck it up! Then I come to your rescue and you're still ungrateful as hell!"

"Go to hell, Lebanon."

"Fuck you, Jackson."

He turns around, lumbers to the door and slams it shut. I return to the bedroom and look at my throat in the mirror. It's red and swollen. It hurts to swallow, but this isn't anything I can't get through. I finish packing.

I got about a seven- or eight-hour drive before I get to Naomi's house. The girl's got to be headed there. Good memories for her. I was born in Tennessee and lived there until Sara moved us back to Chicago when I was about two or three years old.

Last time I stepped foot in Tennessee, Naomi died. Before that, when Alice tried to leave me. She came back though. Alice saw me standing on that porch and all the words she probably set up in her head vanished, just like the courage that got her to the house.

Naomi was always stronger than her daughter, but I never knew where she got it. I never bothered to ask and she hated me so I doubt she would have ever talked to me about it. If she had the strength, she'd probably have killed me. She put up more of a fuss about me being there than Alice. She was a tough ole bird. I'll give her that. A pain in the ass, but tough. The girl is a lot like her.

Won't do much good thinking about all this now. I'll be on the road in a few hours. I'll get the girl and be back by early Tuesday. I can start my life a different way. Not the way I planned, but you roll with the punches. You live your life and you remember to pack goddamn underwear for a road trip to find your prodigal daughter.

LAYLA

The article in Dad's old Bible is dated May 2, 1979. It explains a few things to me that his sermon doesn't. Lebanon served five years in prison for manslaughter; he killed a boy named Syrus Myllstone. An officer named Holden Walters made the arrest but believed there may have been another assailant.

Another assailant. Dad.

His confession, that wrinkled piece of paper now carefully folded in my coat pocket, isn't nearly as aged as the clipping. It was stuck between the pages of that old Bible for a while though. The lives it would destroy at this point wouldn't just be his. It'd be Mom's and J.P.'s and mine. Not to mention the church's.

Now everything becomes clear. This is why Dad's protected Lebanon all these years. You don't leave behind the one person who can expose you. You can either keep him quiet when he leaves prison with a nice job and a sweet girl named Alice, or you can silence him. I guess my dad was only capable of murder once.

Tim's truck rumbles north on the Dan Ryan Expressway. Every few minutes he glances over at me and I stare straight into the windshield.

"Pull over."

"Layla, we're in the middle of—"

"I'm gonna be sick! Pull the hell over!"

Tim turns on his blinker and then his hazards, slowly pulling onto the shoulder along the 63rd Street exit. The whir of passing cars is silenced only by my vomiting and dry heaving. Tim tries to approach me, but I wave him off. Constant bright yellow blinking of hazard lights assaults my peripheral vision. After I've given up anything I've eaten today or yesterday, I finally straighten up. Tim jogs to the truck, going into the glove compartment and retrieving napkins. When I don't feel like I'm going to lose my guts again, we both head back to the truck.

"We'll sit here as long as we need to until you figure out what you should do next," counsels Tim.

Staring again at the windshield, past it, a few miles north of here, peaks of cosmopolitan towers seem like a living organism. Chicago ebbs and flows in architecture, white headlights and red taillights buzzing around its confines—a hive and fat bees attracted to its honey glow.

I rummage through my bag and finally recover my tin of mints and take two of them. The tick of the hazard lights gives me an audible reminder of the time slipping by and my limited options, and at this moment the only person who can help me.

"I need to see Christy."

Tim flicks off the hazard lights, checks the rearview mirror and pulls back into traffic.

"You wanna let me in that head of yours?"

I can't even begin to break down how fixing my father's lies, this horrible act, will help me and Ruby, but I'm going to try to explain. Even if Tim doesn't think it'll work, even if he thinks my idea is stupid, I know he'll help me. He loves me so he'll help me.

"If I want to bring Ruby home, I have to break down this stronghold Lebanon has on my dad. The only way is by exposing Lebanon and my dad to the community. This means revealing secrets, including those of my family. These secrets are keeping me and Ruby from being safe."

"So how does going to Christy help figure out what happened with your dad?"

"The only way I can see doing this is by getting answers from someone who isn't Dad or Lebanon, someone who was there that night in January, but wouldn't have a reason to lie about who else was there. Holden Walters. I don't know who that is, but Christy's dad probably has access to information about cops, past and present."

"It makes sense, but it's a long shot at best."

"It's the only plan I got right now unless you got something better."

"So possibly revealing Reverend Potter killed someone is the way to do that?"

"If Ruby comes back and Lebanon tries to use Dad's past as leverage, I need something, some nuclear option of getting him to leave Ruby alone. And the truth, the naked truth, is the only way I can do this—it's the only way I can save Ruby and myself. If Lebanon sees I'm serious about outing my own dad, that might get him to leave Ruby alone for good."

"If not, if it doesn't stop him?"

"Then I'll buy Ruby another ticket anywhere she wants and I'll…let her go."

Tears blur my vision passing Cermak-Chinatown toward the Circle Interchange. Barreling toward Lincoln Park, I think of what I'll say to Christy, my friend who rarely goes south of 35th Street; my friend who lives in Lincoln Park, one of the richest neighborhoods in the city.

To be fair, I rarely go past the Loop onto the North Side, a part of the city where I feel I don't belong. Rather I sense the whispers and stares of the white people who stroll up and down the blocks; the cute little shops and restaurants and other businesses that wouldn't think of opening or investing in our communities, because, well, this is their community and south of 35th Street isn't anything they really want to think about. And that is why I don't come—it's not that I don't feel worthy, it's because my self-esteem dictates I don't go where I'm not wanted or appreciated. If they don't want to deal with my neighborhood, then I won't deal with theirs. They can have their artisan cupcakes and organic coffee and handmade gelato.

I'll take the South Side with its jagged splendor and unrealized beauty, the tangled ways of survival and the underbelly of violence that seems to color every part of our lives and the community at large. It's an honesty the North Side will never possess.

But right now, I need Christy's help if I want to bring Ruby home.

My left arm is again broken into skinny bumps. I don't want to call Mom or J.P.—not yet. If I must tear apart our lives, I need to make sure I have all the facts. When I was in college my journalism professors taught me many important things, one of them being how to pull apart a story piece by piece and compose the parts again into a narrative that makes sense and is believable.

One thing I know as a proud American is having a rich friend with a powerful father gets you answers quicker than trolling Google.

JACKSON

I returned to the church to pray for answers about Lebanon, to find Layla and reconcile with her. I came to compose a plan to take back my life or some semblance of one without guilt, lies or imaginary obligations. It's a delicious affliction of relief and terror. Who am I without guilt and fear shaping every decision I make, every relationship I build? I'm free to be me, but who is that now?

Harnessing raggedy bits of my hatred for Lebanon into something that looks like empathy, I still continue in thought. How can I reassemble any fragment of love for him? How can I forgive him? All the brokenness that wove itself into the fabric of Ms. Sara's life, her and Lebanon's pain, each can be traced back to the one person put on this earth to protect them.

For now, though it seems nearly impossible, my focus is finding Layla. If she tracks down Ruby and she gets in Lebanon's way, what would he do? Layla will fight for Ruby with everything she's got. Is Lebanon capable of killing my baby girl? He killed Syrus. He likely killed Alice, too.

I rub my right knee again, and limp to my office and open the door. I recognize Alma cleaned the place I left in shambles after my earlier day's tantrum, and though things are neat and orderly the way they should be, something feels out of place.

Earlier, I hoped Layla would come back to the house, abandon this whole crusade. I know better. Now I have to play detective. Think like my daughter. My clever, loyal, beautiful, obstinate, disrespectful, disobedient daughter. Scanning my space, I surmise she'd want to use the computer. I turn it on. Layla taught me how to look up a search history, but I'm drawing a blank.

Our conversation about this computer was, like everything else in our relationship lately, a fight. She insisted I get one. I didn't need one because it was an extra expense for the church, another item to get approved through the board. Plus, I like to write everything by hand. Feeling the pen's weight on the page and the paper giving way to my thoughts is more satisfying. Layla said the church and I needed to step into the twenty-first century, said the church needed a website, mentioned something called "metrics" and social media and websites I never heard of and I just said okay so she'd stop talking.

I'm not sure where to place my fingers and a few of the keys might as well be written in an ancient language. I just learned how to text a few months ago, and all Layla did when I sent her a message was correct my spelling, so I stopped texting her. I stopped texting period.

Layla's right about me not listening, but I didn't fully pay attention because she was harping on one more thing I wasn't doing, one more thing as her father I was miserably falling short on.

Like tonight.

So I got this box with wires and chips and it normally collects dust, but the cover on the screen is removed and the keyboard is placed to the left, not the right. I spend ten minutes clicking away on a mouse until I finally see the search history. She saved the password on the airline's site. Thank God. I wouldn't have otherwise gotten access to the account.

The recent purchase is a flight to Memphis, Tennessee. I call Joanna. She doesn't answer so I leave a brief message. She won't talk to me until I bring Layla back through the door of our home. I try calling my daughter. It goes to voicemail.

So busy with walking through the valley of the shadow of computers, I didn't notice my Bible was opened. I swallow the softball-sized lump in my throat as I flip through the pages hoping to find what I already know is missing.

I don't feel myself collapse in my chair, but I do feel the healthy bounce it gives supporting my sudden weight.

She's read my confession. Layla probably thinks I'm a monster, a murderer, but I'm not. She doesn't know that. She doesn't know that for the past thirty years I served time in a jail with no bars and no walls. That I lived my life scared every step would lead to irreparable exposure. I've been holding this secret for so long, I don't know how my life is shaped without it. I don't know how to exist without withholding some part of me from the people I love, and now I find myself free of this burden. I'm now feeling the weight of another one, the possibility of losing Layla over a secret I was never meant to keep, a label of murderer I was never meant to bear, and a debt to the kind of man I once, long ago, held as dear as a brother.

The only thing left to do now is drive the half hour to Midway Airport and attempt to speak to Layla and have her believe me. Did Layla already tell Joanna about what she found? Is that why no one is answering my calls? Does Joanna hate me? Does J.P.? That feeling of being an outsider in my family would no longer be an intangible fear, but a constant, nasty reminder I never belonged with them and their hearts were never mine to protect. Somehow they knew to never trust me.

Good for them.

Maybe I'm getting ahead of myself. Maybe Layla doesn't know what she has. Maybe she hasn't told Joanna anything. Maybe I still have time to fix this mess, redeem myself.

Maybe I don't.

I don't know if God ever forgave me for lying and still trying to shepherd a community of people who trusted me to do the right thing even when it was the hard thing.

Layla can hate me, but she must know, my family must know, I didn't take a life. I'm not a murderer. I'm a liar and a coward, but not a killer, and that brings me a relief perhaps only God can interpret.

If forgiveness is not an option on the table for my daughter, then I will try meeting the consequences of my past actions with the courage eluding me all these years. Then I can show her how much I love her, how much I wish I was a better man, a better father.

Someone is singing. I can't quite place the origin of the music. Following the sound past my office and another two rooms, I turn right and into the main hall. The church feels downright cavernous when not filled with people. I find Alma. I thought by some miracle it'd be Layla, maybe she forgot something. I should have known better.

Alma prefers the church to be empty while she does her cleaning. She lines her spray bottles of disinfectants, bleaches and waxes from biggest to smallest. The vacuum stands guard at her right side. She reverently croons the same song Thorolese Myllstone's radio played a few hours ago, "Lord, Don't Move the Mountain." Alma serenades an invisible audience, baptizing the dusty air with a pure soprano. It's her devotion before she cleans the church during these brief midnight hours.

"God don't want a dirty home," she likes to say when complimented on the pristine state of the church.

Tonight, Alma begins with the altar. I listen to her a little longer before she spots me.

"Pastor!" she exclaims. "You just standing in the shadows scared me half to death!"

Alma is a match for anyone who'd dare rob the church, or cross its threshold with dirty shoes, but I understand why she's startled. I'm never here at this hour, but my circumstances are far from normal these past few days.

"I wanted to apologize, Alma...for earlier."

She smiles and takes my hand, covering it with hers. "I forgave you when you did it, but act like a three-year-old again, and I'm gonna tan your hide like you're a three-year-old."

Returning her smile, I squeeze her hand. "Okay, Alma, okay."

She laughs but the underlying timbre has a conviction and I know she'd not perform that mercy for me again. Ever.

"Now what are you doing here this time of night, Jackson? I know it's not to help me clean."

She laughs again.

"I apologize, Alma. Thought you might be someone else."

"No, sir. I just got here a moment ago."

I turn to leave, the throbbing in my right knee forcing the slightest limp.

"You okay, Pastor?"

"I'm fine."

Somehow, I seem to attract every human lie detector within a hundred-mile radius.

Momma. Joanna. Layla. Alma Locke.

Her head cocked, eyes narrowed, Alma sizes me up. "Now I'm not one to get in other people's business—" she begins to tell me, which is the introduction of someone about to insert themselves in your business "—but why are you here this time of night and who did you think I was?"

Examining her face and knowing this woman for the better part of twenty-five years, I know whatever I reveal stays between her, myself and God Almighty. Alma doesn't gossip. She just needs the truth and she wants me to be accountable.

"I thought you were Layla."

"Is she okay?"

"I hope so. We had a fight."

"So it was bad."

"Are there any good ones, Alma?"

Her smile vanishes. "She the reason you're limping?"

"No. I just bumped it on the desk is all."

"Mmm-hmm."

Alma guides me to the front pew in the middle aisle, right in front of the pulpit.

"I preach forgiveness, but I don't know if that's an option for me or with us," I say.

"It is. People who love one another always think they have that one fight to end all fights. Have something in their past making them the one person God can't touch. It's happened to me plenty of times, but I'm still here and I still love people and they love me."

"How do you come back from that, Alma?"

"Make a choice to love. That choice ain't easy. It's hard as anything you'll ever do. Love needs action, but I imagine living with hate in your heart is much, much harder."

She says these words with such faith, I wonder if there is part of her I can liquidate and bottle, just like the cleaners lying on top of the altar.

"What if I've pushed her too far? What if Layla doesn't want that? What if she never comes back to me?" This last question lurks all monster and shadow beneath my regrets.

"So you're going to stand on 'what-ifs,' Jackson? The Man of God needs to be stronger than that."

"Am I not supposed to ask myself about possibilities?" I fire back.

"Yes, but you're letting what hasn't happened run your life. You can't make good decisions doing that. You can't lead out of fear."

"I'm just so tired."

Standing up, Alma says, "Better you take yourself down off that cross soon, Jackson. There's only room up there enough for Jesus."

Then she laughs hard and loud and the church doesn't seem so barren a place. A smile creeps at the corners of my mouth. Alma's candor at my dilemma, her bold refusal to allow me to fall into self-pity, solidifies my respect and my trust in her. Making her an elder is one of the best calls I've made for this church and for myself.

"Go find Layla. Something's telling me you know where she may be. Walk through the fear and out the other side. Believe me, you'll have something much more powerful with you and in you."

I feel hope. I feel I need to leave here, let Alma finish what she came here to do, and *finally* start cleaning up my own messes.

CALVARY

Spring 1997

Layla and Ruby spend a lot of time in my basement. It is their special place among the shadows and the boxes of old clothes and seasonal decorations. In my space they talk, laugh and fight as sisters do, even those who don't share blood. The girls hold some intangible connection that, even after all my years of existence, I've yet to decipher. Though I do recall decades ago three girls who shared a similar bond.

These types of connections are ones fortified through merciless circumstance not games of jump rope or hopscotch. Perhaps girls, ones whose skin color defines them more than the depth of their character, unearth a reserve of energy and strength alien to those on the outside, and maybe only other girls who share this trait are able to truly understand one another in a way a city or nation or world at large cannot.

Maybe that's why Layla and Ruby cloister themselves within my confines so others won't intrude on whatever they share with each other. Like the first time Ruby told Layla about what Lebanon did at home. Layla didn't comprehend at first because she's only ten years old, but she recognizes enough to be quiet for once and listen to Ruby as she explained.

"It's like he gets so mad and no one can get him to calm down. So Mom just makes me go in my room and tells me to not come out. That she'll come get me. She says no matter what I hear, don't come out of my room."

Layla didn't know what to do with this except to say, "I can tell my daddy. He can do something!"

Layla grabs Ruby's arm to take her to her father because he could fix it. She's sure of this, but Ruby won't budge. And Layla pulls on her arm and tugs, but Ruby doesn't move, and, finally when she's had enough of Layla pulling at her, Ruby yells at

Layla, "Stop!" And then she cries, it's an ugly sound, one fright-
ening Layla. All she can do is go to Ruby and hug her, and
Ruby, with her skinny arms, holds Layla and clings to her until
her tears won't come anymore.

They sit down on a creaky old pew worn down from worship,
and Layla offers Ruby a piece of candy which Ruby declines.

"If no one's gonna protect you, I'll do it," Layla promises.

"Okay," Ruby agrees. "I believe you."

Ruby puts her head on Layla's shoulder and there they remain on the old pew until Jackson finds them both and walks
them upstairs.

There was a great shift in their sisterhood after that day, one
Layla and Ruby recognized. The next Sunday, Layla begged
for Ruby to come home with her to spend the night. She did
so every Sunday afterward or whenever the girls saw one another. Sometimes Jackson and Joanna agreed and sometimes they
didn't. But when they did, she and Ruby slept in the same room,
in the same bed and Layla clung to Ruby, and tried to think
of a way they could both stay together, where Ruby could be
happy and Layla could feel there was no longer a reason to keep
holding her breath. But this feeling lingered, especially when
Layla looked into Ruby's eyes. And though Ruby loved Layla,
she resented her for always believing she needed to be rescued,
when all she needed was for someone to listen, not scheme or
plot or plan, just listen because Ruby knew, one day, when she
got older, she'd figure out how to escape. But Layla didn't want
Ruby to leave—not without her.

It's no wonder off Layla goes again to save Ruby. Pull her to
some kind of tenuous safety, like she did when they were ten-
year-old girls, entombed in the light and shadow and dust of
my basement.

And I hope Layla finds Ruby. For if she doesn't, I dread to en-
vision what could become of Layla, her family and, if selfishness
is a thing for a conscious collection of brick and mortar, of me.

LAYLA

I stand in front of Christy's condo and hope she isn't pissed it's after midnight. She was a night owl in college, but aren't all students, completing papers or studying for exams? Maybe I woke her out of a good sleep. Tim's hand in mine gives me the smallest measure of hope.

On the third-floor landing, Christy opens the door, and doesn't look at Tim and me with anything other than concern.

"I'm sorry for showing up late like this, girlie, but I—"

"It's fine. It's fine," Christy responds and ushers us in. "I was working on some late-night social media stuff for Dad. He's hopeless with it."

She glides through her living room in gray yoga pants and a Vampire Weekend T-shirt.

Her third-floor condo is laid out like something you'd see in magazines, a light gray sectional, an ivory patterned oversized seat and matching throw rug ornament a sitting area, right off a galley kitchen. A modern painting of an elephant on the east wall perfectly complements the modern furniture and surroundings of her posh living room. Christy and I sit on the sofa. Tim takes the chair.

"I just need a favor…well two," I begin. "We have a flight in the morning, and I can't quite go home right now. So could Tim and I just rest here? We'll be out in a few hours. I promise."

Christy nervously laughs. "Really? Is that all? That's not a problem, Layla. It's a pull-out sofa. Geez, I thought you were going to ask me to do something like help you bury a body."

"Well, I said I needed two favors."

"If you need help with that body, then I might have to change my clothes." She chuckles again, but I don't laugh along with her. Christy's eyes slightly narrow. "What do you have up that sleeve of yours, Layla? What's the actual favor, the one that means something to you?"

"Your dad knows a lot of people. Has access to information that might take me a while to get."

"True," agrees Christy. "Dad has to have dirt on just about everyone. It's his stock and trade."

"Well, I don't need dirt, really just a name and an address. Holden Walters. He was a cop, back in the '70s, probably retired. We think he may have information."

"For Ruby?" guesses Christy.

I glance at Tim, who gestures for me to answer Christy. "Not exactly. It's just something for me, but maybe in the end it can help a lot of people, including Ruby."

"Okay, Layla."

"I owe you, girlie. I really do. I'll owe your Dad too, but I'll figure something out with that."

"You don't owe me. And you don't owe my dad. I'll make sure of that."

I lie awake on the pull-out sofa in Christy's condo. Tim's muscular arm is draped over my waist as he softly snores in my ear. I close my eyes and nod off, but only in brief interludes. When I manage a few moments of rest, I dream about Ruby. Clips of us: playing, running, laughing. Then there's black and her face fading away.

A muffled voice wakes me out of a light slumber. Christy opens her bedroom door and walks toward the kitchen starting the coffee machine. She whispers, "Just put him on the phone, Karen. I know he's there, and not with my mother, and I'm certain he doesn't want my mother to know where he actually is."

I keep my eyes closed. Christy walks back into her bedroom and gently closes the door.

Buzzing around her beautifully decorated condo as if it's the middle of the day and not the early morning, Christy offers us drinks and food. Tim and I continuously decline. I just need resolution, not a strawberry and kale salad she got from Trader Joe's or Whole Foods or some other chic grocery chain that doesn't have a location on the South or West Sides of the city.

Tim stands against the wall leading to the kitchen, the soft gray of the curtains in the living room create a strange, but magnetic contrast to his brown skin. I steal a glance at him, or two or three.

A ping from Christy's BlackBerry steals my attention away from Tim.

"Finally!" exclaims Christy as she makes her way to the laptop sitting on the countertop of her kitchen. She opens her email and the file attached from her father. And there before me is everything I can know about Holden Walters.

There are two pictures: one as a determined dark-eyed officer, full lips frowning with a policeman's cap firmly fixed to his neatly trimmed afro; the other one as a tempered older man. White hair dispersed like errant snow among his onyx mane framing high cheekbones encased in skin the color of mature clay. He's a handsome guy who aged well. Kind of an everyman, Denzel Washington type.

I notice the difference in his eyes. The most striking feature, they're more hopeful than the younger cop in the fuzzy color photo from a few decades before. I don't know why this causes me to smile, but I do. Maybe I'm seeking any light in an otherwise nightmarish few hours.

Also in the folder is information about his organization, Uplifting Chicago Youth. The office is in a Hyde Park street storefront with colorful painted handprints bleeding into the glass of the windows. His home address is also included, and isn't very far from that office, a walkable distance.

"If we leave right now, Tim and I could make it to his house in half an hour," I say. It's not the best wake-up call, but maybe Holden Walters would be getting ready to head out for the day.

Maybe he's an early riser with a few minutes to talk and help me shape a past from the almost forty-year-old picture in my hand.

Before leaving, I give Christy a bone-crushing embrace, hoping it conveys my gratitude for her help and commiseration about the dysfunction between fathers and daughters. She smiles in a bright way with sad eyes.

"Thank you for everything," I say.

"Anytime," she replies.

Outside of the condo, crisp air smells like gasoline. Our flight leaves in a few hours, and our journey finds itself back to the part of my city I know best, the South Side. Of course it's the place where all of this will come together and I will get my answers.

"You ready?" Tim asks.

"Of course not, but I'd rather know something bad than keep pretending there's nothing on the other side of all of this."

We climb into his truck and head toward Hyde Park.

I'm willing to dismantle everything I was taught, everything I know for the truth. Ultimately, this could forever break my church and my family into a million parts. I still have no idea what to do with the information once I have it.

Tim turns on the radio. I hear the unmistakable poetic, bare guitar chords of "Redemption Song" and Bob Marley sings.

"Stop thinking about what you're going to do," Tim says. "Just learn to live with the decision you've already made."

CHAPTER 15

LAYLA

This is a happy place. I can tell just from walking up the steps. The Georgian home stands proud but looks stunted next to the higher apartment building on its left. Matching burgundy shutters on the two top windows lie against sand-colored bricks. Sunlight creeps above wispy clouds, soft raspberry and sherbet hues kiss the rapidly dwindling stagnant puddles on the walkway.

I don't expect a smile when Holden Walters opens the door. I expect grumpiness, maybe a little cursing. He stands beyond the threshold grinning at Tim and me like old friends, like he was expecting us and greets us, "Morning! What can I do for you?"

I try to ease into the conversation so I don't sound as crazy as I feel. I go into my professional voice, the one I use on the phone in the office, the one that makes white people not so afraid of a black person. I'm a representative of myself.

"Sir, I'm Layla Potter and this is Timothy Simmons. I got your name from Samuel Sikorska. I just want to ask you about an event in January 1979. The Syrus Myllstone case. Do you happen to remember it?"

His smile fades as he replies, "I do."

"I have some questions about a newspaper article."

"What questions? You wasn't even born then."

I can't say I've ever had someone stare into my eyes the way he does, sizing up my character, my motivation as easy as someone breathes in and out.

"Mr. Walters…"

"Call me Holden."

"Holden, I think maybe you knew my father, Jackson Potter."

My stomach clenches from calling my father by his first name. Or it could have been the cheap coffee from the gas station we stopped at a few minutes ago.

"You both might wanna come in out this cold," he replies.

The compact living room seems bigger with only a small couch, red patterned chair and a small coffee table. I recognize a print of an old Jackson Pollack painting hanging above the couch. The pony wall to the small eat-in kitchen reveals an older woman standing with a short-cut salt-and-pepper afro, bright eyes and a cup of coffee in her hand.

"This is Tabitha, my wife," Holden introduces.

A few pictures of Holden, Tabitha, family and friends hang on the wall nearest the side door. One picture, the frame bigger than some, smaller than others captures Holden next to a guy with bushy blond-gray hair, Senator Sikorska. He and Holden are fishing and, by the looks of the large swordfish and the smiles, it was a good trip.

"We're sorry to disturb you," I begin. "Tim and I have a flight this morning. I swear we won't take much of your time."

"No bother," he says.

From my pocket I retrieve the yellowed article.

"I'll put some more coffee on," Tabitha says.

"We won't be here long," I reply, but Tabitha only smiles and walks back into the kitchen. She's the same height as Grandma Violet. Possesses the same kind of firm, but gentle gaze like

Momma. She has spoken only a few words since I walked through her door, but I already trust her.

Holden's face sags further. The imprints of caramel skin etch an accepted grief, a sorrow he learned to live with long ago.

"I knew this time would come. That this story wasn't over. You just weren't who I was expecting," says Holden.

"Who were you expecting?" Tim interjects.

He points to the sole picture from the article, a picture of Lebanon. "I was expecting him."

He began the story. The night he arrested Lebanon hiding in a backyard two blocks from the scene, clothes covered in blood. The violence overshadowing an abominably cold night.

Hotness in my belly courses north, sledgehammer-strong pulses knock against my temples. I wait for destruction. I wait for him to mention Dad. I wait to hate my father. Tim squeezes my sweaty hand. There is a cost to the knowledge Holden carries, a burden heavier than two thousand pounds on his shoulders. Hunched over, deflated he relays the last of the tale.

I still have questions. Important ones. "The clip said you believed someone else was there that night."

Holden fidgets with his perfectly starched collar and replies, "Yes."

"Was it my father? Did he kill Syrus?"

"No, sweetheart. I knew someone else was there, but Lebanon didn't let on. The only thing he told me was someone, I'm guessing that might have been your dad, hit Syrus with the pipe and was so scared, he ran off. Syrus was alive. Lebanon confessed he kept hitting Syrus. Killed him."

"But why?"

"All I can do is speculate. Maybe he thought he was helping your dad. Maybe he was tired of feeling powerless and thought killing a man was a way to take power back. Maybe both those things together." Holden stood up and walked to his wall of pictures, staring at none of them in particular. "Lebanon never said *why* he did it and I didn't spend a lot of time with him. When I saw him, he was already beaten to hell. There wasn't a thing I could do for him either. We both had to keep our mouths shut. He didn't talk about your dad and I didn't talk about his bruises. I was a cop first, black second. But, Lebanon, the thing that struck me is he didn't shake or mumble or cry. He took whatever was done to him in those rooms and acted like it was normal. It was disturbing. It was sad and disturbing. I'll never forget that or him. I hoped maybe he got out, did something with his life. I hoped he wasn't dead or in another prison somewhere. I quit being a cop a couple years later, wasn't making the difference I set out to. First time I realized that was looking at Lebanon. I didn't help him. Didn't feel like I could. And I regretted it. All these years."

A tightness spreads across my chest. "So how does my dad play into this? When did you meet my father?"

"Never have. Not face-to-face."

"So how did you recognize his name?"

"Your daddy was the local golden boy! Everyone knew him or about him. Football star. Good student too from what I heard. College bound. Preacher's kid. He had a lot going for him. More so than a lot of other kids then. Which means he had a lot to lose I suppose. Someone like Lebanon can latch on to that. Not hard for someone like him I'd think."

So, Dad didn't murder anyone. He just believes he did.

Lebanon presented himself a martyr, someone who took the blame, and used my father's guilt. He made sure Dad served some type of sentence with a special cage of his very own making.

"Are you okay?" asks Tim.

"I think so. I mean Dad isn't a killer and that's, God I can't tell you how much of a relief that is, but the rest of it. It's crazy, Tim. Crazy and sad."

The blessed aroma of coffee wafts from the kitchen. Excusing myself, I go pour a cup, think about the violent loop we're in.

I realize it isn't just merciless. It's ravenous, consuming everything and everybody.

Light footsteps invade my heavy thoughts. Swirling around ready to ask Tim to give me some space to absorb everything, I instead see Tabitha.

"Sweetie, there are many things we learn in this world," she says. "Those things can make you hard, but you have a choice to not let it. You don't be the rock. You be the river. You hear me?"

"Yes, ma'am."

"Good. Now go do what you need to do. Stay strong. It'll be alright."

She's a great hugger. Just the right amount of squeezing and warmth.

It will be okay. It must be.

Go!

JACKSON

Airports herd people. Countless bodies plodding through lines and metal detectors; my daughter likely somewhere among them. Only a few ways in or out, but I spot Layla zipping through the sliding doors with Tim close behind.

When I call her name, she turns and rushes to me, hugging me so hard. Layla breathes out the word "Daddy." The hateful words we exchanged in the kitchen. What I called her. What she said. I see my daughter smile at me, the way she used to. When her hand barely fit in mine, before she learned fathers make awful mistakes.

"You're not angry with me?"

"I think you've tortured yourself better than I ever did."

How can these small hours since our separation cause such a difference? How is grace in such abundance? It has to be a trick. She should believe I'm a killer, but she grabs hold of me tighter.

"I met Holden Walters," Layla says.

"From the article?"

"Yeah, from the article."

"What did he tell you?"

"Everything I needed to know. Some things I didn't want to know," she confesses.

Taking my hand and squeezing it, Layla reveals the story, the one Holden told her. The one I already know thanks to Thorolese Myllstone, the one where I'm not a murderer. So much time wasted. I suppose many people feel like this at one point in their lives. How a mistake can color every other action.

"I can't tell you how sorry I am, sweetheart," I begin.

Eyes darting to Tim, he stands there the whole time, bearing witness to the clumsy stitching of old wounds, a partial closing of a bitterly deep divide. He is a good man. I treated him horribly.

"For what I said, I have no excuse." Extending my hand, he

shakes it. No hesitation, no animosity. Just forgiveness. Travelers filter around us, whipping blurs of bundled bodies and boarding passes.

"Sorrys don't do much, Pops. It's about action now," Layla says.

"You're right, which is why I'm going with you. Lebanon is after Ruby, too. He's only a few hours away from Tennessee I'm guessing."

The lies and secrets. Protection masquerading as self-perseveration. I can stand in this gap, this abyss where nothing moves.

"Can I get a ticket this late?"

Less than an hour remains before the plane leaves. Two more agents approach the counter and begin taking customers. Thank God! We make it to the front in less than ten minutes. There are three tickets left for the flight, but I snag one. Layla pulls Tim's arm so we can sprint for the gate, but he doesn't move.

"I should stay here," Tim suggests. "You need to do this. Just you and your Dad. Plus, on the small chance Ruby comes back, I can make sure she's safe until you two return."

Layla shakes her head. "No! We should all—"

And Tim kisses her. Right in front of me! I don't know whether to punch him or thank him again.

Tim lets her go and says, "Just say thank you, Layla."

Rolling her eyes, with a begrudging smile spreading across her face, she says, "Thank you."

She hugs Tim. I take her hand and we run for the security line. So winded by the time we make it to the gate, I resolve to start working out with J.P. when we return to Chicago. My right knee still throbs from the earlier run-in with Lebanon.

Layla finds seats near the gate so we can be the first to line up before they begin to board. Layla bites her bottom lip, a nervous tic Joanna made me privy to when she was younger.

"What's wrong?"

She faces me. "We have to figure out how we're going to find her. I don't know Ms. Naomi's address. Maybe Grandma Violet knows, but that's not a definite."

She's right, none of us know the address, but we'll figure something out. We can't leave Ruby behind, let her slip away. Friends shouldn't let each other go.

"Give me your phone, sweetheart."

"Don't go too far, Pops. The plane will probably start boarding in ten minutes or so."

Out of earshot, I call the house. It rings twice and Joanna's voice answers.

"Don't hang up," I plead.

"Jackson, I'm not some teenage girl throwing a tantrum. I save those theatrics for you. Do you have my daughter?"

When Joanna's mad, her words are cold, but damn! Maybe Layla's smart mouth isn't something for which I should take all the credit.

"Layla's with me and we're getting ready to board a plane for Tennessee to find Ruby."

The phone is silent, and I almost think the call dropped until Joanna says, "Now you're going to help Layla find Ruby? I thought you—"

"Long story. Long, long story I swear I'll tell you when I get back, and I mean everything, Joanna, I promise. Right now, I need to speak to Mom. Please."

The phone goes silent again for about ten seconds, then I hear Mom's voice in equal measures of alarm and relief. "Jackson, thank God. Did you find Layla?"

"Yes, I'm with her now. I love you, Mom. But I have questions and I need answers quick."

"Okay, baby."

"What's the address to Ms. Naomi's old house? Layla and I think Ruby is there, and Lebanon is after her and we don't want her to be alone. We don't know what will happen when he confronts her."

The static on my end crackles loudly. I step closer to the boarding area, but still out of earshot of Layla. "You think Lebanon would hurt her? He could be like you, trying to make sure she's okay and won't hurt herself."

"He *is* the one who will hurt her," I counter. "He's not above inflicting pain on those closest to him. Mom, I know you see something good in him and that's fine, maybe there's something there, but even if there's a chance he might hurt Ruby, wouldn't you rather Layla and I be there?"

"Of course, but I don't know if y'all going there will fix what's wrong, what's been wrong for a long time."

"Because of your stubborn granddaughter, I'm finally learning we have a choice, Mom. We aren't prisoners of our past actions."

I glance at Layla. She catches me looking and grins. She always takes pride in her ability to be obstinate. She thinks it's a superpower. The crackling static becomes louder. I move to the left and it worsens, I then move to the right, and it gets better. It probably appears to onlookers I'm doing a really bad version of the electric slide.

"Mom…are you there?"

"It's a small ranch house with a red door. Not far from my house—3729 Cottonwood Road. Just get the girl. Save Ruby."

"We will. I promise."

RUBY

I smell the wood of the floors. I long to smell fresh sunflowers. I stretch my arms and twirl around like I did when I was a little girl. I wanted to be a dancer, stand with learned feet en pointe, creating circles of air, extending my body into impossible angles. I wanted people to marvel as I pirouetted onstage, as I rose and touched brilliance.

My experience of dancers and their struggles was limited to what I saw on television or an occasional movie. Mom could afford lessons, barely, but it was possible. Lebanon laughed, said it didn't make sense to waste the money. "She probably ain't gone be good at it anyway," he prophesied.

But in this place, I pivot and spin, and *I am perfect*. I have no scars and I have no pain or guilt or shame. Movement and motion possess me. My focus, sharp as butcher's blades, keeps me upright as the living room blurs round the edges of my vision.

Maybe I could have been a great dancer. I'll never know.

Promises unfulfilled and dreams deferred or cast aside altogether.

As agile as I am, I tripped walking through the red door a few minutes ago. I forgot the warped floorboard past the threshold. Furniture is covered by dusty white sheets, which I remove.

I thought Mom sold this place years ago. I thought this sanctuary was lost.

Memories tease my head, make me think the times here weren't real, that I was never that happy, that I didn't laugh or make silly faces with Grandma Naomi.

But I did. I was happy with her and sometimes watching Mom sew and make beautiful things from tattered strips of fabric. I think of Mom in her sewing room. I think of how I bumped my leg against her desk and heard the faintest jingle. I opened her drawer and found the deed to my grandmother's home in Mom's name and keys to open the doors. Sanctuary.

We could have left Lebanon when Grandma died; we would have at least had a place to go. But Lebanon would have found us and beat her and me. We would have returned to Chicago.

The same photographs still sit on the fireplace mantle, layers of dust covering each image, including the one in the silver frame, the one with the three girls. Using a sheet to wipe away the filmy residue, I once again study the picture, taking in the faces. One of them is my grandma Naomi, the other Ms. Violet, Layla's grandma, but I never found out the name of the girl in the middle. I asked Grandma Naomi about her when I was younger. Her face confirmed there was a tale too heavy to share with an eleven-year-old. Her eyes misted over with tears and the half-moon wrinkles around her mouth, normally upturned in laughter, sagged in such a way it terrified me.

Grandma Naomi was the person I loved most, and I couldn't bear being the cause of her grief, too. I was already so well acquainted with making people who were supposed to love me, either hate me or feel miserable.

I never asked another question about the picture.

I did think about the three girls together, the girl in the middle, at the oddest moments, folding laundry or answering a call at the office. I wondered who she was, how was she connected to Grandma Naomi, and what happened to her. I thought I saw parts of me in her face or maybe I wanted to because her sadness seemed familiar. No one wanted to talk about her. Over the years, she ceased being a person and became part of discarded memories. Now, she's just a picture with no name.

I wonder if years from now, Layla's children will look on a picture of us and ask about me, and she will hold the same look in her eyes as Grandma Naomi, and her children will know to never ask about me again.

I'll be forgotten.

Save yourself, baby.

Why didn't Mom at least try? Why didn't she sell Grandma's house and take me and the money and disappear? Why didn't she fucking save us? Why didn't she save me? Was I not worth her even trying?

She cried, she begged. She was weak. I was weak. She loved me, but she just wasn't strong enough to love herself. The idea of who Mom was, and my belief in the quiet strength of Grandma Naomi, inhabit two separate and damaged spaces in my heart.

What will happen to me without her?

How can there be a me without her?

Grandma Naomi's home and the sunlight don't lift my spirits as much as I'd hoped, but in some small way, I do feel better.

A freedom from anger and lies and hurt and sadness. A way to leave these things behind. The shape of my journey is no longer this triangle connecting my pain to my mother's failures and Lebanon's anger. It's just a straight line from captivity to freedom. And I no longer need a razor to accomplish this.

All I need is my black purse with the gold buckle.

LAYLA

My ears fill with air then pop, an invisible needle jammed over and over again. I'm hungry and these stale cookies are not satisfying. Dad doesn't remove his eyes from the window, surveying long lines or circles of blue interlocking with patchworks of flat green and brown land gliding by below.

It's weird, almost unsettling to be here with him. The secrets and lies, the pride and spite dividing us was for nothing. Dad kept me at arm's length and I resented him, many of the things I said or did were meant to hurt him, and a chasm formed.

He turns from the window. "How are we going to make Ruby come with us?"

"We have to convince Rue she's safe from Lebanon. The way we do that is by standing up to him. He doesn't have power over you anymore. We have the truth. All he has is fear."

Though fear is a strong force, inescapable for some.

"Do you think that will be enough?" he says.

"We can't make her do anything, but if we're both there, if we show her we won't let Lebanon torment her anymore, torment *us* anymore, we have a chance."

The plane firmly shudders and rocks. The fasten seat belt signs ping on. We jostle, bounce up and down. I squeeze his hand, and smile, I remember what Ms. Tabitha said while I was at her and Holden's home. "You can't be the rock. You have to be the river." I repeat this same statement to Dad.

He stares at me, his eyes as much of an enigma to me as they always have been, because I have no idea what he's thinking. That happens if you close yourself off to someone, but I'll get to know his looks and he'll learn mine.

"What is it, Pops? Because you're freaking me out a little staring at me."

"I'm just proud of you, is all," he says.

I want to say this means little to me, but of course it doesn't. Of course, it means everything! You always want your parents to be proud of you, think you're doing a good job at something; it doesn't matter what that something is. Most importantly I want him to believe, to know I'm a good person, and that's what his smile and his words confirm.

"Proud of me? What does that feel like?"

"Something between joy and fear. I think I'm gonna burst to be honest," he answers. "It could also be indigestion. Maybe that's what pride is, at least when it comes to you, Layla. Joy and fear and a little indigestion."

"I don't think I can argue that, Pops."

He chuckles, and though the lifting of one weight seems to free part of my heart, another part of me is still heavy. That space is occupied by Ruby.

Is she okay? Can I bring her back?

CALVARY

SEVEN DAYS AFTER ALICE KING'S DEATH

Ruby sits alone with her thoughts. The ivory casket gleams. Ruby's pearl-colored dress contrasts with her bronze skin and green eyes. Gardenias are lovingly draped along the ends of the aisles and the smell wafts under her nose. Mourners will be here soon, the family, the friends, the knowing, the curious, the congregation, all together, to sing Zion songs and eulogize a woman they never knew.

Not really.

She rises and walks over to the casket. The mortician put a smile on her Mom's face, a soft one, a believable one, Ruby thinks. It was the same smile she gave when someone complimented her pound cake for a church bake sale or said they liked the quilt she made for the annual church raffle.

"Momma, can you hear me?" Ruby whispers, "Are you in Heaven? Is there a Heaven?"

Alice's face remains placid and smiling, the answers to the questions Ruby asks trapped behind embalming liquid and thick makeup. Ruby reaches down to touch her mother's hands, a Bible firmly clutched in them, and they are mannequin rigid but slightly warmer than Ruby expects.

Layla walks up behind Ruby and hugs her. "Sister Johnson brought that tuna noodle casserole no one's gonna eat."

Ruby sighs. "It's like eating fish-flavored plastic."

Layla laughs out loud and smiles. It vanishes when she looks at Alice's casket. "Your mom wanted you to be happy. She loved you."

"I know."

"You got this, Rue. You do. I'm here."

Jackson walks down the aisle. "People are beginning to arrive. Ruby, where's your father?"

She shrugs and looks back at the casket again.

Lebanon enters my hall from the east clad in an alabaster suit, an indigo tie, and a gardenia pinned to his left breast pocket.

"I'm here. Looking damn good if I say so myself."

"You smell like beer and flowers," says Ruby.

"Had a little drink in honor of your mom. So what? I don't have to explain myself to you, girl, *ever*. Remember that."

Ruby scowls and Lebanon glares at her.

Layla stands between them and clenches her fists. "Shouldn't you be making your way to the people who want to give their condolences?"

"Get your girl, Jackson," Lebanon growls, "before she says something she regrets or I do something I'll regret."

"Let's *all* make our way to the front," Jackson orders in a tight voice.

And they leave. Ruby and Layla arm in arm, Jackson following, and Lebanon bringing up the rear.

A small breeze from no open window slightly bends the gardenias.

Alice, is that you?

RUBY

Lebanon never knocks on doors. He pounds on them, breaks them, splinters the wood, bends the hinges into abstract forms no longer able to hold things in frame. He treats doors like he treats people. All things can be broken. In my life, I've realized people can become the easiest of all to destroy.

Nine years ago, as I slid a knife down the canal of brown skin on my arms, I decided to end myself in the bathroom of the house. I figured it'd be more considerate to do it in the bathroom. Getting blood out of tile I assumed was easier than hardwood. I thought Mom would've probably been the one to clean up the mess. But I found out it was Lebanon who did the cleaning and I found some satisfaction in that. Point is I wanted to make less work for Mom. It would have been my last act as a good daughter.

As crimson seeped from me, I thought God or maybe the Devil since I was taking my own life, had come to collect me. At that point, I didn't much care. I just wanted away, from Lebanon and Mom, from seeing happiness every damn day, but never knowing it.

But it was Layla. She saved me. I didn't ask her to. I sound ungrateful as hell, but she would have been fine without me. The world would have kept spinning. Lebanon would have kept terrorizing. Mom would have kept crying. I thought it was my one chance at glory, at freedom, to find out if what even half of what they talked about in church was true.

Gone!

Layla always wanted to rescue me and I do love her for it. But was I worth it? To have someone love you so much they'll move heaven and earth for you—I only know about this all-consuming love through her. I worry she is too closely bound to me. When I'd spend the night over at her house, she'd hold on to me, tight.

And I could hear her thoughts though she didn't speak them out loud. She wanted to get me away from my home and have a home there with her, and I'd wanted that more than anything, but then Mom would be left alone with him. The complicated lines and knots of love are difficult to untangle, they coil again into something unmanageable and not easily pulled apart.

Cotton candy skies swirl across the horizon in Grandma Naomi's backyard. Even the weeds slowly overtaking the grass are beautiful. Green claws through brick pavers underneath my feet.

Everything's prettier in Tennessee.

It's cool. Too cool to keep sitting out here like it's summer, but I stretch my body and gaze at the sky just the same. Cold air whips in gusts against me, goose bumps rise along my scars, dotting my damaged flesh. Leaving the patio, I grab the black purse with the gold buckle and walk back through the kitchen. I hear the creak of the old red door. I didn't lock it.

Save yourself, baby.

He walks through the door. If only it'd been him who came home first.

I reach into my black purse with the gold buckle and find the item I need to make this plan work. This time no mistakes. He dies or I die. In either outcome, I win.

"I came to get you," Lebanon says.

His voice has a slight quiver to it, a slight uncertainty. Maybe it's being in this house. Maybe it's the dust or the memories. Maybe it's the gun I take from my purse and point in his face.

It could be that, too.

CHAPTER 16

LEBANON

That girl points the gun right at my head.

"You really want to do this? I'm all you have left. You're all I got left."

"Shut up," she yells. Hands shake slightly. If I keep talking, and time myself just right, I can take the piece away from her, stop this foolishness and bring her back home. She'll learn there's only one place for her. With me.

"I know what happens to murderers. I know about being locked up. Do you, little girl?"

"I read that file those detectives left. Doesn't surprise me, you being a killer."

"Apparently, it's in the blood and if you don't watch it, you won't have anything left, unless you're smart like me, unless you got heart like me. I can teach you about that."

"I don't want anything from you! That was Mom."

"You wanted my help that night and I gave it to you. Without hesitation."

"You want me to say 'Thank you'?"

It's hard to swallow. Could be from Jackson's little brawl. Could be something else. I inch over toward her. If she shot now, the bullet might hit my shoulder, but not my head.

"I want you to come home with me and work this out."

"Home?" A scowl spreads across her face. She pulls back the slide of the gun with her free hand. "That place was never a home and you, Mom and me were never a family."

"I see what you do to family," I fire back. "Even after all that, I protected you. I hid the gun—"

"It was your gun! You're not even supposed to have one!"

"I kept it for protection, for the bakery." Felons aren't supposed to have guns, but they're as easy to purchase as a cheeseburger.

"I should've used it sooner to protect me and Mom from you. I should've done it a lot sooner. I could've been happier a lot sooner."

"I get angry, yeah. But it's not like I wanted to hurt you or your Mom. I just get beside myself and in my head. I can't explain it. I never wanted to do what I did. I didn't like it."

"Oh well that makes it better!"

"The only way we're gonna make it better is if we stick together. It can be better between us. I promise."

"Like you promised to not hit Mom."

She won't let this go. I don't blame her. But I'm bigger than my mistakes. I did what I did that night for her, for me too, but mainly for her.

"Damn it! I'm trying to change this! Don't you get it? That's why I did what I did. The bakery, helping you that night with your mom, all of it!"

"You did that for yourself, not out of love! You don't have it to give."

"This talk about love, it's not hugs and kisses and words. It's protecting a friend even when he don't acknowledge you. It's taking money for a bakery to provide for you and Alice. It's driving hundreds of miles to bring you home! It's getting shit done for people no one else is gonna do. No one!"

She scoffs. "Why couldn't you have just come home like you always do? I had it all set up."

"You did. It was a good plan," I admit. "I wouldn't have seen you in that corner. The problem is you couldn't see either but pulled the trigger just the same. If you just focused, *really took your shot*, maybe Alice would be in this dusty-ass house with you, but you didn't and here we are."

She shakes her head. "No...no...no."

"See, maybe it's about mercy. Maybe you did a good thing for your mom, but no one's gonna understand that, but me," I say. "Everyone else is gonna say you're a murderer. Crazy. Not me. I get it. I get it."

A glimmer of understanding dances behind her eyes. I move another inch toward her, her gun almost in my reach.

Just a few more steps.

"Don't try to shake those memories. You'll never be able to anyway. Remember what you felt, what you saw. It'll drive you. What was your momma saying when you was holding her? Can you remember that?"

"'Save yourself, baby,'" she whispers.

"Save yourself from who?"

"I don't know. You probably."

If I wasn't focused on what I need to do, if words were more important than legacy, if I was weaker like Jackson, maybe what she said would've hurt. It didn't. I'm built different and so is the girl.

"People like you and me, no one gets us, not really. You feel invisible. You feel like something's breaking apart inside, but you can't quite figure out what it is. I see that in you...now I do."

"I—I..." she stutters.

The girl's eyes pop wide, dirty green ponds of surprise.

Sounded like a herd of buffalo came running through from all them footsteps. Thought it was the police.

Can't say I was expecting Jackson and Layla.

Definitely wasn't expecting Layla to stand in front of me.

"Get out of the way," the girl orders.

"We were afraid Lebanon might find you, hurt you again or that you'd hurt yourself again. Where did you get that gun?" says Layla.

"I'm not gonna kill myself!"

A look of relief then confusion snakes its way across Layla's face.

"Me and the girl were just conversating about some plans, that's all," I say.

"Conversating on how you can keep her quiet for good. Keep her trapped with you," Layla fumes.

The girl's arm remains straight as an arrow.

"You don't know a damn thing," I reply.

Layla turns from me. "Look, Rue, we won't let Lebanon hurt you anymore."

"Ruby, there's a way back from this," Jackson counsels, stepping in front of Layla. "There's been enough death. You can stop this. Just put the gun down."

The girl's breathing slows. She moves her arm slightly to the right and pulls the trigger. Splinters of wood ricochet, a geyser of small oak strips explode from the door frame.

Everything was under control. She was finally starting to listen, maybe even understand me a little, and just like clockwork the Potters come and screw everything up.

She steps closer to Jackson, placing the gun square against his temple. "Now you want to protect me? Now you grow a backbone against Lebanon? Why the hell should I even listen to you or Layla? You deserve a bullet in your head just as much as he does. You stood by and did nothing. You're a damn coward!"

"You're right," Jackson says, his breath uneven. "You have

no reason to trust my word, and you should be able to trust it. But I swear to you, we just want to help."

"Tell me, Pastor, does God forgive murderers?"

Jackson glances over at me. "Yes, Ruby. I'm sure he does. God forgives us all. No matter what happened between Alice and him the night she died, no matter what Lebanon did, God loves him, too."

"Just walk away," I warn. "For once in your damn life don't try and be a hero. You fail every time you try."

"Your father gave me the weapon. The one he used that night. We can go to the police. We can make this right," Jackson says.

Layla's eyes go wide and she stares at her father in awe, in anger, maybe pride. I can't distinguish her look.

"Come with us. Dad can make this right. Lebanon can go away. The police will have the weapon with his prints—" begs Layla.

"Then they'll have mine, too," the girl interrupts.

"What are you saying?"

"Jesus, Jackson. Isn't your daughter the smart one out of your kids?" I say.

Jackson turns to me and scowls. He might choke me again, he might leave me to the girl, but he won't leave without Layla.

"Your prints on the gun? What happened? With your mom... Did you? It wasn't..." Layla trails off.

"No, it wasn't him. I just. I didn't see Momma come through the door. Thought it was him."

The girl moves her arm and the gun once aimed at Jackson's head is now aimed at mine. Layla steps forward again, in front of Jackson.

"You want my life for yours, Rue?"

"I want you to leave! Take your dad with you. I'll deal with mine."

The girl's voice is even and low, like Sara used to sound.

Maybe she *could* kill Layla or me or all of us. Maybe I should give her more credit. Alice always said I underestimated her.

"Just…go, Layla. What happened with Mom was a mistake. A horrible mistake. I never meant to hurt her. Let me deal with this, once and for all."

"Jesus!" Jackson's voice whispers.

"He ain't here!" I reply.

Sirens make their way down the street. Someone probably heard the gunshot. Quiet neighborhood like this, a gunshot probably sounds like a cannon.

"You're right, Rue, I want to save you and I get how arrogant that sounds, but it's because I know you're worth so much more. You've always *been* so much more, and I'm sorry I didn't see it before. Now. *Right now*, before everything is taken away. We're sisters. We're *us!*"

"I don't have anything left. I can make the world a better place without Lebanon in it. Otherwise, what I suffered, Mom… It's for nothing. All of it."

"Jesus, Rue! I need you to see your worth before a bunch of uniforms come in and write your story for you! You still have power. You can still save yourself!"

"What?" The girl's lips start trembling. The gun shakes in her hand. One small move and the girl might accidentally kill again. "Say what you said again, Layla," the girl commands.

"You can save yourself. *Save yourself, Rue*," Layla begs. Her voice is cracking.

Blue lights cut through dusty white curtains. Voices outside. That shouting with authority, without consequence and a lotta malice.

"What about…Mom?"

"We'll figure that out together. But it will be together. Always and forever," Layla's voice whispers, spiderweb thin. "We need to end this. We can't keep hiding behind the past or God or guns or Bibles or self-preservation. It revisits us again and again. I'm tired of this. Aren't you?"

"Ruby, please. *Please,*" Jackson begs.

The girl's time is running short. If she's gonna shoot us, then she better do it now. If not, then she best put that piece down before the cops shoot her.

The girl lowers her arm. Seconds later, cops run through the door and shout orders.

Police have the girl in the back seat of their car. She stares straight ahead. She isn't crying. She rocks back and forth. Back and forth. Layla talks to one of the cops. After all this mess, I deserve a square. My stash is still lying in the glove compartment of my car.

I feel Jackson behind me before he even says a word. I light my square and take a long drag. The tobacco dances around my lungs before I blow it into the southern air. "How's your knee?"

"Sore. How's your throat?"

"I'll live." I take another toke and blow it in his face.

He waves the smoke away. "Mmm–hmm. How fortunate for all of us."

"Well, that comment was petty as hell, Jackson."

"I didn't come over here to get in it with you. Ruby is ours, good, bad and ugly—but she's ours. We'll figure out what to do. Whatever your journey from here on out is, it's on your own," Jackson tells me. "If Ruby hears so much as a peep from you, everyone will know about the gun and how you got that bakery, Lebanon. How you *actually* got it."

I choke and cough so hard my lungs bang back and forth in my chest.

"Alice gave me the papers," he continues. "Said she couldn't help cover up your sins anymore."

"You threatening me?"

"I suppose I am."

One of the cops comes over to me and Jackson, gives us the address of the precinct where they're keeping the girl for now. "So you wanna go over? Say goodbye? She might be in awhile before they can set bail and such." The cop has a slight accent, a twang at the ends of his words, spreading them out like honey over warm toast.

Jackson glares at me. He's not bluffing, not like the other night when he had the wrench in his hand. He has nothing to lose by taking everything from me. I have nothing to gain if I try to keep the girl. The decision is made for me, I suppose.

"Anything for the girl, talk to him." I point to Jackson.

Turning to Jackson the cop says, "Okay, sir, here's my card and information. Let me finish getting your statement, and we'll talk about what happens next."

"Yes, Detective, I'll be over in a bit."

The detective saunters back across the street.

"Didn't think you had it in you, but you've surprised me in these last hours," I say.

"You surprised?"

"Kinda proud, actually."

"It takes courage to do the right thing, Lebanon. Even if it might come too late. I hope it hasn't.

"There's something else I have to tell you," he murmurs.

Sunlight burns my skin as Jackson finishes the story Sara told about my father. Maybe Sara not telling me was her only way to protect me. Maybe it wasn't love she had for me, but it wasn't hate either. She couldn't love me like a mom or hug me like one, but considering what she went through, the fact she still kept me, guess I can't ask for much more. Can't say I'll ever forgive her, but I understand more now.

Jackson makes his way across the street and leaves me alone under an oak tree with a half-finished cigarette. Guess it didn't make much sense to come here, to try and keep the girl; try and make something out of life since Alice is gone. It'd be like trying to get the rotten out from fruit. You cut out the brown spots, but the decay, it's somewhere beneath. You can never really enjoy the fruit because you're always wondering if the fruit is good or if it'll make you sick.

The girl doesn't have much use for me or apologies, so I'll offer none. But maybe not being there is best. Sara was around and a lot of good that did for me, or anyone else. Best thing a parent can do for their child is let them go. Figure out their own shit. She's in handcuffs now, but maybe the girl, maybe Ruby, can be free like I never was. Maybe I owe her by staying away. Maybe I owe myself.

LAYLA

I fix my gaze on Dad and Lebanon speaking across the street. After the dust settled, after we gave our statements to the police and detectives, Dad pulled me aside and told me what Ms. Sara confessed in the hospital, about Lebanon. He said he didn't want any more secrets between us. I told him what Holden told me. This exchange of truth and tragedy, of hurt and heartbreak, connected us in a way I never believed possible. So now, watching across the street, Lebanon's stance, the slumped posture of his frame, I know the story Dad told a man who once was as close to him as a brother.

Ruby's head presses against the window of the detective's car. The police quickly took control of the scene after they came through the door of Ms. Naomi's home. Their guns raised first, we all heard them shout orders and we obeyed, but with the distinct fear all of us have when it comes to police, that no matter the level of compliance, we might still have our caramel-colored bodies riddled with bullets nonetheless. They rushed Ruby out of the house and into the back seat of a dusty brown sedan and there she's remained for the better part of an hour. I just need to say a few words. I just need a little more time with her.

Just a few minutes.

One of the detectives, a stocky bull of a man with a pear-shaped nose and pink skin, stands next to the brown sedan with my friend in the back seat. Asking him to speak to Ruby, he briefly sizes me up, silently making his judgments about my merits and intent. He goes into the car, behind the driver's seat and rolls down her window. I grab her hand. It's so cold.

"I want you to know, Momma forgave me, even though I killed her," Ruby whispers.

I'm still having a hard time processing this information. I'm not mad at her for what she did to Dad. I can understand how easy, how gratifying it'd feel to take some kind of power back, to wrestle it from those who'd stolen it from you. It's not right to feel this way, but feelings aren't a matter of right or wrong, they're a matter of acknowledgement or denial.

There's no right way to respond to her confession. "Why didn't you tell me?"

"And say what, Layla, I killed my mom while trying to kill my dad? What could you have done?"

"Whatever I had to do, Rue."

"And that's why I didn't tell you. You'd have done something you can't take back, like me. I couldn't let you sacrifice yourself. You can't be that hero for me, Layla. You gotta live with that. Like I gotta live with this." She raises her handcuffed wrists.

There's an acceptance in Ruby's voice. One that's chilling. Who she is and who I am are wrapped up in two identities: survivor and protector.

Ruby endured a mom bound to a man she swore to love; a community and church willing to look the other way; she had to endure me, a friend, so caught up in my own battles to be right that I lost sight of the promise I made to her in a church basement, to protect her.

Ruby was lost in all of it. So lost, the only way she saw out was to kill Lebanon.

The only true words I can think of leave my lips, "Your mom loved you."

"She did her best. It wasn't always good enough, but I loved her so much. I can't believe she's gone, because of me."

"But it was a mistake. Like you said, she forgave you," I reply.

"There's no making this right, Layla. No amount of praying or church. No perfect sermon." She squeezes my hand harder. I don't pull away. "I told them…about what happened in Chicago, to Mom. I suppose a happy ending isn't for me. There wasn't for her."

"You're not your mom. You're not Lebanon either. Life doesn't give us our happy endings. We take them and sometimes we take too much, but I gotta believe there's more for us."

Ruby marks the veracity of my statement and looks at me with those pretty green eyes. "Momma told me to save myself before she died."

"So do that," I answer.

Her eyes take in the whole of the car's worn, musty interior. "How?"

"I don't know, Rue. But you're taking responsibility for what happened and that has to count for something."

Holding on to Ruby's hand even tighter. "There has to be some kind of justice."

"There is, and that justice is happening now, and that's why I have to go. Maybe you're right. Maybe Mom was right, too. Maybe the only way to save myself was to tell them about what really happened so what isn't said doesn't have power over me anymore, over any of us."

"Yeah, that makes sense." My heart rattles around my rib cage and my heartbeat almost drowns out Ruby's next words to me.

"Just don't forget me, okay."

The pear-shaped-nose detective comes around the car and looks down at my bent frame. "Miss, we're taking her. You need to wrap this up. Now."

I need more time. Just a few more minutes, seconds with my friend. These people have made their judgments about her after a mere hour, but they don't know who she is, why she is. I barely know Ruby in the way I thought I knew her, but there's a history between us and our fathers, and it's led us here, with me crouching next to a brown car with my friend in the back seat.

"I won't forget you because I'll be with you every damn step of the way. I promise."

The detective gets behind the driver's side again and starts the engine. The window squeaks as it rolls back up, and I hold on to Rue's hand for as long as I can before we must let go of one another. The brown car whisks Ruby away from me and I stand in front of Ms. Naomi's house. Most of the gawking neighbors retreat into their homes. Lebanon's car ambles in the opposite direction to the highway and back to Chicago. I don't cry.

My dad and I head back inside for a last look and to lock up. In this moment of quiet, I almost collapse when I recognize Ms. Naomi, my grandma and another girl in a photo. Ms. Naomi was one of the Three Women in my dream. Alice took some time. It came to me standing on this porch looking at her daughter through the glass of the detective's sedan. I didn't recognize the smile. I didn't take in her youth. The picture next to Ruby's bed in her room, *that* was Alice as she always should have been, but never became in *this* life. A protector. I still can't identify the third woman. She was beautiful with light skin and bright eyes, almost gold. I've never seen eyes like that. Maybe she was an angel.

The Three Women: Naomi, Alice, and The Woman with the Gold Eyes. My cheerleaders from the Other Side. When I needed their guidance the most, they pointed me to Ruby. They showed me the way.

My thoughts and hope and regret all come together inside me. The only certainty is that I will keep my promise to my friend. Turning around I ask Dad, "How long before we can get to the police station?"

"About ten minutes or so," he answers.

"Let's go."

CALVARY

Doors are closed and locked and I am empty.

Sunlight warms my spine of pews. Cold batters my bulky limestone skin and though there is a temporal absence of chattering bodies and music and movement, I don't feel alone. Solitude is a beacon for genuine reflection.

Quiet moments allow me to lay out all that is behind and all that is to come, never allowing fear to weaken my being or soul, if there is such a thing for the likes of me. I take solace in the fact good things are built to last. It's our choice to preserve or neglect them.

Family. Sisterhood. Brotherhood. Time. Life. A Church.

Each of these and more can stand as indestructible and abiding as God, but it takes care and vigilance. It takes love and courage and selflessness. It takes other fruits of a spirit not listed in the Bible.

All have the potential to discover peace, turn it into something everlasting. But humans carry their sorrow and disappointment, their trials and tragedies. They drag them with them, ugly, battered luggage, opened and rummaged through for the sheer purpose of torturing themselves with unfortunate past actions.

Our history can shape the future, but it doesn't define it. Our present is anchored by those around us, those we allow in our lives and those who, by default or shared blood, walk a road with us. What we choose to do with that companionship is up to us.

Past, present and future communing together, the joining of this holy trinity. Who humans are, and what the world is, live in these three things.

Remember this, always.

LEBANON

I used to think Sara was too mean to die. I was wrong. She died in her sleep two weeks ago with Auntie Violet holding her hand. I stayed at the bakery and made a pineapple upside-down cake. Auntie Vi gathered her belongings from the hospital including the picture of her, Sara and Ms. Naomi.

In Sara's belongings was a dinged-up tin box decorated in roses and a bunch of letters from when she lived in Memphis, from a man named Jonas. There are letters from Sara to him, too. They are hopeful and sweet. There was also a journal in the tin box, but I haven't read it yet. Sara started writing in it after I was born. It might have something about me, something I'm not ready to take on.

Sara's death was supposed to bring peace, but I have more questions than answers. She never told me my father and my grandfather were the same person. She never told me what she endured. I didn't understand her way with me, why she had no patience for my shortcomings, why she hit me, why she couldn't look me in the eye.

Her way of surviving, drinking and men and such, always seemed a punishment for me. Who I am, or at least part of it, is because of something horrible that happened to her, and now things make sense, or at least part of her makes sense.

I didn't go to the homegoing. Jackson delivered the eulogy. Auntie Vi said it was a nice service, that Sara would've liked it. I got dressed up that day and sat on my bed, in my nicest suit, indigo with a red satin lining, a Christmas gift from Alice a few years ago. I think Sara's favorite color was blue, but I can't really be sure of it. I'd like to think I knew her favorite color, but I don't.

I do know Sara loved roses.

Today, I'm at Restvale Cemetery, and I brought a dozen of them to her grave, all freshly cut, most in full bloom with a lush red embedded in every petal.

Yeah, Sara would like these.

There isn't much to say to her except I wish I could've known you, *really* known you, Sara. I wish you would've saw fit to love me despite how I came into this world. I'm glad you knew love for a short time in Memphis, even if that love didn't come from me. I want both of us to find peace in this world or, for you, in the next one.

A westward wind blows a few petals off the roses onto Sara's plot. I'm not naive enough to believe it's some cosmic sign she's watching. I know I'm only speaking to dirt and a patch of struggling grass. But maybe my words in the air can find you, wherever you are. Maybe I want to say I'm sorry and I think you'd say you're sorry, too.

But I won't ever know that so best get on with it.

RUBY

FOUR YEARS AFTER ALICE KING'S DEATH

I walked a mile to Walmart after the bus dropped me off. A pink backpack with a fairy on it was the first thing I've bought in almost five years that wasn't from the commissary. I count twenty-four different cereals lined up side by side on the shelves. Twenty-four different cereals to choose from. Funny, the things you miss. I missed Frosted Flakes. I also missed clothes without numbers, someone calling *my name* and not "Inmate" with that practiced sharpness. I'm not a number anymore. I'm not faceless.

Didn't realize I spent twenty minutes in the cereal aisle. I'll buy Frosted Flakes next time. The $56 in my pocket isn't gonna last if I spend it on brand-name cereal, but a $5 pink backpack with a fairy is worth it. I can throw away the white sack with black airbrushed numbers.

The first person to speak to me after I left prison was a Walmart cashier. Her name was Darla and she told me to never smoke. Said she's been trying to give it up for at least fifteen years but hasn't been able to stop. She said it's a horrible habit and it's expensive, too.

"Trust me. Cigarettes are the devil. You know I could have bought at least two cars with what I spent on those things? I don't care how much stress you got, don't smoke! You're a pretty girl, too pretty to do that anyway," she preached.

Darla was once a pretty girl. Maybe smoking took that away or maybe it was something life does to some of us. And though we're not always left looking pretty, we have a ragged beauty, one that shows strength instead of a perfect nose or sculpted cheekbones.

I smile and reply, "Thanks."

I wait for Layla on a bench where fresh air caresses my face, but crawls along my scars. They've faded over time or I think they have, willing my body to somehow start to forget. My eyes still haven't adjusted to the plain squat buildings making up this town. They search for skyscrapers in the distance and instead find barren green pastures and skinny asphalt roads with rumbling trucks blaring country music.

A little brown girl looks at me, curious with flashing dark eyes, almost black, wearing a pretty green dress. Her mom scolds her for staring, takes her hand and ushers her across the parking lot to their blue car.

And I see her. Layla. Smiling. She's gonna ask me if I'm okay and I might be, at least more okay than I was a day ago, and the week before that and so on. She's gonna smile at me and hope I return the smile. Isn't freedom, *my freedom*, cause for celebration? Isn't friendship, *her friendship*, enough to tug at the sides of my mouth in a bright arc?

I go to her silver car, me and my pink backpack with the fairy on it. She hugs me across the divide of a gear shift and cup holders, and I let her. Hazard lights blink. *Tick. Tick. Tick.* I don't pull away. I put my arms around her. I take in someone who wants me to be here, someone who's happy to see me despite who I am and my mistakes. Kinda like what people at church said God was supposed to be like. A friend driving hours to pick up another friend, maybe that's God, too.

Layla smells of soap and cinnamon. I don't know how I smell. I hope it's good. Someone honks their car horn. Layla lets me go before I let her go.

And we drive.

"You got a new car? It's nice," I offer.

Layla's glances at me sheepishly. "I've had this car for a few years."

Which is code for I got this while you were in prison, but I don't want to make things any more awkward than they are. "It still smells new though," I say.

She smiles apologetic and hesitant.

The silence is nice for a time. I think about Mom and what she'd be doing right now. How would that quilt have turned out? Who would she have given it to? I think about her a lot especially during sunset. And that thing happens when I think of Mom, some dark part in the back of my mind grudgingly dredges up Lebanon, my thoughts about him an unfixable, leaky faucet.

Lebanon never showed up to any of the hearings. The ones that determined I was at first a danger to myself, when I spent days in a cell with nothing to hang or cut myself with. A dirty mattress on the floor with no bedding was the only furniture in the room, but they gave me a cell with a window. Cold eyes scanned my small space every fifteen minutes or so to make sure I was still alive. Pale yellow walls became my clock and measure of hours. The sun splashed lower and lower against concrete blocks laid in rows until the moon made the cell bone white. Or, when there was no moon, I sat in the dark until the sun came out and I again began to count the days.

I did this for a week.

I wasn't going to kill myself. Me dead would make Lebanon's life easier and why would I want to help him out? Me living is revenge enough. I wish I would've recognized that before everything.

Jackson and Layla never missed a court date. They were there every step of the way like Layla promised that night by the police car. The public defender pleaded my case down. Said I was depressed. Wasn't thinking straight. Thought it was a burglar. Was so scared I hid the gun. I didn't tell him it was Lebanon who hid it or that it was his gun. It would've been so easy to implicate him, have him behind bars, but he had tried to help me by hiding the gun. That was the closest thing to fatherly I ever saw him do for me, and maybe that meant in some deep recess of his heart he loved me, or at least that's what I chose to believe and that's why I kept my mouth shut.

The detectives, the big one and the one with red hair were there too, but never testified. They just came to make sure their case was closed out. That their job was done. The judge looked at me or maybe through me. I couldn't tell. He said my mistakes would cost me five years. Then I signed some paperwork with my lawyer. I liked my lawyer. He didn't remind me of the slick guys at my old job. He listened. To him I wasn't invisible, and he was good at what he did. I could've spent the rest of my life staring at the sun and moon on a bare concrete wall, but I spent only four and a half years doing this. Let off early for good behavior. It's hard for me to wrap my mind around good behavior after I took a life.

I suppose there's nowhere else to go but up from here.

And we drive.

Gentle bumps on the road give way to mild concrete craters and then back to gentle bumps, then deeper craters. Layla glances over from time to time but lets me be until she can't anymore.

"He doesn't come around the church. I don't think he and Dad have talked since that night. So, you're safe."

"From him? Yeah, I'm safe from him now."

My vision grows blurry for a second. Dull green and even duller brown become some swirl of color, like my eyes, while the sky matures to a darker blue and the clouds a starker white.

"You want to ask me what happened while I was gone, but there's nothing to tell, Layla. I appreciated the letters you sent though."

"Why didn't you want us to visit?"

"What purpose would it have served? Small talk. Forced jokes. Your Dad reading a Bible verse or two or twelve. It's worse for me to see you knowing the world's going on without me. That you're going on without me."

It's hard to breathe now; the plush confines of the car slowly feel suffocating. Chicago's skyline dimly glows from a distance and suddenly bursts forth with all the noise and life and dirt I remember.

"I'm not trying to be a bitch, Layla."

"No, you're not *trying*," she retorts and then she chuckles. It's a warm sound. "I can't say I know your feelings, Rue. I don't, and I know I push—"

"Yeah, but I'm thankful for it."

"Well, thank you, too."

"For what?"

"Not giving up."

And we drive.

EPILOGUE

LAYLA

Sirens carve city air into meaty strips. Countless bodies carrying shopping bags emblazoned with designer names shadow the sun-saturated sidewalks.

Dad is always late when it's his turn to pick the venue for our hangout. He's at least gotten better about trying new things. The Art Institute is a newish thing for him. He fell in love with the museum after they featured a show of up-and-coming artists, and J.P. was selected to participate. J.P.'s art on those walls, the mingling of his colors on a canvas, his talent displayed for all to see, astounded and humbled us, but there was something deeper for Dad. And even though the exhibition was a temporary one, even though there was no promise J.P.'s work would ever be shown there again, there's abiding faith it will be.

Lebanon hasn't stepped foot in Calvary Hope Christian Church since Tennessee. Some of the congregation still frequent his bakery. They say it's nice. I don't go. Neither does Dad.

But Dad does visit Ms. Sara's grave when Grandma Violet comes back every summer from Tennessee. Every visit, Grandma takes a bouquet of roses. Grandma Violet made sure Ms. Sara was buried at Restvale Cemetery, on the other side of her mother, Sophia. Grandma Violet said Sophia had the prettiest eyes, almost golden in the sunlight.

I found my third angel.

Ruby visited Sara's grave once, after she got back. She said she didn't remember Sara, that she saw her only once when she was really young, and that Lebanon never talked about her. Before Ruby left, she said a prayer and hasn't been back since.

Grabbing my phone with the sole purpose of tracking down my father, my engagement ring snags the lining of my coat pocket. I'm still learning how to gracefully reach into purses and pockets without destroying them or breaking a finger. After Tennessee, there was no pretense between Tim and me, no hesitant declaration of feelings or intent, we just knew what we wanted and moved forward. Somehow, it's still weird being engaged to Tim. It's weird and wonderful, and I have this part in my heart, that even on my worst days, still glows.

Glancing at my screen I find a missed a text from Ruby who's making sure I'll pick her up from Midway Airport after church tomorrow.

Too many emojis. There are five smileys, an airplane, and three yellow hearts. I don't know how she became that person who sends texts with all these emojis. When we speak, which is just about every night, the voice on the phone, her voice, is joyful, like I've never heard before.

She's happy in the Tennessee sunlight, hidden in its indigo dreams. She repainted the red door of her home a bright green. Walks her rescue dog, a pit mix named Beau. Takes a dance class Tuesdays and Thursdays. Loves her job as a social worker. Keeps the house filled with a vase of sunflowers or lilies or gardenias next to the picture in the silver frame, and the picture of her and Alice.

Step by step Ruby and I moved on, pushed past costly personal mistakes and parental failures. We fashioned a new peace, uneven and imperfect, but a peace that's ours and ours alone.

Scanning the horizon of skyscrapers and rumbling buses, I catch my father jogging up the stairs.

"Ready to get some culture, baby?"

"I've always had it. I'm my mother's child," I say back.

He laughs. It's a lot easier for him now.

The cavernous museum seems unending. So easy to get lost in paintings and sculptures and history, we lose track of our location, but we keep walking. One of the halls offers a bench. Dad and I take a moment to get our bearings. I people watch, let my mind drift to the presentation on Monday, the one which determines if I make senior associate or not. Trying not to overwhelm myself. I breathe deep, once again immersing myself in beautiful surroundings. Dad is no longer sitting beside me, and I'm pulled to a painting holding his attention like no other piece of art we've seen thus far.

The card below reads *Pond in the Woods*, 1862. It's a pretty forest meadow with a small body of water surrounded by thick trees. There's blue sky and clouds and sun providing a path forward out from the inconstant shadow.

"It's a nice painting," I say. "There's some darkness, but it's supposed to be there. It's something we need. Makes you appreciate the light more."

I would ask Dad what he's thinking, but I won't.

He's smiling.

★ ★ ★ ★ ★

ACKNOWLEDGMENTS

There wouldn't be a single word on paper without the encouragement, faith and tough love of my momma, Georgia Virginia Willis-West; my awesome big-little brother, Gerald West, Jr., and my father, Gerald West, Sr.

Thanks to my courageous and ah-mazing agent Beth Marshea of Ladderbird Literary Agency. I don't believe I'd be here if you didn't take a chance on me. Everlasting gratitude, hugs and tacos to my fantastic editor Laura Brown of Park Row Books. Your faith in this story and your exceptional skill in helping me make it better is the stuff of legend!

Also thank you to my wonderful friends who are more like the additional annoying brothers I didn't know I needed: Branden Johnson (Probie); Kevin Savoie (Mellow); Andrew Dolbeare (Drew); Michael Burgner (Burgner); and Michael Cody (Cody). You guys know where the bodies are buried because you helped me bury them and would help me bury more if I called you in the middle of the night.

Lastly, to my grandma Viola Willis, and my great-grandmother

Georgia Whitaker. I don't know all the parts of your stories, what you sacrificed, so a black girl from the South Side of Chicago could become a writer. I wish I did. I do know there's no way to repay you, so I will pay it forward. I will make you proud.

Thank you.